Penguin Great Books of the 20th Century

SAUL BELLOW, *The Adventures of Augie March* (1953)

WILLA CATHER, *My Ántonia* (1918)

J. M. COETZEE, *Waiting for the Barbarians* (1980)

JOSEPH CONRAD, *Heart of Darkness* (1902)

DON DELILLO, *White Noise* (1985)

FORD MADOX FORD, *The Good Soldier* (1915)

GABRIEL GARCÍA MÁRQUEZ, *Love in the Time of Cholera* (1985)

WILLIAM GOLDING, *Lord of the Flies* (1954)

GRAHAM GREENE, *The Heart of the Matter* (1948)

JAMES JOYCE, *A Portrait of the Artist as a Young Man* (1916)

FRANZ KAFKA, *The Metamorphosis and Other Stories* (1915)

JACK KEROUAC, *On the Road* (1957)

KEN KESEY, *One Flew Over the Cuckoo's Nest* (1962)

D. H. LAWRENCE, *Women in Love* (1920)

TONI MORRISON, *Beloved* (1987)

MARCEL PROUST, *Swann's Way* (1913)

THOMAS PYNCHON, *Gravity's Rainbow* (1973)

SALMAN RUSHDIE, *Midnight's Children* (1980)

JOHN STEINBECK, *The Grapes of Wrath* (1939)

EDITH WHARTON, *The Age of Innocence* (1920)

Franz Kafka

THE METAMORPHOSIS
AND OTHER STORIES

TRANSLATED FROM THE GERMAN
BY MALCOLM PASLEY

PENGUIN BOOKS

PENGUIN BOOKS

Published by the Penguin Group

Penguin Group (USA) Inc., 375 Hudson Street, New York, New York 10014, U.S.A.

Penguin Group (Canada), 90 Eglinton Avenue East, Suite 700, Toronto,
Ontario, Canada M4P 2Y3 (a division of Pearson Penguin Canada Inc.)

Penguin Books Ltd, 80 Strand, London WC2R 0RL, England

Penguin Ireland, 25 St Stephen's Green, Dublin 2, Ireland (a division of Penguin Books Ltd)

Penguin Group (Australia), 250 Camberwell Road, Camberwell,
Victoria 3124, Australia (a division of Pearson Australia Group Pty Ltd)

Penguin Books India Pvt Ltd, 11 Community Centre, Panchsheel Park, New Delhi – 110 017, India

Penguin Group (NZ), cnr Airborne and Rosedale Roads,
Albany, Auckland 1310, New Zealand (a division of Pearson New Zealand Ltd)

Penguin Books (South Africa) (Pty) Ltd, 24 Sturdee Avenue,
Rosebank, Johannesburg 2196, South Africa

Penguin Books Ltd, Registered Offices: 80 Strand, London WC2R 0RL, England

This edition published in Penguin Books 2000

15 16 17 18 19 20

These selections are from the volume, *The Transformation ("Metamorphosis")
and Other Stories*, translated by Malcolm Pasley, Penguin Books, 1992.

ISBN 0 14 02.8336 6

Printed in the United States of America
Set in Janson

Contents

MEDITATION	1
Children on the Country Road	1
Unmasking a Confidence Trickster	5
The Sudden Walk	7
Resolutions	8
The Excursion into the Mountains	9
The Fate of the Bachelor	10
The Businessman	11
A Stray Glance from the Window	13
The Way Home	14
The Men Running Past	15
The Passenger	16
Clothes	17
The Rejection	18
For the Consideration of Amateur Jockeys	19
The Window on the Street	20
Longing to be a Red Indian	21
The Trees	22
Unhappiness	23
THE JUDGEMENT. *A Story*	27
THE STOKER. *A Fragment*	38

THE METAMORPHOSIS	64
IN THE PENAL COLONY	111
A COUNTRY DOCTOR. *Little Tales*	137
The New Advocate	137
A Country Doctor	139
Up in the Gallery	145
A Leaf from an Old Manuscript	146
Before the Law	148
Jackals and Arabs	150
A Visit to the Mine	154
The Next Village	157
A Message from the Emperor	158
A Problem for the Father of the Family	159
Eleven Sons	161
A Fratricide	166
A Dream	168
A Report to an Academy	170
THE COAL-SCUTTLE RIDER	179
A FASTING-ARTIST. *Four Stories*	182
First Sorrow	182
A Little Woman	185
A Fasting-artist	192
Josefine, the Songstress or: The Mouse People	201

THE METAMORPHOSIS
AND OTHER STORIES

MEDITATION

Children on the Country Road

I COULD HEAR THE CARTS driving past the garden fence, sometimes I even caught sight of them through the gently shifting gaps in the foliage. How the wood of their spokes and shafts creaked in the summer heat! Labourers were coming in from the fields and laughing so that it was a scandal.

I was sitting on our little swing, just having a rest among the trees in my parents' garden.

Beyond the fence there was never a pause. Children running by were past in a moment; harvest waggons with men and women perched on the sheaves and round them darkened the flower-beds; towards evening I saw a gentleman with a walking-stick out for a stroll, and a party of girls coming arm-in-arm the other way stepped aside into the grass as they greeted him.

Then birds flew up like a shower of sparks, I followed them with my eyes and saw how they rose in a single breath, until they seemed no longer to be rising but I to be falling, and holding fast to the ropes I began to swing a little out of faintness. Soon I was swinging more strongly as the air grew cooler and in place of the flying birds trembling stars appeared.

I was given my supper by candle-light. Often I had both my arms on the wooden board and I was already weary as I bit into my bread and butter. The wide-mesh curtains billowed in the warm wind, and now and then someone going by outside would hold them fast with both hands if he wanted to see me better and speak to me. Usually the

candle soon went out and the midges which had gathered went on cir-
cling for a while in the dark candle-smoke. If someone asked me
something from the window I would look at him as if I were staring at
the mountains or into thin air, not that he much cared about an answer anyway.

But if one of them jumped over the window-sill and announced
that the others were waiting in front of the house, then indeed I did
get up with a sigh.

'Come on now, what are you sighing for? Whatever's happened? Is
it some specially awful, fatal disaster? Shan't we ever be able to get
over it? Can really all be lost?'

Nothing was lost. We ran out to the front of the house. 'Thank
heavens, there you are at last!'—'You're always late!'—'Why pick on
me?'—'Because it's always you, stay at home if you don't want to
come.'—'No mercy!'—'What? No mercy? What kind of talk is that?'

We plunged into the evening headfirst. There was no day-time and
no night-time. Now our jacket-buttons were clicking against one another like teeth, now we kept a steady distance between us as we ran,
breathing fire like tropical beasts. Like cuirassiers in ancient wars,
stamping and leaping high, we chased one another down the short village street and then, carried by our legs, up along the main country
road. Some of the party dropped off singly into the roadside ditch;
hardly had they vanished against the dark embankment when there
they stood up on the field path like strangers, looking down.

'Come on down!'—'First you come up!'—'So you can push us
down, not likely, we're not that stupid.'—'You mean you're too scared.
Come on up, come on!'—'Scared? Of you? Push us down, will you?
Some hope.'

We made our attack, got a push in the chest, and collapsed into the
grassy ditch, falling of our own free will. Everything had the same
mildness, we felt neither warmth nor chill in the grass, just weariness
setting in.

If you turned on your right side and put a hand under your ear, you
felt like falling asleep. And yet you wanted to struggle to your feet
again with your chin in the air, but only so as to fall into a deeper
ditch. And you wanted to go on like that for ever.

What it might feel like to stretch right out, stretching your legs
above all, for a proper sleep in the final ditch, that was something you

barely thought of as yet as you lay on your back like an invalid, half inclined to tears. You blinked whenever one of the boys, with his elbows
tucked in, leapt across you with his dark soles from the bank to the
roadway.

You could already see the moon quite high in the sky; in its light a
mail-coach drove past. All around a gentle breeze got up, even in the
ditch you could feel it and the forest nearby began to rustle. And you
no longer wanted so much to be alone.

'Where have you got to?'—'This way!'—'Everyone collect!'—
'What are you hiding for, don't be a fool!'—'Don't you know the mail-
coach has gone by already?'—'Oh no! Gone already?'—'Of course, it
went past while you were asleep.'—'Me asleep? What rubbish!'—'Oh
shut up, anyone can tell you were.'—'No, honestly.'—'Oh come on!'

We kept closer now as we ran, many of us held hands; we couldn't
hold our heads up high enough, for now it went downhill. Someone
whooped an Indian war-cry, our legs found a gallop as never before,
the wind gave a lift to our hips as we sprang in the air. Nothing could
have checked us; we were going so strongly that even when overtaking
we could fold our arms and look calmly around us.

At the bridge over the mountain stream we halted; those who had
run ahead came back. Below us the water dashed against the stones
and rocks as if it were not already late evening. There was no reason
why one of us shouldn't jump on the parapet of the bridge.

In the distance a railway train emerged from behind a clump of
trees, all the carriages were lit up and no doubt the windows were
down. One of us started to sing a popular song, but then we all wanted
to sing. We sang much faster than the train was going, we swung our
arms because our voices weren't enough, we got our voices into a
scrum that delighted us. When you mix your voice with others you are
caught like a fish on a hook.

So we sang, with the forest at our backs, for the ears of the distant
travellers. In the village the grown-ups were still awake; our mothers
were preparing the beds for the night.

Now it was time. I kissed the boy standing nearest me, just gave
my hand to the next three, and set off on the way home, nobody called
me back. At the first cross-roads where they could no longer see me I
turned off, and ran by field paths back into the forest again. I was making for that town in the south of which it is said in our village:

'They're strange folk there! Just think, they never sleep!'
'And why's that?'
'Because they don't get tired.'
'And why's that?'
'Because they're fools.'
'Don't fools get tired?'
'How could fools get tired!'

Unmasking a Confidence Trickster

A T LAST I ARRIVED, about ten in the evening, outside the grand house where I was invited to a party, accompanied by a man who was already slightly known to me from earlier occasions and who had attached himself to me again out of the blue, dragging me through the streets for two whole hours.

'Well now!' said I, and clapped my hands to indicate the absolute necessity of parting company. I had made a number of less decisive efforts before. By now I was tired out.

'Are you going straight on up?' he asked. From his mouth came a sound like the chattering of teeth.

'Yes.'

After all, I was invited, I had told him that at the outset. But I had been invited to mount the steps to where I now so dearly wished to be, not to stand down here outside the gate staring past the ears of my opposite number. Nor indeed to fall silent with him now, as if we had determined on a prolonged occupation of this spot. It was a silence, moreover, in which the surrounding houses at once took part, and the darkness above them right up to the stars. And the footsteps of invisible strollers, whose routes one had no desire to guess, the wind that kept pressing itself against the other side of the street, a gramophone that was singing up against the closed windows of some room,—these made themselves heard out of this silence as if it belonged to them for all time past and to come.

And my companion submitted to all this on his own behalf, and— after a smile—on mine too; he stretched out his right arm along the top of the wall and rested his cheek on it, closing his eyes.

But I never saw that smile through to the end, for shame suddenly whirled me round. It had taken that smile for me to recognize that the man was a confidence trickster, nothing more. And yet I had been in this town for months by now, had supposed I knew these confidence tricksters through and through; the way they come out of side-streets at night to meet us, with their arms outstretched like innkeepers, the way they sidle round the advertising pillar by which we're standing as if playing hide-and-seek, and spy on us round the curve of the column with at least one eye, the way that they suddenly, when we become nervous at a street-crossing, hover in front of us on the edge of our pavement! For I understood them so well, indeed they had been my first acquaintances in the town's small taverns, and to them I owed my first glimpse of an obduracy which by now formed so much a part of my world that I was beginning to detect it in myself. How persistently they went on facing you, even when you had long since eluded them, so that there was nothing left for them to trick! How they refused to sit down, how they failed to collapse, but instead kept on sending you those looks which still remained compelling, if only from a distance! And their methods were always the same: they planted themselves in front of us, as broad as could be; tried to head us off from where we wanted to go; offered us in exchange a dwelling in their own breasts; and if our pent-up feelings finally burst out, they received them like an embrace into which they flung themselves face foremost.

And this time it had taken me so long in the man's company to spot the old games. I rubbed my finger-tips firmly together to undo the disgrace of it.

But meanwhile this fellow of mine was still propping himself up here as before, still regarding himself as a confidence trickster, and satisfaction with his lot glowed pink on his exposed cheek.

'Found out!' said I, and gave him a gentle tap on the shoulder. Then I hurried up the steps, and in the ante-room above the groundless devotion on the servants' faces rejoiced my heart like a pleasant surprise. I looked at them all in turn, while they took my coat and dusted off my boots. Then with a sigh of relief and drawing myself up to my full height I strode into the hall.

The Sudden Walk

'WHEN YOU SEEM finally to have made up your mind to spend the evening at home, when you have put on your smoking-jacket and settled down after supper with a light on the table to the piece of work or the game that usually occupies you till bedtime, when the weather outside is so unpleasant that it makes staying at home the obvious thing to do, when by now you have been sitting quiet at the table for so long that to go out would cause general astonishment, when the staircase is anyhow dark now and the front door locked, and when despite all this you get to your feet in a sudden fit of restlessness, change your jacket, promptly reappear dressed for the street, explain that you have to go out and after a brief word of good-bye actually do so, estimating the degree of irritation you may have left behind from the force with which you slam the flat door, when you then rediscover yourself down in the street, your limbs responding with particular agility to the unexpected freedom you have procured for them, when you feel all your decisiveness concentrated within you as a result of this one decisive act, when it strikes you with more than usual significance that your power to effect the swiftest of changes with ease and to cope with it outstrips your need to do so, and when in such mood you go striding down the long streets,—then for the space of that evening you have completely broken out of the ranks of your family, which veers off into the void, while you yourself, firm as can be, black with your sharpness of outline, slapping the back of your thighs, rise up to your true stature.

All this is intensified still further if at so late an hour of the evening you look up a friend to see how he is.

Resolutions

To RAISE ONESELF out of the depths of misery must be easy, even with a studied display of energy. I will wrench myself out of my chair, trot round the table, loosen up my head and neck, inject a gleam into my eyes, tauten the muscles surrounding them. Defy all my natural feelings, give A. an enthusiastic welcome if he comes, tolerate B. amicably in my room, swallow down everything that is said at C.'s place in long draughts, despite the labour and pain it costs me.

Yet even if I can manage all that, each false step—and they're bound to occur—will make the whole enterprise, easy or difficult, falter; and I shall have to turn back to the point where I began.

So in the end it remains advisable to accept whatever comes, to behave like an inert mass even if one feels oneself being swept away, not to be lured into a single unnecessary step, to regard others with the gaze of an animal, to feel no remorse, in short to crush with one's own hand any ghost of life that subsists, that is, to intensify the final quiet of the grave still further and let nothing beyond that endure.

A characteristic gesture in such a condition is to run one's little finger along one's eyebrows.

The Excursion into the Mountains

'I DON'T KNOW,' was my soundless cry, 'I really do not. If nobody comes, well then, nobody comes. I've done nobody harm, nobody's harmed me, yet nobody wants to help me. Just nobody. But that's not quite how it is. It's simply that nobody helps me—, apart from that, just Nobody would be fine. I'd really quite like to make an excursion—and why not—with a party of just Nobodies. Into the mountains, of course, where else? How these Nobodies crowd together, all these manifold arms, stretched out crosswise and linked together, all these manifold feet with tiny paces between them! It goes without saying that they all wear evening dress. We don't get along too badly, the wind blows through the gaps that we and our limbs leave open. Our throats become clear in the mountains! It's a wonder we don't start singing.'

The Fate of the Bachelor

IT SEEMS SO DREADFUL to remain a bachelor, to become an old man who must beg for hospitality with such dignity as he can muster each time he wants to spend an evening in human company, to be ill and stare for weeks on end at an empty room from your bed in the corner, always to have to say your goodbyes outside the front door, never to scurry upstairs with your wife at your side, to have in your room only side-doors that lead into other people's flats, to carry home your supper in your hand, to have to gaze in wonder at strange children and not be allowed constantly to repeat 'I do not have any', to model yourself in appearance and behaviour on one or two bachelors remembered from your youth.

That's how it will be, except that there you will stand in stark reality, each very day and from that day forward, with a body and a real head, that's to say a forehead too, for you to beat upon with your hand.

The Businessman

IT IS POSSIBLE that some people may feel sorry for me, but I see no sign of it. My small business fills me with worries that make my forehead and my temples ache, but without these offering any prospect of satisfaction, because my business is small.

Hours in advance I have to make my dispositions, I have to keep refreshing the storekeeper's memory, warn against mistakes that I fear may be made, and calculate each season the fashions of the next one, not as these may hold among the people of my circle but among inaccessible tribes of folk in the country.

My money is in the hands of strangers; their circumstances must remain a mystery to me; I cannot foresee what disaster might befall them; how could I avert it! Perhaps they have grown extravagant and are giving a banquet in some garden restaurant, and others are stopping off at this party before making good their escape to America.

When I come to lock up my premises at the end of a working day, and suddenly see hours stretching ahead of me in which I shall be able to do nothing to meet the incessant demands of my business, then the excitement which I had projected so far into the future that morning comes flooding back into me like an incoming tide, but it cannot contain itself there and sweeps me away again aimlessly with it.

And yet I can turn this mood to no purpose and can only go home, for my face and hands are dirty and sweaty, my coat stained and dusty, I am wearing my working cap and my boots are all scratched with the nails of crates. I move off then like a man afloat, snapping the fingers of both my hands and stroking the hair of the children I meet.

But the way is too short. I am home in no time, I open the door of the lift and step in.

I find that I'm now, quite suddenly, alone. Others who have to climb stairs get a bit tired as they climb; they have to wait with panting breath for someone to open the door of their flat, which gives cause for irritation and impatience; now they enter the hall where they hang up their hat, and it's not until they have got down the passage past several glass doors and into their room that are they alone.

But I am alone in the lift right away, and propped on my knees I gaze into the narrow mirror. As the lift begins to ascend I say:

'Now keep still, all of you; now stand back; would you like to disappear into the shade of the trees, behind the drapery at the windows, into the vaulted arcade?'

I am talking to my teeth, and the banisters of the staircase float down past the panes of frosted glass like a waterfall.

'Fly away then; may your wings, which I have never yet seen, carry you off to the country valley or off to Paris if you feel so inclined.

But make the most of the view from the window, when the processions converge out of three streets at once, not giving way but threading through one another and letting the square open out again between their parting ranks. Wave your handkerchiefs, be appalled, be touched, praise the beautiful lady driving past.

Cross over the stream by the wooden bridge, nod to the children bathing, and gasp at the cheer that rises from a thousand sailors on the distant warship.

Just you follow the inconspicuous little man, and when you have pushed him into a doorway, rob him and then watch him, each with your hands in your pockets, as he goes sorrowfully on his way down the left-hand street.

The scattered police on their galloping horses rein in their mounts and force you back. Let them; the empty streets will dishearten them, I know. What did I tell you, they're riding off in pairs already, slowly round the street corners, flying across the squares.'

Then I have to get out, send the lift down again, ring the doorbell, and the maid opens the door while I wish her good evening.

A Stray Glance from the Window

WHAT SHALL WE DO in these spring days that are fast coming on? Early this morning the sky was grey, but now if you go to the window you are surprised, and lean your cheek against the window-latch.

Down below you can see the rays of the sun, though it's setting already, on the face of the young girl who's just strolling along and looking about her, and at the same time you see her caught in the shadow of the man who comes striding up faster behind her.

Then the man has already passed by and the face of the child is quite bright.

The Way Home

HOW PERSUASIVE in its power is the air after a thunderstorm! My merits become apparent and overwhelm me, though admittedly I put up no resistance.

I march along and my pace is the pace of this side of the street, of the whole of this street, of this whole quarter. I am rightly responsible for all knocks on all doors and all raps on all tables, for all the toasts that are drunk, for the lovers in their beds, in the scaffolding of new buildings, pressed against walls in dark alleys, on the ottomans of the brothels.

I weigh my past against my future but find both of them excellent, can give neither the preference and have nothing to criticize save the injustice of a providence that favours me so.

Only when I enter my room do I feel a little reflective, though without having found anything worth reflecting on while climbing the stairs. It is no great help to me when I throw the window wide open and hear music still playing in a garden.

The Men Running Past

IF ONE IS WALKING along a street at night and a man who can be seen a long way off—for the street slopes uphill ahead of us and the moon is full—comes running towards us, then we shan't lay hands on him, even if he's feeble and ragged, even if someone else is running after him and shouting, but we'll let him run on.

For it is nighttime, and we can't help it if the street does slope uphill ahead of us in the full moon, and besides, perhaps these two have organized the chase for their own amusement, perhaps they are both of them pursuing a third man, perhaps the first man is being unjustly pursued, perhaps the second man intends to kill him and we would be implicated in the murder, perhaps the two know nothing of each other and each is simply running home to bed on his own initiative, perhaps they are sleepwalkers, perhaps the first man is armed.

And after all, haven't we a right to be tired, haven't we drunk so much wine? We're glad that we can't see the second man any more either.

The Passenger

I AM STANDING ON THE platform of the tram and am entirely uncertain as to my place in this world, in this town, in my family. Not even approximately could I state what claims I might justifiably advance in any direction. I am quite unable to defend the fact that I am standing on this platform, holding on to this strap, letting myself be carried along by this tram, and that people are getting out of the tram's way or walking along quietly or pausing in front of the shop windows.—Not that anyone asks me to, but that is immaterial.

The tram approaches a stop and a girl takes up her station near the step, ready to alight. She appears to me as distinctly as if I had run my hands over her. She is dressed in black, the pleats of her skirt are almost motionless, her blouse is tight-fitting and has a collar of white fine-mesh lace, her left hand is held flat against the side of the tram, the umbrella in her right rests on the second step from the top. Her face is brown; her nose, slightly pinched at the sides, is broad and round at the tip. She has a mass of brown hair, with some stray wisps blown over her right temple. Her small ear is close-set, but since I'm standing near her I can see the whole back of the right ear and the shadow at its root.

I wondered at the time: How is it that she is not astonished at herself, that she keeps her lips closed and says nothing of that kind?

Clothes

OFTEN WHEN I SEE CLOTHES with various pleats, frills and flounces which fit so beautifully on to a beautiful figure, I reflect that they never stay like that for long, but get creases that can't be ironed out, collect dust that lies so thick in the trimmings it can't be removed, and that no woman would wish to make herself so pathetic and ridiculous as to put on each morning and take off each evening the selfsame costly dress.

And yet I see girls who are certainly pretty, and have lots of delightful muscles and little bones and smooth skin and masses of fine hair to show, and they do, nonetheless, appear daily in this one natural fancy dress outfit, always laying the same face in the palms of the same hands and letting it be reflected from their looking-glass.

Only sometimes, in the evening, when they come back late from a party, does it seem to them in the glass to be threadbare, puffed up, dusty, too familiar to everyone and hardly wearable any longer.

The Rejection

WHEN I MEET a pretty girl and beg her: 'Please be so kind and come along with me,' and she goes by without saying a word, what she means is:

'You are no duke with extravagant name; no broad American, built like a Red Indian, with level imperturbable gaze, whose skin has been massaged by the winds of the prairies and the waters of the rivers flowing through them; you have made no journeys to the great lakes and voyaged there, wherever these exactly may be found. So why, I ask you, should a pretty girl like me go along with you?'

'You forget that no limousine carries you in long thrusts swaying through the street; nor can I see your escort of gentlemen, pressed into their suitings, following behind you in a strict semi-circle and murmuring their blessings on your head; your breasts are indeed neatly ordered in your bodice, but your thighs and your hips make up for that restraint; you're wearing a taffeta dress with pleats, like those which delighted every one of us last autumn, and yet—with this mortal danger upon you—you smile from time to time.'

'Yes, we are both quite right; and to keep us from being irrefutably aware of it we'd better, don't you think, go our separate ways home.'

For the Consideration of Amateur Jockeys

THERE IS NOTHING that can tempt one, if you think it over, to want to be the winner of a race.

The glory of being hailed the best rider in the country is a pleasure too heady, when the band strikes up, for remorse not to follow the next morning.

The envy of our opponents, wily and rather influential folk, is bound to distress us as we now ride in, through the narrow lane of the welcoming crowd, after that plain which soon lay empty ahead of us save for the puny figures of a few lapped riders charging the line of the horizon.

Many of our friends are in haste to collect their winnings, and can only shout their hurrahs to us over their shoulders from the far-off bookmakers' stalls; but our best friends never even betted on our horse, for they feared they must be angry if we lost; and now that our horse has come in first and they've not won a thing they turn away as we go past and rather contemplate the stands.

Our competitors behind us, firmly in the saddle, are trying to get the measure of the misfortune that has overtaken them and of the injustice that has somehow been inflicted on them; they assume a brisk expression, as if a new race were about to start and a serious one after this child's play.

To the eyes of many ladies the winner appears ridiculous, because he's swelling with pride and yet just cannot cope with the endless handshaking, saluting, bowing-and-scraping and distant waving, while the losers are keeping their mouths shut and giving their mounts, which are most of them whinnying, casual pats on the neck.

And finally from the now overcast sky it even begins to rain.

The Window on the Street

WHOEVER LEADS A SOLITARY life and yet now and then feels the need for some kind of contact, whoever wishes, in view of the never-ending changes in the hour of day, in the weather, in business affairs and so forth, just to have some arm or other that he might cling to within sight, such a man will not get by for long without a window on the street. And even if his state is such that he is not seeking anything at all and merely steps to the window-ledge as a weary man, letting his eyes wander up and down between the public and the sky, and he is reluctant to look and has his head tilted back a little, yet for all that the horses down below will drag him into the train of their waggons and their tumult and so in the end towards the harmony of man.

Longing to be a Red Indian

O H TO BE A RED INDIAN, instantly prepared, and astride one's galloping mount, leaning into the wind, to skim with each fleeting quivering touch over the quivering ground, till one shed the spurs, for there were no spurs, till one flung off the reins, for there were no reins, and could barely see the land unfurl as a smooth-shorn heath before one, now that horse's neck and horse's head were gone.

The Trees

FOR WE ARE like the trunks of trees in the snow. Apparently they rest smoothly on the surface and with a gentle push we should be able to shift them. No, that one cannot, for they are firmly attached to the ground. But see, that too is only apparent.

Unhappiness

WHEN IT HAD already become unbearable—once towards evening in November—and I went pacing down the strip of carpet in my room as if on a race-track, and then turned back in alarm at the sight of the brightly lit street, to find a fresh goal at the opposite end of the room in the depths of the wall mirror, and I screamed out loud, only to hear the scream which meets with no answer and which nothing can diminish in its power, so that it goes on rising without a counterbalance and cannot even stop after its sound has gone,—then from out of the wall the door burst open, with such great haste because haste was sorely needed, and even the carthorses down in the street were rearing up like horses crazed in battle, with their throats exposed.

From the pitch-dark corridor where the lamp was not yet lit, a small ghost of a child sallied forth, and stopped on its toes on a faintly swaying floorboard. Dazzled all at once by the half-light in the room, it made as if to bury its face in its hands, but then suddenly found relief in a glance to the window where beyond the bars the haze of the streetlights, rising from below, finally came to rest beneath the cover of darkness. There it stood, in front of the open door, with its right elbow propped against the wall, letting the draught from outside play round its ankles and brush over its neck and its temples.

I stared for a moment, then I said 'Good evening' and took my jacket from the fire-screen, not wanting to stand there half naked. For a short space I kept my mouth open to let my agitation escape that way. I had a nasty taste in my mouth and felt my eyelashes quivering; in fact this visit, though admittedly expected, was just about the last thing I needed.

The child was still standing on the same spot by the wall; it held its right hand pressed against the plaster and was lost in wonder, its cheeks bright pink, that the white-washed surface was grainy and chafed its fingertips. I said: 'Is it really me you're after? Isn't there some mistake? Nothing easier than to make a mistake in this big building. My name's So-and-so and I live on the third floor. So am I the person you want to see?'

'Hush, hush!' said the child over its shoulder, 'it's all quite in order.'

'Then come on in further, I'd like to close the door.'

'I've just this moment closed it. There's no need to trouble. Just keep entirely calm.'

'It's not a question of trouble. But a lot of people live on this corridor, I know them all of course; most of them get home from work about now; if they hear voices in one of the rooms they think they've a perfect right to march in and see what's going on. That's the way it is. These people have got their day's work behind them; who would they be likely to submit to in the evening, in the time that's provisionally their own! But you know that as well as I do. Allow me to close the door.'

'What do you mean? What's wrong with you? The whole house can come in as far as I'm concerned. And to repeat: I've already closed the door, do you think you're the only one who can close it? I've even turned the key.'

'That's all right then. That's all I want. There wasn't any need to lock it as well. And now that you're here, just make yourself comfortable. You are my guest. You can trust me completely. Don't be afraid to make yourself at home. I shan't force you either to stay or to leave. Do I have to tell you that? Do you know me so little?'

'No. You really didn't have to tell me that. What's more, you shouldn't have told me. I'm a child; why put on so much of a show for me?'

'There's no harm done. Of course, a child. But you're not so very small. You're quite well-grown already. If you were a girl it would hardly be right to lock yourself into a room with me like this.'

'We don't have to worry about that. I just wanted to say: my knowing you so well doesn't protect me much, it merely spares you the effort of telling me stories. And you're paying me compliments just the same. Do stop it, I really must ask you to stop it. And for another thing, I don't know you everywhere and all the time, especially not in this darkness. It would be much better if you were to light up. No, perhaps not. At any rate I'll bear it in mind that you've threatened me.'

'What's that? Threatened you? Come now. I'm simply delighted that you're here at last. I say "at last" because it's now quite late. I can't understand why you've come so late. So perhaps my delight at seeing you made me mix up what I was saying, and that's why you took it as you did. I'll admit ten times over that I did get mixed; all right, I threatened you with anything you like.—Let's not quarrel, for heaven's sake!—But how could you believe it? How could you hurt me so? Why are you so set on spoiling this brief little visit of yours? A mere stranger would be more inclined to meet me halfway than you are.'

'Now there I agree; that's no great discovery. However close any stranger might come to you, I'm as close to you as that by nature. And what's more you know it, so why this lamenting? If you want to put on an act, just say so, and I'll be off right away.'

'I see. So you even dare to tell me that? You are getting a little too bold. Don't forget, it's my room that you're in. It's my wall that you're rubbing your fingers against like mad. My own room, my own wall! And besides, what you say is not just impudent, it's ridiculous. You say your nature compels you to speak to me in this fashion. Really? Your nature compels you? That's nice of your nature. Your nature is mine, and if I'm being friendly by nature to you then you're not allowed to be otherwise.'

'Is that supposed to be friendly?'

'I'm talking about earlier on.'

'And do you know how I'll be later on?'

'I don't know a thing.'

And I walked over to the bedside table and lit the candle. At that time I had neither gas nor electric light in my room. Then I sat for a while at the table until I got tired of that too, put on my overcoat, picked up my hat from the sofa and blew out the candle. On my way out I tripped over the leg of a chair.

On the stairs I met a tenant from the same floor.

'Going out again, you old scoundrel?' he asked, pausing on his way with his legs astride two steps.

'What can I do?' I said, 'I've just had a ghost in my room.'

'You sound as much put out as if you'd just found a hair in your soup.'

'You can make fun of it. But I tell you, a ghost is a ghost.'

'True enough. But supposing one doesn't believe in ghosts anyway?'

'You don't think I believe in ghosts, do you? But how can my not believing help me?'

'Very simple. Then you don't need to be scared when a ghost actually comes.'

'Yes, but that's only a trivial fear. The real fear is the fear of what caused the apparition. And that fear won't go away. I'm full of it now, in all its splendour.' In my nervous state I began to search through all my pockets.

'But since the apparition itself didn't scare you, you could easily have asked what caused it!'

'Obviously you haven't ever spoken to ghosts. You can never get a straight answer out of them. It's all shilly-shallying. These ghosts seem more uncertain about their own existence than we are, which seeing how frail they are is no wonder.'

'I've heard that one can feed them up, though.'

'There you're well informed. That can be done. But who's likely to do it?'

'Why not? If it's a female ghost, for example,' said he, swinging himself up on to the higher step.

'Oh I see,' said I, 'but even then it's not worth it.'

I considered the matter. By now my neighbour had climbed so far that he had to lean out from a curve in the stair-well to see me. 'All the same,' I called out, 'if you take that ghost of mine up there away from me, then it's all over between us, for good.'

'Oh, I was only joking,' he said, withdrawing his head again.

'That's all right, then,' said I, and now there was really nothing to stop me taking a quiet walk. But because I felt so extremely forlorn I went back up the stairs and there to my bed.

THE JUDGEMENT

A Story

IT WAS A SUNDAY MORNING in the height of spring. Georg
Bendemann, a young businessman, was sitting in his own room on
the first floor of one of the small, lightly built houses which stretched
out in a long row beside the river, hardly distinguishable from one another except in height and colour. He had just finished a letter to an
old friend of his who was now living abroad, toyed with it for a while
as he slowly sealed it, and then, resting his elbow on his desk, he
looked out of the window at the river, the bridge and the rising ground
on the far bank with its faint show of green.

He recalled how many years ago this friend of his, dissatisfied with
his progress at home, had quite simply decamped to Russia. Now he
was carrying on a business in St Petersburg, which after a most encouraging start had apparently been stagnating for some time, as his
friend always complained on his increasingly rare visits. So there he
was, wearing himself out to no purpose in a strange land; his full,
foreign-looking beard only partially obscured that face which Georg
had known so well since childhood, with its yellowish skin that seemed
to indicate the growth of some disease. By his own account he had no
real contact with the colony of his fellow-countrymen out there, and
indeed hardly any social intercourse with Russian families, so that he
was resigning himself to becoming a permanent bachelor.

What should one write to such a man, who had so obviously taken
the wrong turning, whom one could be sorry for but could do nothing
to help? Should one perhaps advise him to come home again, to trans-

fer his business here, resume all his old personal connections—for there was nothing to prevent that—and rely for the rest on the support of his friends? But that would amount to telling him in so many words, and the more gently one did it the more offensive it would be, that all his efforts so far had failed, that he should finally abandon them, come back home, and be gaped at on all sides as a prodigal who has returned for good, that only his friends understood things and that he himself was a great baby who must simply do as he was told by these friends of his who had stayed put and been successful. And besides, was it even certain that all the pain that one would have to inflict on him would serve any purpose? Perhaps it wouldn't even be possible to get him back at all—he said himself that he had quite lost touch with affairs at home—and so he would just stay on out there in his remoteness, embittered by the advice offered to him and even further estranged from his friends. But if he really did follow their advice, only to find himself driven under on his return—not as the result of any malice, of course, but through force of circumstance—if he failed to get on either with his friends or without them, felt humiliated, and so became homeless and friendless in all earnest, wouldn't it be far better for him, in that case, to stay abroad as he was? Could one really suppose, in the circumstances, that he would make a success of life back here?

For these reasons it was impossible, assuming one wanted to keep up the correspondence with him at all, to send him any real news such as could be given unhesitatingly to even the most distant acquaintance. It was now more than three years since his friend had last been home, and he attributed this rather lamely to the uncertain political situation in Russia, which apparently was such as to forbid even the briefest absence of a small businessman while it permitted hundreds of thousands of Russians to travel around the world without a qualm. Precisely in the course of these last three years, however, Georg's own life had changed a lot. News of the death of Georg's mother—this had occurred some two years back, since when he and his aged father had kept house together—was something that had still reached his friend, and from the dry wording of his letter of condolence one could only conclude that the grief caused by such an event was impossible to imagine at a distance. Since then, in any case, Georg had applied himself to his business with greater determination, just as to everything else. Perhaps it was that his father, by insisting on running the business in his own way, had prevented him from taking any initiative of his own during his mother's lifetime, perhaps since her death his father, while still active in the business, had kept himself more in the background, perhaps—indeed this was highly probable—a series of fortunate accidents had played a far more important part, at all events the business had developed in a most unexpected way during these two years, the staff had had to be doubled, the turnover had increased fivefold and a further improvement undoubtedly lay ahead.

But Georg's friend had no inkling of this change. Earlier on he had tried—perhaps the last occasion had been in that letter of condolence—to persuade Georg to emigrate to Russia, and had enlarged on the prospects that were open in St Petersburg for precisely Georg's line of trade. The figures were minimal compared with the scale that his business had now assumed. But Georg had felt no inclination to write to his friend of his commercial successes, and if he were to do so now in retrospect it would certainly look peculiar.

As a result Georg merely contented himself with writing to his friend of such unimportant events as collect in one's mind at random when one is idly reflecting on a Sunday. His sole aim was not to disturb the picture of the home town which his friend had presumably built up during the long interval and had come to accept. Thus it happened that three times in three quite widely separated letters Georg had announced the engagement of some indifferent man to some equally indifferent girl, until quite contrary to his intentions his friend began to develop an interest in this notable occurrence.

However, Georg greatly preferred to write to him about things like these than confess that he had himself become engaged, a month ago, to a Fraulein Frieda Brandenfeld, a girl from a well-to-do family. He often talked to his fiancée of this friend of his, and of the special relationship which he had with him owing to their correspondence. 'So he won't be coming to our wedding,' said she, 'and yet I have a right to get to know all your friends.' 'I don't want to disturb him,' Georg replied, 'don't misunderstand me, he probably would come, at least I think so, but he would feel awkward and at a disadvantage, perhaps even envious of me, at all events he would be dissatisfied, and with no prospect of ever ridding himself of his dissatisfaction he'd have to go back again alone. Alone—do you realize what that means?'

'Yes, but may he not hear about our wedding in some other way?' 'I can't prevent that, certainly, but it's unlikely if you consider his circumstances.' 'If you've got friends like that, Georg, you should never have got engaged.' 'Well, we're both of us to blame there; but I wouldn't have it any other way now.' And when, breathing faster under his kisses, she still objected: 'All the same, it does upset me,' he thought it really couldn't do any harm to tell his friend the whole story. 'That's how I'm made and he must just take me as I am,' he said to himself, 'I can't fashion myself into a different kind of person who might perhaps make him a more suitable friend.'

And he did in fact report to his friend as follows, in the long letter which he wrote that Sunday morning, about the engagement that had taken place: 'I have saved up my best news for the end. I have become engaged to a Fraulein Frieda Brandenfeld, a girl from a well-to-do family which only settled here some time after you left, so that you are unlikely to know them. There will be opportunity later of giving you further details about my fiancée, but for today just let me say that I am very happy, and that as far as our mutual relationship is concerned the only difference is that you will find in me, in place of a quite ordinary friend, a happy friend. Furthermore you will acquire in my fiancée, who sends you her warm greetings and will shortly be writing to you personally, a genuine friend of the opposite sex, which is not wholly without its importance for a bachelor. I know there are many considerations which restrain you from paying us a visit, but would not my wedding be precisely the right occasion for flinging all obstacles aside? But however that may be, act just as seems good to you and entirely without regard.'

With this letter in his hand Georg had been sitting for a long time at his desk, his face turned to the window. He had barely acknowledged, with an absent smile, the greeting of a passing acquaintance from the street below.

At last he put his letter in his pocket and went out of his room across a little passage-way into his father's room, which he had not entered for months. There was indeed no call for him to go there in the normal course of events, for he saw his father regularly in the warehouse, they took their midday meal together in a restaurant, and while for the evening meal they made their separate arrangements they usually sat for a while afterwards in their common sitting-room, each with his own newspaper, unless Georg—as usually happened—went out with friends, or more recently went to call on his fiancée. Georg was amazed to find how dark his father's room was even on this sunny morning. What a shadow that high wall cast, rising up on the far side of the narrow courtyard. His father was sitting by the window, in a corner decked out with mementoes of Georg's lamented mother, reading a newspaper which he held up to his eyes at an angle so as to compensate for some weakness of vision. On the table stood the remains of his breakfast, not much of which appeared to have been consumed.

'Ah, Georg!' said his father, and rose at once to meet him. His heavy dressing-gown swung open as he walked, and the flaps of it fluttered round him. 'What a giant my father still is,' thought Georg.

'It's unbearably dark in here,' he then said.

'Yes, it is dark,' replied his father.

'And you've shut the window as well?'

'I prefer it like that.'

'Well, it's quite warm outside,' said Georg, as a kind of appendix to his previous remark, and sat down. His father cleared away the breakfast things and put them on a cabinet.

'I really just wanted to tell you,' Georg continued, his eyes helplessly following the old man's movements, 'that I've now written off to St Petersburg after all with the news of my engagement.' He drew the letter a little way out of his pocket and let it drop back again.

'To St Petersburg?' asked his father.

'To my friend, you know,' said Georg, seeking his father's eye.—In the warehouse he looks quite different, he thought, how he spreads himself out here in his chair and folds his arms across his chest.

'Indeed. To your friend,' said his father with emphasis.

'Well, you know, father, that I wanted to keep my engagement from him at first. Out of consideration for him, that was the only reason. You know yourself he's a difficult man. I said to myself, he may perhaps hear about my engagement from some other source, even though it's hardly probable in view of the solitary life he leads—I can't prevent that—but at all events he shan't hear about it from me.'

'And now you've had second thoughts?' asked his father, laying his great newspaper on the window-sill, and on top of that his spectacles, which he covered with his hand.

'Yes, now I've had second thoughts. If he's a true friend of mine, I said to myself, then my being happily engaged should make him happy too. And so I hesitated no longer about announcing it to him. But before I posted the letter I wanted to let you know.'

'Georg,' said his father, drawing his toothless mouth wide, 'listen to me! You have come to me in this matter to consult me about it. That does you credit, no doubt. But it means nothing, it means worse than nothing, if you don't now tell me the whole truth. I have no wish to stir up matters that don't belong here. Since the death of our dear mother certain rather distasteful things have occurred. Perhaps the time will come to speak of them too, and perhaps it will come sooner than we think. In the business there are a number of things which escape me, perhaps they aren't actually kept from me—I won't assume for the moment that they are kept from me—I'm no longer as strong as I was, my memory's failing, I can't keep track of so many different matters any more. That's the course of nature in the first place, and secondly the death of dear mother was a much greater blow to me than it was to you.—But since we're just on this particular matter, this letter, I beg you Georg, don't lie to me. It's a trivial thing, it's hardly worth mentioning, so don't lie to me. Have you really got this friend in St Petersburg?'

Georg rose to his feet in embarrassment. 'Never mind my friends. A thousand friends can't take the place of my father. Do you know what I think? You're not looking after yourself properly. But age needs to be treated with care. I can't get on in the business without you, you know that perfectly well, but if the business were to endanger your health I'd close it down tomorrow for good. This won't do. We'll have to make a change in your daily routine. A real, thorough change. Here you sit in the dark, and in the sitting-room you'd have plenty of light. You peck at your breakfast instead of taking proper nourishment. You sit with the window shut, and the air would do you so much good. No, father! I'll get the doctor to come and we'll follow his orders. We'll change our rooms round; you shall take the front room and I'll move in here. It won't mean any upset for you, all your belongings can be moved across too. But there's time enough for that, just lie down in your bed for a bit, you really must have some rest. Come, I'll help you off with your things, you'll soon see how well I can manage. Or if you'd rather go straight into the front room you can lie down in my bed for the time being. That would really be the most sensible thing.'

Georg stood close beside his father, who had let his head with its shaggy white hair sink on his chest.

'Georg,' said his father softly, without moving.

Georg knelt down by his father at once, and in his tired face he saw the over-large pupils staring at him fixedly from the corners of his eyes.

'You haven't any friend in St Petersburg. You always were a joker, and you've not even shrunk from playing your jokes on me. How could you have a friend out there of all places! I simply can't believe it.'

'Just cast your mind back, father,' said Georg, lifting his father out of his chair and taking off his dressing-gown as he stood there now quite feebly, 'it must be almost three years ago that this friend of mine was here visiting us. I still remember that you didn't particularly care for him. At least twice when you asked after him I denied his presence, though in fact he was sitting with me in my room all the time. As a matter of fact I could quite understand your dislike of him, my friend does have his peculiarities. But then later on you got on with him pretty well after all. At the time I felt really proud that you were listening to him, nodding to him and asking him questions. If you think back you're sure to remember. He used to tell the most incredible stories of the Russian Revolution. For instance, how he was on a business trip to Kiev, and during a riot he saw a priest on a balcony who cut a broad cross in blood on the palm of his hand, and then raised this hand and called out to the mob. You've even repeated that story once or twice yourself.'

Meanwhile Georg had succeeded in lowering his father into his chair again and carefully removing the knitted drawers he wore over his linen underpants, as well as his socks. The sight of these not particularly clean underclothes made him reproach himself for having neglected his father. It should certainly have been part of his duty to keep an eye on his father's changes of underclothes. Up till now he had not explicitly discussed with his fiancée what arrangements they were to make for his father's future, for they had silently assumed that he would remain on his own in the old flat. But now without more ado he resolved quite firmly to take his father with them into his future establishment. It almost looked, on closer inspection, as if the care he meant to devote to his father there might come too late.

He carried his father in his arms to the bed. During his few steps towards it he noticed with a terrible sensation that his father, as he lay against his breast, was playing with his watch-chain. He could not put him down on the bed straight away, so firmly did he cling to this watch-chain.

But no sooner was he in bed when all seemed well. He covered himself up and then drew the blanket extra high over his shoulders. He looked up at Georg with a not unfriendly eye.

'There you are, you're beginning to remember him now, aren't you?' Georg asked, nodding at him encouragingly.

'Am I well covered up now?' asked his father, as if he couldn't quite see whether his feet were properly tucked in.

'So you're feeling quite snug in bed already,' said Georg, and arranged the bedclothes more firmly round him.

'Am I well covered up?' asked his father once more, and seemed to await the answer with special interest.

'Don't worry, you're well covered up.'

'No!' shouted his father, sending the answer resounding against the question, flung back the blanket with such force that for an instant it unfurled flat in the air, and stood up erect on the bed. He just steadied himself gently with one hand against the ceiling. 'You wanted to cover me up, I know that, my young scoundrel, but I'm not covered up yet. And even if I'm at the end of my strength, it's enough for you and more than enough. Of course I know your friend. He would have been a son after my own heart. That's why you've been playing him false all these long years. Why else? Do you imagine I haven't wept for him? And that's why you lock yourself up in your office, no one's to disturb you, the master's busy—just so that you can write your deceitful little letters to Russia. But luckily no one has to teach a father to see through his son. And just when you think you've got him under, so firmly under that you can plant your backside on him and he won't move, then my fine son decides to get married!'

Georg gazed up at the nightmare vision of his father. The friend in St Petersburg, whom his father suddenly knew so well, touched his heart as never before. Lost in the vastness of Russia he saw him. At the door of his empty, plundered warehouse he saw him. Among the ruins of his stacks, the shreds of his wares, the falling gas-brackets, he was still just able to stand. Why had he had to go away so far?

'Now attend to me!' cried his father, and Georg, hardly aware of what he was doing, ran towards the bed to take everything in, but then stopped short half-way.

'All because she lifted her skirts,' his father began to flute, 'because she lifted her skirts like so, the repulsive little goose,' and to demonstrate it he hitched up his shirt so far that the scar of his war wound could be seen on his thigh, 'because she lifted her skirts like so and like so and like so, you made your pass at her, and so as to take your pleasure with her undisturbed you have besmirched your mother's memory, betrayed your friend, and stuck your father into bed so that he can't move. But can he move or can't he?' And he stood up quite unsupported, kicking his legs. He was radiant with insight.

Georg stood in a corner, as far away from his father as possible. A long time since he had firmly resolved to observe everything with the utmost attention, so that he should not somehow be surprised, outflanked, taken from the rear or from above. Just now he recalled this long-forgotten resolve, but it slipped from his mind again like a short thread being drawn through the eye of a needle.

'But your friend hasn't been betrayed after all!' cried his father, and his wagging forefinger confirmed it. 'I've been representing him here on the spot.'

'You comedian!' Georg couldn't restrain himself from calling out, then realized at once the harm done, and with starting eyes he bit—too late—on his tongue, so hard that the pain made him cringe.

'Yes, of course I've been playing a comedy! A comedy! Just the word for it! What other comfort was left to your old widowed father? Tell me—and for the space of your answer you shall be still my living son—what else was left to me, in my back room, hounded by disloyal staff, decrepit to the marrow of my bones? And my son went about the world exulting, concluding deals that I had prepared, falling over himself with glee, and stalking away from his father in the stiff mask of an honourable man! Do you suppose that I didn't love you, I from whom you sprang?'

Now he'll lean forward, thought Georg, what if he fell and smashed himself to pieces! These words went hissing through his brain.

His father leaned forward, but he did not fall. Since Georg failed to approach as he had expected, he straightened up again.

'Stay where you are, I've no need of you! You think you still have the strength to come over here, and that you're just hanging back of your own accord. Don't be too sure! I'm still the stronger by far. Perhaps on my own I might have had to give way, but as it is your mother has passed on her strength to me, I've formed a splendid alliance with your friend, I've got your clients here in my pocket!'

He's even got pockets in his shirt! said Georg to himself, supposing that with this phrase he could make him a laughing-stock in the eyes of the whole world. Only for a moment did he think so, for all the time he kept forgetting everything.

'Just link arms with your bride and try coming my way! I'll soon sweep her away from your side, you wait and see!'

Georg made grimaces as if he didn't believe it. His father merely nodded towards Georg's corner, confirming the truth of his words.

'How you amused me today, coming and asking me if you should tell your friend about your engagement. He knows it all already, you stupid boy, he knows it all! I've been writing to him, you see, because you forgot to take my writing things away from me. That's why he hasn't been here for such years now, he knows everything a hundred times better than you do yourself, he crumples up your letters unread in his left hand while he holds up my own letters to read in his right!'

He waved his arm over his head in his enthusiasm. 'He knows everything a thousand times better!' he cried.

'Ten thousand times!' said Georg, to make fun of his father, but in his very mouth the words turned to deadly earnest.

'For years I've been waiting for you to come out with this question! Do you suppose I concern myself with anything else? Do you suppose I read newspapers? There!' and he threw Georg a sheet of newspaper that had somehow found its way into bed with him. An old newspaper, with a name that was already quite unknown to Georg.

'How long you've delayed before coming to maturity! Your mother had to die, she was unable to witness the happy day, your friend is decaying in that Russia of his, three years ago he was already yellow enough for the scrap-heap, and as for me, you can see what condition I'm in. You've eyes enough for that!'

'So you've been lying in wait for me!' cried Georg.

In a pitying tone his father observed casually: 'I expect you meant to say that earlier. It's not to the point any more.'

And in a louder voice: 'So now you know what else there's been in the world besides you, until now you've known of nothing but yourself. You were an innocent child, it's true, but it's even more true that you've been a devilish human being!—And so hearken to me: I sentence you now to death by drowning!'

Georg felt himself driven from the room, the crash with which his father collapsed on the bed behind him still sounded in his ears as he ran. On the stairs, down which he sped as if skimming down a slope, he collided with the charwoman who was on her way up to the flat to do the morning cleaning. 'Jesus!' she cried and covered her face with her apron, but already he was gone. Out of the front door he sprang, across the roadway, towards the water he was driven. Already he was grasping at the railings as a starving man grasps at food. He swung himself over, like the outstanding gymnast who had once been his parents' pride. Still holding on, with a weakening grip, he spied through the railings a motor-bus that would easily cover the noise of his fall, called out softly: 'Dear parents, I did always love you,' and let himself drop.

At that moment the traffic was passing over the bridge in a positively unending stream.

THE STOKER

A Fragment

A S THE SIXTEEN-YEAR-OLD Karl Rossmann, who had been sent off to America by his poor parents because a maidservant had seduced him and had a child by him, sailed into the harbour of New York on the now slowly moving liner, he saw the Statue of Liberty, which he had been watching from far off, suddenly stand out as if in stronger sunlight. The arm with the sword stretched up as if newly /raised, and round the figure the free winds blew.

'So high!' he said to himself, and without any thought of leaving the ship he was gradually forced against the rail by the swelling crowd of the porters pushing past him.

A young man whom he had got to know slightly on the voyage called out in passing: 'Well, don't you feel like going ashore yet?' 'Oh, I'm quite ready,' said Karl with a laugh, and out of sheer high spirits and being a strong young lad he hoisted his trunk on to his shoulder. But as he cast an eye over his acquaintance, who was already moving off with the others and giving a twirl or two to his stick, it struck him with dismay that he had forgotten his own umbrella down below. He hastily begged his acquaintance, who did not seem any too pleased, to be kind enough to wait by his trunk for a moment, just paused to check his position so as to be sure of finding his way back, and went hurrying off. Once he got below he was sorry to discover that a gangway, which would have shortened his route considerably, was now for the first time barred, probably in connection with the disembarking of all the passengers, and he had to find his way with difficulty through a host of little rooms, down short stairways which kept following one another, along corridors with endless turnings, through an empty room with a deserted writing-desk, until in the end, since he had only been this way once or twice before and always with a crowd of others, he found himself completely lost. In his bewilderment, and since he came across no one and could hear nothing but the constant shuffling of the thousand human feet above him, and from the distance, like a gasp, the final heavings of the shut-off engines, he began without thinking to hammer on a little door by which he had chanced to stop in his wanderings.

'It's not locked,' came a shout from within, and Karl opened the door with a genuine sigh of relief. 'Whatever are you hammering so madly on the door for?' asked a huge man, with hardly even a glance at Karl. Through some kind of overhead hatch a glimmer of murky light, long since stale from its use on the decks above, fell into the miserable cabin in which a bunk, a cupboard, a chair and the man stood packed close together, as if stored away there. 'I've lost my way,' said Karl, 'I never really noticed it during the voyage, but it's a terribly big ship.' 'Yes, you're right there,' said the man with a certain pride, and went on fiddling with the lock of a little chest, which he kept pressing to with both hands to hear how the catch snapped home. 'Come on in, then!' the man went on, 'you don't want to stand around out there!' 'Aren't I disturbing you?' asked Karl. 'Good Lord no, no fear of that!' 'Are you a German?' Karl asked to reassure himself, for he had heard a lot about the perils which threatened newcomers to America, especially from the Irish. 'That I am, that I am,' said the man. Karl still hesitated. Then the man abruptly seized the door-handle, and pulling the door to with a jerk he swept Karl into the cabin towards him. 'I can't stand people staring in at me from the gangway,' said the man, now working away at his chest again, 'every man-jack who walks by peers in, I'd like to know who'd put up with it!' 'But the gangway's quite empty,' said Karl, who was standing uncomfortably squeezed against the end of the bunk. 'Yes, it is now,' said the man. 'But it's now we're talking about,' thought Karl, 'it's hard to communicate with this man.' 'Why not lie on the bunk, you'll have more room there,' said the man. Karl crawled in as best he could, and laughed out loud at his first unsuccessful attempt to swing himself across. But hardly was he properly in when he cried: 'For heaven's sake, I've quite forgotten my trunk!' 'Why, where is it then?' 'Up on deck, someone I met is

keeping an eye on it. Now whatever's his name?' And he fished out a
visiting-card from the secret pocket that his mother had sewn for him,
especially for the voyage, into the lining of his jacket. 'Butterbaum,
Franz Butterbaum.'

'Do you need your trunk so badly?' 'Of course I do.' 'Well then,
why did you give it to a stranger?' 'I'd left my umbrella below and ran
off to fetch it, but I didn't want to lug my trunk along with me. And
then I lost my way, too.' 'Are you on your own? No one travelling with
you?' 'Yes, I'm on my own.' 'Perhaps I ought to stick to this man,' it
occurred to Karl, 'where am I going to find a better friend all at once.'
'And now you've lost your trunk as well. Not to mention the umbrella.' And the man sat himself down on the chair as if Karl's affair
had now acquired a certain interest for him. 'But I don't believe the
trunk really is lost yet.' 'You can believe what you like,' said the man,
giving a vigorous scratch to his thicket of short dark hair, 'but on
board ship the morals change with the ports. In Hamburg maybe your
Butterbaum might have looked after your trunk, here there's most
likely no trace of either of them any more.' 'But then I must go up and
check at once,' said Karl, looking round to see how he could get out.
'You just stay where you are,' said the man, and he put a hand against
Karl's chest and pushed him quite roughly back into the bunk. 'But
why?' Karl asked crossly. 'Because there's no point in it,' said the man,
'I'm going myself in just a moment, and then we can go together. Either the trunk's stolen and then there's no help for it, or the fellow's
still watching over it, in which case he's a fool and had better carry on
watching, or else he's simply an honest man and has left it where it
was, and then we'll find it all the more easily when the ship's quite
empty. And the same goes for your umbrella.' 'Do you know your way
around the ship?' asked Karl suspiciously, and it seemed to him that
there must be a hidden snag in the otherwise plausible notion that his
things would be easier to find on the empty ship. 'But I'm a stoker,'
said the man. 'You're a stoker!' cried Karl delightedly, as if this sur-
passed all his expectations, and propping himself up on his elbows he
looked at the man more closely. 'Just outside the little compartment
where I slept with the Slovaks there was an opening made in the wall
through which you could see into the engine-room.' 'Yes, that's where
I've been working,' said the stoker. 'I've always been so interested in
mechanical things,' said Karl, pursuing his own particular line of
thought, 'and I'd certainly have become an engineer later on if I

hadn't had to leave for America.' 'Why did you have to leave, then?' 'Oh, that!' said Karl, dismissing the whole business with a wave of his hand. At the same time he looked at the stoker with a smile, as if asking his indulgence for what he had not even admitted. 'There was some reason, I suppose,' said the stoker, and it was hard to tell whether he was encouraging Karl to explain it or not. 'Now I could become a stoker too,' said Karl, 'my parents don't care a bit now what I become.' 'My job's going to be free,' said the stoker, and in his full consciousness of the fact he stuck his hands into his trouser pockets and flung his legs, in their creased and leathery iron-grey trousers, up on the bunk to stretch them. Karl had to move over closer to the wall. 'Are you leaving the ship?' 'That's right, we're moving off today.' 'But why's that? Don't you like it?' 'Well, it's the circumstances, you see, it isn't always a matter of whether you like the job or not. Actually you're right, I don't like it either. I don't suppose you're seriously thinking of being a stoker, but that's just when it's easiest to become one. So I advise you strongly against it. If you wanted to study in Europe, why don't you want to here? The American universities are infinitely much better than the European ones.' 'Maybe they are,' said Karl, 'but I've hardly got any money for studying. I did once read about someone who worked in a shop all day and studied at night, until he got a doctor's degree and became a mayor I think, but that needs a lot of perseverance, doesn't it? I'm afraid I haven't got that much. Anyhow I wasn't particularly good at school, I really wasn't a bit sorry to leave. And perhaps the schools here are even stricter. I hardly know any English at all. And anyway people here have got a prejudice against foreigners, I believe.' 'So you've come up against that too, have you? That's all right, then. Then you're my man. Look, here we are on a German ship, it belongs to the Hamburg–America Line, so why aren't we all Germans here? Why is the chief engineer a Rumanian? He's called Schubal. It's beyond belief. And this miserable swine grinds us Germans down on a German ship. Don't you imagine'—he had to pause for breath, he flapped about with his hand—'that I'm complaining just for the sake of it. I know you've got no influence and you're just a poor lad yourself. But it's too bad!' And he thumped the table several times with his fist, keeping his eye fixed on it with every thump. 'I've served my time on so many ships'—and he reeled off twenty names one after the other like a single word, Karl felt quite dizzy—'and I've distinguished myself, I've been praised, my work's always been just what the captain wanted, I even served some years on the same merchantman'—he rose to his feet, as if this had been the high point of his life—'and here on this tub, where everything's done by the book and you need no wits at all, here I'm no good, here I'm always in Schubal's way, I'm a slacker, I deserve to be slung out and only get my pay as a favour. Can you understand that? I can't.' 'You mustn't put up with that,' said Karl in great excitement. He had almost lost all sense of being on the unsure ground of a ship, off the coast of an unknown continent, so much did he feel at home down here on the stoker's bunk. 'Have you been to the captain? Have you asked him to see that you get your rights?' 'Oh, get away with you, get away. I don't want you here. You pay no attention to what I say, and then you give me advice. How am I supposed to go and see the captain!' And the stoker sat down again wearily and laid his face in his hands.

'There's no better advice I can give him,' said Karl to himself. And it seemed to him that he would have done altogether better to have fetched his trunk than to stay down here offering advice that was merely considered stupid. When his father had handed the trunk over to him for good he had asked him jokingly: 'How long will you keep it?' and now this precious trunk was perhaps already lost in earnest. The only consolation was that his father could hardly learn of his present situation, even if he did make inquiries. The last news the shipping company could give was simply that he had got as far as New York. But Karl did feel sorry that he had hardly used the things in the trunk yet, despite the fact that he ought, for example, to have changed his shirt long before now. So that really had been a false economy; just now, right at the start of his career when it was so essential to turn up neatly dressed, he would have to appear in a dirty shirt. Otherwise the loss of his trunk would not have been too dreadful, for the suit he had on was in fact better than the one in the trunk, which was actually only a spare one for emergencies that his mother had had to patch up for him just before he left. Then he also remembered that there was still a piece of Veronese salami in his trunk, which his mother had put in as a special extra, but he had only eaten the smallest bit of it, for he had been quite without appetite during the voyage and the soup that was served out in the steerage had been amply sufficient for him. But now he would have been glad to have the salami at hand, so as to present it to the stoker. For such people are easily won over if one slips them some trifle; Karl had learnt that from his father, who won over all the minor employees with whom he had business by distributing cigars. All that Karl had got left to give away at present was his money, and if his trunk was perhaps already lost he did not want to touch that for the time being. Again his thoughts returned to the trunk, and he now really failed to understand why he had watched over it during the voyage so closely that the watch had almost cost him his sleep, if he had now allowed this same trunk to be removed from him so easily. He remembered the five nights during which he had permanently suspected a little Slovak, who was lying two berths away to his left, of having designs on his trunk. This Slovak had merely been waiting for the moment when Karl, overcome by weakness, should finally doze off for a second so that he could use a long pole, which he was always playing with or practising with during the day, to draw the trunk over to him. By day this Slovak looked innocent enough, but hardly had the night come when he kept getting up from his berth and casting melancholy glances in the direction of Karl's trunk. Karl was able to see this quite clearly, for there was always someone here or there who with the restlessness of the emigrant lit some little light, though this was forbidden by the ship's regulations, and attempted to decipher the incomprehensible brochures of the emigration agencies. If a light of this kind was close at hand then Karl could doze off for a little, but if it was in the distance or if all was dark then he had to keep his eyes open. The strain of this had quite exhausted him, and now perhaps it had been all in vain. Oh, that Butterbaum, if ever he should come across him again somewhere!

At that moment the silence outside the cabin, which up to then had been total, was broken by sounds coming from the far distance, a series of little short taps like the tapping of children's feet; these came nearer, growing steadily louder, and now it was the calm tread of marching men. They were evidently moving in single file, as was natural in the narrow gangway, and a clinking could be heard like the clink of weapons. Karl, who had been on the point of stretching out in the bunk for a sleep undisturbed by all worries about trunks and Slovaks, started up and gave the stoker a nudge to alert him urgently, for the head of the procession seemed to have just reached their door. 'That's the ship's band,' said the stoker, 'they've been playing up on deck and now they're going off to pack. All's clear now and we can go. Come along!' He grabbed Karl by the hand, took down at the last moment a little framed Madonna from the wall above the bunk, which he

stuffed into his breast pocket, then he seized his chest and led Karl
rapidly with him out of the cabin.

'Now I'm going to the office and I'll give those gentlemen a piece
of my mind. The passengers have all gone, so I don't have to mind
what I say.' The stoker kept on repeating this with variations, and as
he went along he kicked out sideways to stamp on a rat that was crossing their path, but he merely drove it faster into its hole which it had
just reached in time. He was altogether slow in his movements, for
though his legs were long they were just too heavy.

They passed through a part of the kitchen, where some girls in
dirty aprons—they splashed them deliberately—were washing dishes
in great tubs. The stoker called a girl by the name of Line over to him,
put an arm round her hips and led her along with him a little way,
while she kept saucily pressing herself against his arm. 'It's pay-out
time now, do you want to come along?' he asked. 'Why should I
bother, you bring the money here,' she replied, slipping out from under his arm and running off. 'Where did you pick up the pretty boy,
then?' she called out after him, but without waiting for an answer. A
burst of laughter could be heard from all the girls, who had interrupted their work.

But they went on and came to a door which had a little pediment
above it, supported by little gilded caryatids. For a ship's fitting it
looked positively extravagant. Karl realized that he had never set foot
in this part of the ship; probably during the voyage it had been reserved for the first- and second-class passengers, whereas the parti-
tions had now been taken out to prepare for the great swabbing down.
Indeed they had already met some men with brooms on their shoulders who had greeted the stoker. Karl was amazed at the great amount
of activity, which of course he had hardly been aware of down below.
There were also wires of electrical installations running along the
gangways and a little bell kept constantly ringing.

The stoker knocked respectfully at the door, and when someone
called 'Come in!' he indicated to Karl with a wave of the hand that he
should step bodly in. This he did, but once inside the door he stopped.
Out beyond the three windows of the room he beheld the waves of the
sea, and as he watched their buoyant movement his heart leapt, as if he
had not been looking at the sea continuously for five long days. Great
ships crossed one another's course, yielding to the swell only so far as
their weight allowed. If one half closed one's eyes these ships seemed

to be staggering under their own sheer weight. At their masts they bore slim but elongated flags which were drawn taut by the ship's way and yet flapped to and fro a little. Salute volleys, probably fired by warships, could be heard; one such ship was passing quite close and its gun-barrels, gleaming with the sunlight on their steel casing, were as if caressed by its sure and smooth though undulating progress through the water. The smaller ships and boats were, at least from the door, only visible in the distance, as they darted in swarms through the gaps between the great ships. But behind all this stood New York and looked at Karl with the hundred thousand windows of its skyscrapers. Yes, in this room one knew where one was.

At a round table three gentlemen were sitting, one of them a ship's officer in blue ship's uniform, the other two officials of the harbour authority in black American uniforms. On the table lay a great pile of various documents, which the officer first glanced over with pen in hand before passing them on to the others, who now perused them, now made excerpts, now tucked them away in their folders, except when one of the two, who was constantly making little noises with his teeth, dictated something to his colleague for the record.

At a desk by one window there sat a smaller gentleman, with his back to the door, who was busying himself with great ledgers that were ranged on a stout book-shelf at head height in front of him. Beside him stood an open cash box, which at least at first glance appeared to be empty.

The second window was clear and provided the best view. But near the third stood two gentlemen, conversing in low tones. One of them, leaning against the wall by the window, also wore ship's uniform and was playing with the hilt of his sword. The man he was speaking to was facing the window, and now and then some movement of his revealed part of the row of decorations on the other man's breast. He was in civilian clothes and carried a thin bamboo cane which, since he kept both his hands firmly on his hips, also stuck out like a sword.

Karl did not have much time to take all this in, for soon a steward came up to them and asked the stoker, giving him a look as if he had no business here, what it was he wanted. The stoker replied, as softly as he had been asked, that he wanted to speak to the chief purser. The attendant dismissed this request for his own part with a wave of his hand, but all the same he went on tiptoe, giving the round table a wide berth, to the gentleman with the great ledgers. This gentleman—one could see it clearly—positively froze at the steward's words, but at last he turned round to face this man who wished to speak to him, and proceeded to gesticulate in a sternly dismissive manner towards the stoker, and for safety's sake at the steward too. Thereupon the steward returned to the stoker and said in the tone of one passing on a confidential message: 'Clear out of this room at once!'

On hearing this response the stoker looked down at Karl, as if Karl were his heart to which he was silently bewailing his sorrow. Without stopping to think Karl launched himself forward, he ran straight across the room and even brushed against the officer's chair in passing; the steward set off too, at a crouching run, with his outspread arms ready to grab, as if he were pursuing some kind of vermin; but Karl was the first to reach the chief purser's desk, to which he held on tight in case the steward should try to drag him away.

Naturally the whole room sprang to life at once. The ship's officer at the table had leapt to his feet; the officials from the harbour authority were looking on calmly but attentively; the two gentlemen at the window had moved shoulder to shoulder; the steward, who considered himself out of place where the high and mighty were already showing interest, stepped back. The stoker by the door waited tensely for the moment when his help should be needed. And finally the chief purser swung himself round emphatically to the right in his armchair.

Karl rummaged in his secret pocket, which he had no qualms about exposing to these people, and drew out his passport which he laid open on the desk in lieu of further introduction. The chief purser appeared to think this passport irrelevant, for he twitched it aside with two fingers, whereupon Karl, as if this formality had been satisfactorily concluded, returned it to his pocket.

'May I be allowed to say,' he then began, 'that in my opinion an injustice has been done to this stoker gentleman. There's a certain man called Schubal aboard who treats him badly. He has served on a great many ships, all of which he can name for you, and has given complete satisfaction; he is hard-working, he takes his job seriously, and it's really hard to see why on this particular ship, where the duties aren't so excessively onerous as they are for instance on merchantmen, he shouldn't be able to perform them properly. So it can't be anything but slander that is blocking his advance and robbing him of the credit that he would most definitely be getting otherwise. I have only given a general outline of this matter; he can give you an account of his spe-

cific complaints himself.' Karl had addressed this speech to all the gentlemen present, because in fact they were all listening, and because it
seemed much more likely that one just man should be found among
the whole number than that this just man should happen to be the
chief purser. Karl had also cunningly concealed the fact that he had
only known the stoker for such a short time. But he would also have
spoken a great deal better if he had not been distracted by the red face
of the gentleman with the bamboo cane, which was visible to him for
the first time from where he now stood.

'It's all true, every single word,' said the stoker, before anyone had
asked him anything or indeed even looked in his direction. This over-
hastiness on the stoker's part would have been a great mistake, had not
the gentleman with the decorations, who as it now suddenly dawned
on Karl was without doubt the captain, evidently already made up his
mind to give the stoker a hearing. For he stretched out his hand and
called to the stoker: 'Come here!' with a voice firm enough to strike
with a hammer. Now everything depended on how the stoker con-
ducted himself, for as far as the justice of his cause was concerned Karl
had no doubts whatever.

Fortunately it became clear at this point that the stoker was a man
who had seen a good deal of the world. With exemplary calm he drew
out of his little chest, with an unerring hand, a small sheaf of papers
together with a notebook; he then walked over with these to the captain, as if this were the obvious course and completely ignoring the
chief purser, and spread out his pieces of evidence on the window-
ledge. The chief purser had no alternative but to make his own way
across. 'The man is a notorious complainer,' he said by way of explanation, 'he spends more time in this office than he does in the engine-
room. He's driven Schubal, that calm fellow, almost to distraction.
Now just you listen!'—here he turned to the stoker—'This time
you're really taking your impertinence too far. How many times have
you been slung out of the pay-rooms already, as you richly deserve,
with your wholly, completely and invariably unjustified demands!
How many times have you then come running here to the purser's
office! How many times have you been told in a friendly way that
Schubal is your immediate superior, and that he and he alone is the
one you have to come to terms with! And now you actually come
along here when the captain's present, and unashamedly pester even
him; and for good measure you have the effrontery to bring this young

lad with you, whom you've trained as the mouthpiece for your taste-
less accusations, a lad whom I've never so much as seen on the ship
before!'

Karl forcibly restrained himself from springing forward. But the
captain had already intervened by saying: 'Let us hear what the man
has to say. Schubal is in any case becoming a great deal too independent for my liking, though by that I don't mean to imply anything in
your favour.' This last remark was addressed to the stoker; it was only
natural that he couldn't take his side at once, but everything seemed to
be going the right way. The stoker began to state his case, and he controlled himself at the outset so far as to give Schubal the title of 'Mis-
ter'. How Karl rejoiced beside the chief purser's abandoned desk,
where he kept pressing down the letter-scales for sheer pleasure.—Mr
Schubal is unfair! Mr Schubal favours the foreigners! Mr Schubal ordered the stoker out of the engine-room and made him clean lavato-
ries, which certainly wasn't the stoker's job!—On one occasion Mr
Schubal's competence was even called in question, it being allegedly
more apparent than real. At this point Karl looked at the captain intently, in a confiding manner as if he were a colleague of his, just to
ensure that he should not become influenced against the stoker by his
somewhat unfortunate manner of expressing himself. But the fact remained that nothing definite emerged from the torrent of words, and
even though the captain still stared fixedly ahead of him, his eyes expressing the resolve to hear the stoker this time through to the end,
the other gentlemen were growing impatient, and soon the stoker's
voice no longer held undisputed sway in the room, which was an omi-
nous sign. First the gentleman in civilian clothes brought his bamboo
cane into play and began tapping, though gently, on the parquet floor.
The other gentlemen naturally looked his way from time to time; the
harbour officials, who were clearly pressed for time, took up their documents again and began, if only somewhat absently, to glance through
them; the ship's officer moved closer to his table again, and the chief
purser, who by now believed he had won the day, heaved an ironic
sigh. This general dispersal of interest seemed to affect everyone but
the steward, who could sympathize to some extent with the sufferings
of the poor man surrounded by the great and nodded earnestly to Karl
as if he wanted to explain something.

Meanwhile the life of the harbour was proceeding outside the windows; a flat cargo boat with a mountain of barrels, which must have

been wonderfully stowed for them not to start rolling, moved slowly past and plunged the room into near darkness; little motorboats, which Karl might have observed more closely if he had had time, whisked straight as arrows through the water, obeying the slightest touch of the man standing erect at the wheel; here and there curious floating objects bobbed of their own accord out of the restless waves, only to be submerged again at once and sink before his astonished eyes; boats from the ocean liners were pulled past by sailors straining at the oars, full of passengers who were sitting still and expectant, just as they had been squeezed in, even though some of them could not refrain from turning their heads to gaze at the shifting scenery. A movement without end, a restlessness passed on from the restless element to the helpless human beings and their works!

But everything called for haste, for clarity, for the most accurate description, and what was the stoker doing! He was certainly talking himself into a lather, he had long since been incapable of holding in his trembling hands the papers laid out on the window-ledge, from every point of the compass complaints about Schubal kept flooding into his head, each single one of which should in his opinion have been enough to bury this Schubal for good, but all he was able to produce for the captain was a pathetic jumble of the whole lot mixed together. For some while now the gentleman with the bamboo cane had been whistling softly up at the ceiling; the harbour officials had managed to anchor the ship's officer at their table and showed no sign of ever letting him go again; the chief purser was evidently only being restrained from bursting out by the calmness of the captain; the steward was standing to attention, waiting to receive his captain's orders regarding the stoker at any moment.

At this point Karl could remain inactive no longer. He therefore advanced slowly towards the group, turning over in his mind all the more rapidly how he might tackle the situation as adroitly as possible. It really was high time; only a little while longer and they might both of them be thrown out of the office. The captain might indeed be a good man, and he might in addition, or so it seemed to Karl, have some special reason at present for showing himself as a just master, but after all he was not some instrument that one could hammer away at until it fell apart—and that was exactly how the stoker was treating him, though admittedly out of the boundless indignation of his heart.

So Karl said to the stoker: 'You must tell the story more simply, more clearly, the captain can't appreciate it properly the way you are telling it now. Do you suppose he knows all the engineers and the ship's boys by name, let alone by their first names, so that you only have to pronounce one of these names for him to know who you mean? Sort your complaints out a bit, explain the most important ones first and then the others in descending order, then perhaps it mayn't even be necessary to mention most of them. You've always explained it so clearly to me!' If one could steal trunks in America one could also tell an occasional fib, so he thought to excuse himself.

If only this might have helped! But perhaps it was already too late in any case? The stoker did indeed break off at once when he heard the familiar voice, but his eyes were so blinded with the tears of wounded pride, of dreadful memories, of his most extreme present distress, that he was hardly capable of recognizing Karl any more. And how could he at this stage—Karl silently acknowledged this as he faced his now silent friend—how could he at this stage suddenly change his whole way of putting things, when it seemed to him that he had already said all there was to say without getting the slightest response, and on the other hand that he had not yet even started and could hardly now expect these gentlemen to hear the whole thing through from the beginning. And at a time like this along comes Karl, his sole supporter, and wants to hand out good advice, but instead merely succeeds in showing him that all is utterly lost.

'If only I'd come forward sooner instead of gazing out of the window,' Karl told himself, lowering his eyes before the stoker, and he stood to attention, clapping his hands to his sides as a sign that all hope was gone.

But the stoker misunderstood this, he probably scented in Karl's behaviour some kind of secret reproach directed against him, and with the honest intention of talking him out of it he now proceeded to crown his misdeeds by starting to wrangle with Karl. Now of all times, when the gentlemen at the round table had long since become exasperated by the futile babble that was disturbing their important work, when the chief purser was gradually beginning to find the captain's patience incomprehensible and threatened to explode at any moment, when the steward, by now fully restored to the sphere of his masters, was measuring the stoker with wild looks, and when finally the gentleman with the bamboo cane, to whom the captain himself sent a friendly glance from time to time, being already completely stultified and indeed repelled by the stoker drew out a little notebook and began, with his mind obviously on quite other matters, to let his eyes wander to and fro between the notebook and Karl.

'Yes I know, I know,' said Karl, who was having difficulty in resisting the torrent that the stoker was now directing at him but still managed in the heat of the dispute to let a smile of friendship shine through, 'you're in the right, you're in the right, I've never once doubted it.' He would have liked to hold the stoker's flailing hands for fear of being struck by them, but he would have liked even more to press him into some corner so as to whisper a few soothing words to him that no one else need hear. But the stoker was past all bounds. Karl now even began to find some comfort in the thought that if need be the stoker could overwhelm all the seven men present with the strength of his desperation. On the desk, however, as a glance in that direction revealed, lay an attachment with an array of far too many push-buttons, connected to electric wires; a single hand pressed down on that would be enough to have the whole ship, with all its gangways full of hostile men, up in arms.

Here the gentleman with the bamboo cane, who had been displaying so little interest, stepped up to Karl and asked, not too loudly but audibly enough above all the stoker's shouting: 'What is your name, may I ask?' At that moment, as if someone behind the door had been awaiting this remark by the gentleman, there came a knock. The steward looked across at the captain; the captain nodded. At this the steward went to the door and opened it. Outside stood a man of medium build, dressed in an old frock-coat; to judge from his appearance he was not exactly cut out for work on the engines but nevertheless he was—Schubal. If Karl had not realized this from the look in everyone's eyes, which expressed a certain satisfaction from which even the captain was not exempt, it must have become clear to him, to his horror, from the stoker, who clenched his fists at the end of his outstretched arms with such force that this clenching seemed to be the most essential part of him, for which he was ready to sacrifice all the life in his body. His entire strength, even the strength that kept him upright, was now concentrated there.

And so here was the enemy, all fresh and sprightly in his formal dress, with an account book under his arm that probably contained the records of the stoker's work and pay, and he made it unashamedly clear, by scanning all the faces in turn, that his first aim was to assess

the mood of each individual. The seven were already his friends in any
case, for even if the captain had previously harboured—or perhaps
only pretended to harbour—certain reservations about him, he could
probably, after all the pain that the stoker had inflicted on him, no
longer find the slightest fault with Schubal. In the case of a man like
the stoker no measures could be too severe, and if Schubal could be
reproached for anything, it was for not having subdued the recalci-
trance of the stoker sufficiently in the course of time to prevent him
from daring to appear before the captain now.

But one might perhaps still have assumed that the confrontation of
the stoker and Schubal could not fail to have the same effect upon men
as it would warrant before a higher tribunal, for however cunning
Schubal might be at disguise there was no reason to suppose that he
could keep it up to the end. A single flash of his evil nature would be
enough to make it obvious to these gentlemen, and Karl intended to
see to that. He already had a rough idea of the perceptiveness, the
weaknesses, the moods of the individual gentlemen, and from that
point of view the time he had already spent here had not been wasted.
If only the stoker had been in better shape, but he seemed to be completely out of action. If someone had held Schubal in front of him, he
could probably have cracked open his hated skull with his fists. But
even to take those few steps across to him was probably more than he
could manage. Why then had Karl not foreseen what could have been
foreseen so easily, that Schubal was bound to turn up in the end, if not
of his own accord then summoned by the captain. Why had he not
on his way here with the stoker discussed a precise plan of campaign,
instead of simply walking in when they came to a door, as they had
in fact done, hopelessly unprepared? Was the stoker still capable of
speech at all, of saying yes and no, as he would have to when cross-
examined, if indeed cross-examination was not too much to hope for?
There he stood with his legs apart, his knees a little bent, his head
slightly raised, and the air passed in and out of his open mouth as if
there were no longer any lungs within to deal with it.

On the other hand Karl himself felt more vigorous and alert than
he had perhaps ever felt at home. If only his parents could see him
now, fighting for a good cause in a foreign land, before persons of
standing, and even though not yet triumphant holding himself in
complete readiness for the final conquest! Would they revise their

opinion of him? Set him between them and praise him? Look just once, just once, into his eyes so filled with devotion? Uncertain questions, and the most unsuitable moment to ask them!

'I have come here because I believe the stoker is accusing me of some sort of dishonesty. A girl from the kitchen told me she'd seen him on his way here. Captain, sir, and all you other gentlemen, I am ready to refute every charge from my own documents, and if necessary by the statements of impartial and unprejudiced witnesses who are waiting outside the door.' So far Schubal. It was certainly a clear and manly statement, and from the change that came over the faces of the listeners one might have thought these were the first human sounds they had heard for a long time. They failed however to notice that even this fine speech did not hold water. Why was the first significant word that occurred to him 'dishonesty'? Should the accusation perhaps have begun there, rather than with his national prejudices? A girl from the kitchen had seen the stoker on his way to the office and Schubal had immediately understood? Wasn't it a sense of guilt that had sharpened his understanding? And he had at once brought witnesses along with him and called them impartial and unprejudiced into the bargain? Barefaced trickery, sheer barefaced trickery! And the gentlemen put up with it and even accepted it as proper conduct? Why had he evidently allowed such a very long time to elapse between the kitchen-maid's report and his arrival here? Wasn't the sole purpose of that to let the stoker weary the gentlemen to such an extent that they gradually lost their powers of clear judgement, from which Schubal had most to fear? Had he not, obviously after standing for a long while behind the door, knocked only when he heard that gentleman asking his casual question, which gave him reason to hope that the stoker was already done for?

It was all quite clear, and that was how Schubal had unwittingly presented it, but it had to be brought home to the gentlemen in a different, more palpable way. They had to be shaken up. Come on then, Karl, quick, at least make the best of every minute you have before those witnesses appear and swamp everything!

But just at that moment the captain stopped Schubal by raising his hand, whereupon the latter—since his affair seemed to have been adjourned for a while—promptly stepped aside and began a muttered conversation with the steward, who had attached himself to him from the outset, a conversation that was accompanied by many sidelong glances at the stoker and Karl as well as by the most emphatic gestures. Schubal appeared to be rehearsing his next great speech.

'Wasn't there something you wanted to ask the young man, Mr Jakob?' said the captain to the gentleman with the bamboo cane, amid general silence.

'Why, yes,' said the other, acknowledging this courtesy with a little bow. And he inquired of Karl again: 'What is your name, may I ask?'

Karl, who thought that the all-important matter at stake would be best served by getting this incident of the stubborn questioner out of the way fast, answered briefly, and without introducing himself as was his custom by showing his passport, which he would have had to hunt for: 'Karl Rossmann.'

'Well really!' said the gentleman who had been addressed as Jakob, and first took a step backwards with an almost incredulous smile. The captain too, and the chief purser, the ship's officer, indeed even the steward, all showed signs of utter astonishment on hearing Karl's name. Only the harbour officials and Schubal remained indifferent.

'Well really,' Mr Jakob repeated and walked somewhat stiffly up to Karl, 'then I'm your uncle Jakob and you are my dear nephew. I suspected it all along!' said he turning to the captain, before embracing and kissing Karl, who suffered all this in silence.

'And what is your name?' asked Karl after he had been released again, most politely but wholly unmoved, making every effort to estimate the consequences which this new development might have for the stoker. For the moment there was no indication that Schubal might be able to extract any advantage from it.

'You don't appear to realize your good fortune, young man,' said the captain, in the belief that Karl's question had offended Mr Jakob's personal dignity, for this gentleman had moved to the window, evidently to conceal from the others the agitation on his face, which he also kept dabbing with a handkerchief. 'It is Senator Edward Jakob who has just made himself known to you as your uncle. There awaits you henceforth, no doubt in stark contrast to your previous expectations, a brilliant career. Try to grasp this as far as you can in the first shock of the moment, and pull yourself together!'

'I do have an uncle Jakob in America, it's true,' said Karl, turning to the captain, 'but if I've understood rightly Jakob is only the senator's surname.'

'That is so,' said the captain expectantly.

'Well, my uncle Jakob, who is my mother's brother, has Jakob for his first name, while his surname must of course be the same as my mother's, whose maiden name was Bendelmayer.'

'Gentlemen!' cried the senator in reaction to Karl's statement, returning cheerfully from his break for recuperation by the window. All present, with the exception of the harbour officials, burst out laughing, some as if moved, others impenetrably.

'But what I said wasn't all that ridiculous,' thought Karl.

'Gentlemen,' the senator repeated, 'you are taking part, against my own wishes and yours, in a little family scene, and so I cannot avoid giving you an explanation, since I think only the captain'—this reference was followed by an exchange of bows—'is fully informed of the circumstances.'

'Now I really must pay attention to every word,' Karl told himself, and was delighted to see from a sideways glance that life was beginning to return to the figure of the stoker.

'I have during all the long years of my sojourn in America—though sojourn is hardly the right word to apply to an American citizen, which I am with all my heart and soul—during all these long years, as I say, I have been living without any kind of contact with my European relations, for reasons which in the first place do not belong here and in the second would really be too painful for me to relate. I even dread the moment when I may be forced to relate them to my dear nephew, for I fear that in doing so it will be impossible to avoid some plain speaking about his parents and their immediate connections.'

'He's my uncle all right,' said Karl to himself, listening intently, 'probably he's changed his name.'

'Now, my dear nephew has been quite simply—let us not hesitate to use the appropriate term—he has been quite simply cast off by his parents, just as one might fling a cat out of the house when it misbehaves. I do not wish by any means to gloss over what my nephew did to incur such punishment, but his fault is of such a kind that one merely has to name it for it to be excused.'

'That sounds fair enough,' thought Karl, 'but I don't want him to go telling everyone about it. Anyway, he can't possibly know. Who could have told him?'

'The fact is,' continued his uncle, rocking gently forward now and then on his bamboo cane that he had propped in front of him, by

which means he did in fact succeed in avoiding any unnecessary
solemnity which the matter would have otherwise been bound to assume, 'the fact is that he was seduced by a maidservant, Johanna
Brummer, a person of some thirty-five years of age. By using the word
"seduced" I by no means intend to insult my nephew, but it is difficult
to find another, equally suitable word.'

Karl, who by now had moved quite close to his uncle, turned
round at this point in order to gauge the reaction to this story from
the faces of those present. No one was laughing, all were listening pa-
tiently and earnestly. After all, one does not laugh at the nephew of a
senator at the first available opportunity. The most that could be said
was that the stoker was smiling at Karl, though only very faintly, and
that was in the first place encouraging as a renewed sign of life, and
secondly it was excusable, because down in the stoker's cabin Karl had
tried to make a particular secret of this affair which was now being
made so public.

'Now this Brummer,' Karl's uncle went on, 'had a child by my
nephew, a healthy boy, who was baptized by the name of Jakob, evidently with my humble self in mind, since my nephew's no doubt
casual references to me must have been enough to make a deep impression on the woman. Fortunately, I may add. Because once the
boy's parents, in order to avoid having to pay alimony or being involved in any further personal scandal—I should emphasize that I
know nothing of how the law stands over there nor of how the parents
are placed in other respects—once they had shipped their son, my
dear nephew, off to America, so pitifully ill-provided for, as we can see,
the young lad would soon—save for the wonders that do still happen,
at least in America—in all probability, being left to his own resources,
have met with a shameful fate in some back-alley of New York harbour, were it not for the fact that this maidservant had sent me a letter,
which came into my possession after lengthy wanderings the day before yesterday, in which she informed me of the whole story, together
with a personal description of my nephew and, very sensibly, the name
of the ship as well. If it were my purpose to entertain you, gentlemen,
I could read one or two passages from that letter'—he drew two enormous, closely written sheets of notepaper out of his pocket and flour-
ished them—'aloud for your benefit. It could hardly fail to affect you,
for the letter is written with a certain simple but also well-intentioned
artfulness, and with much love for the father of the child. But I have

no wish either to entertain you for longer than is necessary to put you in the picture, or perhaps to wound, at this first moment of my nephew's reception, any feelings that he may possibly still retain; the letter is for him to read, if he so wishes, in the seclusion of the room that already awaits him, for his own edification.'

But Karl had no feelings for that woman. Among the crowded figures of an ever-receding past she sat there in her kitchen beside the dresser, with her elbows propped on the slab. She would look at him whenever he came into the kitchen to fetch a glass of water for his father or to pass on some instructions from his mother. Sometimes she would be writing a letter, sitting in her awkward position at the end of the dresser, and would draw inspiration for it from Karl's face. Sometimes she had her hand over her eyes, and then no word could get through to her. Sometimes she would be kneeling in her little room next to the kitchen, praying to a wooden crucifix; Karl would then just observe her shyly as he went past, through the crack of the slightly open door. Sometimes she would chase about in the kitchen and start back, laughing like a witch, if Karl should get in her way. Sometimes she shut the kitchen door after Karl had come in, and held on to the door-handle until he begged her to let him out. Sometimes she fetched things that he didn't want at all and pressed them silently into his hands. But once she called him 'Karl', and led him, still in his state of surprise at this unexpected familiarity, with much grimacing and sighing into her little room, which she proceeded to lock. She flung her arms round his neck, almost choking him, and while begging him to take her clothes off she actually took off his own, and laid him down in her bed as if she meant never to let him go again, but instead to caress him and cherish him to the end of the world. 'Oh, Karl, oh my Karl!' she cried, as if she were gazing at him to confirm that he belonged to her, whilst he couldn't see the slightest thing and merely felt uncomfortable in all the warm bedclothes that she seemed to have heaped up specially for his benefit. Then she lay down beside him and wanted to get some kind of secrets out of him, but he couldn't tell her any, and she was annoyed by that, either in fun or in earnest; she shook him, she listened to his heart-beat, she offered her own breast for him to do the same, which Karl however could not bring himself to do; she pressed her naked belly against his body, felt with her hand between his legs, so repulsively that Karl shook his head and neck out of the pillows, and then thrust her belly against him a few times; it seemed to him that she was a part of himself, and perhaps for that reason a terrible feeling of helplessness had overcome him. It was in tears that he finally reached his own bed, after many entreaties on her side that he should come again. That had been all it amounted to, and yet his uncle had managed to make a great story out of it. And so that cook had also been thinking of him, and had let his uncle know about his arrival. That had been very kind of her and he hoped he would be able to repay her one day.

'And now,' cried the senator, 'I want you to tell me plainly whether I am your uncle or not.'

'You are my uncle,' said Karl, kissing his hand, for which he received in return a kiss on the forehead. 'I'm very glad to have met you, but you're wrong if you think that my parents only speak badly of you. But even apart from that there were several mistakes contained in your speech, that's to say, what I mean is, it didn't all really happen like that. But you really can't judge things so well from this distance, and I think anyway that it won't do any special harm if the gentlemen are not quite accurately informed about the details of a matter that really can't interest them very much.'

'Well spoken,' said the senator, leading Karl up to the captain, who was visibly sympathetic, and asking: 'Have I not got a splendid nephew?'

'I am happy,' said the captain, with the kind of bow that only people with military training can produce, 'to have made the acquaintance of your nephew, Mr Senator. It is a particular honour for my ship that it should have been able to provide the scene for such a meeting. But the voyage in the steerage must have been quite an ordeal; it's really so hard to tell just who's being carried down there. Of course we do whatever we can to make the voyage as tolerable as possible for our steerage passengers, far more for example than the American lines, but to turn such a voyage into a pleasure is admittedly more than we have been able to manage as yet.'

'It's done me no harm,' said Karl.

'It's done him no harm!' repeated the senator with a loud laugh.

'There's just my trunk that I'm afraid I must have mis—' and with that it all came back to him, all that had happened and all that still remained to be done; he looked around him and saw all those present struck dumb with respect and astonishment in their previous positions, with their eyes fixed upon him. Only the harbour officials, inso-far as their severe, self-satisfied faces were legible, betrayed regret at having come at such an inopportune moment, and the pocket watch which they now had lying on the table in front of them was probably more important to them than anything that was going on or might perhaps still happen in the room.

The first person, after the captain, to express his sympathetic feel-ings was curiously enough the stoker. 'I congratulate you heartily,' he said and shook Karl by the hand, trying to make this gesture express something like appreciation as well. When he then turned to address the senator with the same words the senator drew back, as if the stoker were exceeding his rights; the stoker then at once desisted.

But the others now realized what was required of them and imme-diately formed a huddle round Karl and the senator. So it happened that Karl even received congratulations from Schubal, which he ac-cepted and thanked him for. The last to come up, once calm had returned, were the harbour officials, who said a couple of words in English, which made a ludicrous impression.

The senator was now in the mood to savour this delightful occa-sion to the full by recalling some of the more incidental details for the benefit of himself and others, which was of course not merely toler-ated but received with interest on all sides. Thus he drew attention to the fact that he had entered Karl's most striking distinguishing marks, as enumerated by the cook in her letter, in his notebook, so that he might be able to consult them at short notice if necessary. And then he had, during the course of the stoker's rantings and solely in order to distract himself, taken out this notebook and tried for the sake of amusement to compare the cook's descriptions, which were of course not wholly sound from a detective point of view, with Karl's appear-ance. 'And that's how one finds one's nephew!' he concluded, in a tone of voice that seemed to be inviting a fresh round of congratulations.

'What is going to happen to the stoker now?' asked Karl, passing over his uncle's latest anecdote. In his new situation he felt entitled to express everything that came into his head.

'The stoker will get what he deserves,' said the senator, 'and what the captain considers proper. I think we have had enough and more than enough of the stoker, and I am sure that every one of the gentle-men present will agree with me.'

'But that's not the point when it's a matter of justice,' said Karl. He was standing between his uncle and the captain and felt, perhaps influenced by this position, that he had the decision in his own hands.

And yet the stoker himself appeared to have abandoned all hope. He had his hands stuck halfway into his trouser belt, which had come into view, together with a strip of patterned shirt, as a result of his agitated movements. That did not worry him in the slightest; now that he had poured out all his woes, they might as well see the few rags that covered his body and then they could carry him away. He envisaged the steward and Schubal, being the two lowest-ranking persons present, as those who should perform this final act of kindness for him. After that Schubal would have his peace and no longer be driven to distraction, as the chief purser had put it. The captain would be free to take on Rumanians only, Rumanian would be the language spoken everywhere, and perhaps things really would work better like that. No stoker would be heard ranting in the purser's office any more, only his final rantings would be quite kindly remembered, since as the senator had expressly declared these had been the indirect cause of his nephew's recognition. This nephew had in any case made a number of previous efforts to assist him, and thus long since more than fully rewarded him for his services in the recognition scene; it did not even occur to the stoker to ask anything further from him now. Besides, even if he might be the nephew of a senator, he was far from being a captain, and it was from the captain's mouth that the dread verdict would fall.—And in accordance with this opinion the stoker did his best to avoid looking at Karl, though in this room full of enemies there was unfortunately nowhere else for his eyes to rest.

'Do not misunderstand the situation,' said the senator to Karl, 'perhaps it may be a matter of justice, but at the same time it is a matter of discipline. Both matters, and most particularly the latter, are in this case for the captain to decide.'

'That's right,' murmured the stoker. Those who could hear this and understand it, smiled uneasily.

'But we have in any case been obstructing the captain for far too long in his official duties, which no doubt must pile up enormously just after arriving in New York, so it is now high time for us to leave the ship, without making things worse by turning this petty squabble between two engineers into a matter of importance through any kind of quite unnecessary interference on our part. I can perfectly understand your mode of conduct, my dear nephew, but that is precisely what gives me the right to take you away from here with all speed.'

'I'll have a boat lowered for you right away,' said the captain, without—to Karl's astonishment—raising the slightest objection to the words of his uncle, although these might certainly be regarded as amounting to self-abasement. The chief purser went rushing off to his desk and telephoned the captain's order through to the boatswain.

'Time's running out fast,' said Karl to himself, 'but short of offending everyone there's nothing I can do. I really can't desert my uncle now, just after he's found me again. The captain is certainly polite, but that's as far as it goes. When it comes to discipline his politeness fades away, and I'm sure my uncle was voicing exactly what the captain feels. I'm not going to speak to Schubal; I'm sorry I even shook hands with him. And all the other people here simply don't count.'

And with these thoughts in his mind he went slowly over to the stoker, drew his right hand out of his belt and weighed it gently in his own. 'Why don't you say anything?' he asked. 'Why do you take it all lying down?'

The stoker merely furrowed his brow, as if searching for some way to express what he had to say. Meanwhile he gazed down at Karl's hand and his.

'You've been wronged, more than anyone else on the ship; I know that for certain.' And Karl ran his fingers to and fro between the fingers of the stoker, who looked about him with shining eyes as if he were experiencing a bliss that no one ought to begrudge him.

'But you have to defend yourself, to say yes and no, otherwise people will have no idea of the truth. You must promise to do as I tell you, because I'm very much afraid, and for good reason, that I shan't be able to help you myself any more.' And now Karl was sobbing as he kissed the stoker's hand, and he took that cracked and almost lifeless hand and pressed it to his cheeks like a treasure that must be given up.—But already his uncle the senator was at his side, and with only the gentlest of pressures he led him away.

'The stoker seems to have put you under a spell,' he said, and glanced knowingly towards the captain over Karl's head. 'You felt lonely, you found the stoker, and now you're grateful to him; that's all entirely to your credit. But don't take these things too far, if only for my sake, and try to understand your position.'

Outside the door a hubbub arose; shouts could be heard, and it

even sounded as if someone were being brutally shoved against the
door. A sailor entered in a somewhat dishevelled state, with a girl's
apron tied round his waist. 'There's a crowd of people out there,' he
cried, sweeping round with his elbow as if he were still being jostled.
Finally he managed to collect himself and was about to salute the
captain when he noticed the apron, which he tore off and flung to
the ground, exclaiming: 'That's a foul thing to do, they've tied a girl's
apron round me.' But then he clicked his heels and saluted. Someone
tried to laugh but the captain said sternly: 'High spirits, indeed. Who
are these people outside?'

'They're my witnesses,' said Schubal, stepping forward, 'I humbly
beg pardon for their improper conduct. When the crew have got the
voyage behind them they sometimes go a bit wild.'

'Call them in here at once!' ordered the captain, and then turning
immediately round to the senator he said, politely but hastily: 'May I
respectfully ask, Mr Senator, that you be so good as to accompany this
sailor with your nephew? He will escort you to the boat. I need hardly
say what a pleasure and an honour it has been, Mr Senator, to make
your personal acquaintance. I can only hope that I may soon have the
opportunity to resume with you, sir, our interrupted conversation
about the state of the American fleet, and perhaps to be interrupted
once again in so pleasant a manner as today.'

'This one nephew will be enough for the time being,' said Karl's
uncle with a laugh. 'And now please accept my best thanks, and
farewell. It is by no means impossible, after all, that we, on our next
voyage to Europe'—he embraced Karl warmly—'may perhaps be able
to spend a longer time in your company.'

'That would give me great pleasure,' said the captain. The two
gentlemen shook hands; Karl could only extend a hand to the captain
in silent haste, for the latter was already preoccupied with the fifteen
or so people who were streaming into the room under Schubal's direction, slightly intimidated but still with a great deal of noise. The sailor
asked the senator to be allowed to lead the way and then opened a
path through the crowd for him and Karl, who passed easily between
the bowing ranks. It seemed that these people, who were indeed a
good-humoured lot, regarded Schubal's quarrel with the stoker as a
joke, which did not cease to be amusing even in the presence of the
captain. Among them Karl noticed the kitchen-maid Line, who with a

cheerful wink or two in his direction was tying on the apron that the sailor had flung down, for it was hers.

Still following the sailor, they left the office and turned into a small gangway which brought them after a few paces to a little door, from which a short ladder led down to the boat that had been made ready for them. The sailors in the boat, into which their guide leapt with a single bound, rose to their feet and saluted. The senator was just warning Karl to be careful about descending the ladder when Karl, still on the topmost rung, burst into violent sobs. The senator put his right hand under Karl's chin, holding him tightly against him and stroking him soothingly with his left hand. Thus they slowly descended, step by step, and clinging together they entered the boat, where the senator found a good seat for Karl immediately facing him. At a sign from the senator the sailors pushed off from the ship and set to at once, rowing at full stretch. Hardly were they more than a few yards from the ship when Karl made the unexpected discovery that they were on the side of the ship overlooked by the windows of the purser's office. All three windows were occupied by witnesses of Schubal's, who were saluting and waving in the friendliest manner; even Karl's uncle raised a hand in acknowledgement, and one of the sailors managed to perform the feat of blowing them a kiss without actually breaking his even stroke. It was really as if there were now no stoker any more. Karl looked more closely at his uncle, whose knees were almost touching his own, and he began to feel doubts as to whether this man would ever be able to take the stoker's place. And his uncle avoided his eyes and looked out at the waves on which their boat was tossing.

THE METAMORPHOSIS

WHEN GREGOR SAMSA AWOKE one morning from troubled dreams he found himself transformed in his bed into a monstrous insect. He was lying on his hard shell-like back and by lifting his head a little he could see his curved brown belly, divided by stiff arching ribs, on top of which the bed-quilt was precariously poised and seemed about to slide off completely. His numerous legs, which were pathetically thin compared to the rest of his bulk, danced helplessly before his eyes.

'What has happened to me?' he thought. It was no dream. His room, an ordinary human room, if somewhat too small, lay peacefully between the four familiar walls. Above the table, on which an assortment of cloth samples had been unpacked and spread out—Samsa was a commercial traveller—there hung the picture which he had recently cut out of a glossy magazine and put in a pretty gilt frame. It represented a lady complete with fur hat and fur stole, who was sitting upright and extending to view a thick fur muff into which the whole of her forearm had vanished.

Gregor's eyes turned next to the window, and the dull weather—raindrops could be heard beating on the metal window-ledge—made him feel quite melancholy. 'Suppose I went back to sleep for a little and forgot all this nonsense,' he thought, but that was utterly impracticable for he was used to sleeping on his right side and in his present state he was unable to get into that position. However vigorously he swung himself to the right he kept rocking on to his back again. He must have tried it a hundred times, he shut his eyes so as not to have to watch his struggling legs, and only left off when he began to feel a faint dull ache in his side which was entirely new to him.

'O God,' he thought, 'what an exhausting job I've chosen! On the move day in, day out. The business worries are far worse than they are on the actual premises at home, and on top of that I'm saddled with the strain of all this travelling, the anxiety about train connections, the bad and irregular meals, the constant stream of changing faces with no chance of any warmer, lasting companionship. The devil take it all!' He felt a slight itching up on his belly; slowly pushed himself on his back nearer the top end of the bed so as to be able to lift his head better; found the itching place, which was covered with a mass of little white spots that he was unable to interpret; and then tried to examine the place with one of his legs, but at once drew it back, for the first touch sent cold shivers through him.

He slid back again into his original position. 'This early rising makes one quite stupid,' he thought. 'A man needs his sleep. Other travellers live like harem women. For instance, when I go back to the hotel during the morning to write up the orders I've taken, these gentlemen are still sitting over their breakfast. If I tried that with my chief I'd be sacked on the spot. And who knows if that wouldn't be the best thing for me. If I didn't have to hold back for the sake of my parents I'd have handed in my notice long since, I'd have marched in and given the chief a piece of my mind. I'd have made him fall off his desk! That's an odd way to behave in any case, sitting up on his desk and talking down to his staff from on high, especially when one has to come right up close because he's hard of hearing. Ah well, I haven't given up all hope yet; once I've got the money together to pay back what my parents owe him—that should be managed in five or six years—I'll do it without fail. I'll make a clean break. For the moment, though, I had better get up, for my train goes at five.'

And he looked across to the alarm-clock which was ticking away on the bedside table. 'Father almighty!' he thought. It was half past six and the hands were moving quietly on, in fact it was after half past, it was nearly a quarter to seven. Could the alarm not have gone off? One could see from the bed that it had been set correctly for four; surely then it must have gone off. Yes, but could one sleep calmly through that din that was enough to shatter the furniture? Well, he hadn't in fact slept calmly, but probably all the sounder for that. But what had he better do now? The next train went at seven; to catch that he would have to make frantic haste and his samples weren't even packed up yet; nor was he feeling by any means specially fresh and active himself. And even if he did catch that train he couldn't avoid a blast from the chief, because the messenger would have met the five o'clock train and long since reported him absent. He was a mere tool of the chief, spineless and stupid. Well, suppose he reported sick? But that would be very awkward and look suspicious, for Gregor hadn't gone sick once during the five years of his employment. The chief would be sure to come along with the doctor from the health-insurance, would reproach his parents for the idleness of their son, and would cut short all excuses by referring to the insurance doctor, for whom of course the world was composed exclusively of perfectly healthy but work-shy individuals. And besides, would he have been so wholly wrong in this instance? Gregor did in fact feel quite well, apart from a drowsiness that was really quite superfluous after such a long sleep, and he even felt exceptionally hungry.

As he was thinking all this over at top speed, without being able to make up his mind to get out of bed—the alarm-clock was just striking a quarter to seven—there came a cautious knock at the door behind the head of his bed. 'Gregor,' called a voice—it was his mother—'it's a quarter to seven. Weren't you going to catch the train?' That gentle voice! Gregor gave a start when he heard his own voice coming in answer; it was unmistakably his own voice as of old, but mixed in with it, as if from below, was an irrepressible, painful squeaking; and this only left the sound of the words clear for a moment, before distorting them so much that one could not tell if one had heard them properly. Gregor had intended to answer at length and explain everything, but in the circumstances he confined himself to saying: 'Yes, yes, thank you mother, I'm just getting up.' The alteration in Gregor's voice was apparently not noticeable outside because of the wooden door, for his mother, reassured by these words, went shuffling off. But as a result of this brief exchange the other members of the family had become aware that Gregor, contrary to expectations, was still at home, and already his father was knocking at one of the side-doors, gently but with his fist. 'Gregor, Gregor,' he called, 'what's up?' And after a little while he repeated his admonishment in a deeper voice: 'Gregor! Gregor!' Meanwhile from the other side-door came the soft, plaintive voice of his sister: 'Gregor? Aren't you well? Is there anything you want?' 'I'm just coming,' said Gregor, by way of reply in both directions, doing his best to make his voice sound as normal as possible by articulating most carefully and leaving long pauses between each word. And indeed his father went back to his breakfast, but his sister whispered: 'Do open up, Gregor, please do.' But Gregor had no intention of opening up, and congratulated himself insted on the prudent habit he had acquired as a commercial traveller of locking all his doors at night, even when at home.

The first thing he meant to do was to get up in peace and quiet, get dressed, and most important of all have breakfast; only then would he think about the next steps, for it was clear to him that he would come to no sensible conclusions by meditating in bed. He remembered that often enough previously he had experienced some slight discomfort in bed, perhaps as a result of lying in an awkward position, which had turned out, once he got up, to be pure imagination, and he was eager to see how this morning's fancies might gradually dissolve. That the alteration of his voice was merely the first sign of a bad chill, that standing complaint of commercial travellers, he was not in the slightest doubt.

Disposing of the bed-quilt was quite simple; he had only to inflate himself a little and it fell off automatically. But after that things became difficult, especially since he was so uncommonly broad. He would have needed arms and hands to raise himself to a sitting position; but instead he only had these numerous legs, which were constantly executing the most varied movements and which moreover he was unable to control. Whenever he tried to bend one of them, that was the first to straighten itself; and if he finally succeeded in getting this leg to do what he wanted, in the meantime all the others began working away, as if set free, in the highest state of painful agitation. 'It's simply no use lying idle in bed,' said Gregor to himself.

First of all he tried to get the lower part of his body out of bed, but this lower part, which in fact he had not seen yet and could not even visualize very clearly, proved too cumbersome; he made such slow progress; and when at last, becoming almost frantic, he summoned up all his strength and thrust himself recklessly forward, he found he had misjudged the direction and bumped hard against the bottom end of the bed; and the searing pain he felt informed him that it was precisely this lower part of his body that was perhaps the most sensitive at present.

So he tried getting the upper part of his body out first, and cautiously swivelled his head towards the edge of the bed. This proved easy enough, and eventually his main bulk, despite its breadth and weight, slowly followed the movement of his head. But when at last he had got his head out over the side of the bed in the air, he became alarmed about proceeding further, for after all if he let himself fall like that it would be a positive miracle if his head wasn't injured. And he couldn't on any account afford to lose consciousness just now; he would rather stay in bed where he was.

But when after a similar exertion he lay gasping with relief in his original position, and he once more observed his diminutive legs struggling with one another, if anything more fiercely than ever, and could see no way of reducing their anarchy to any sort of order, he again told himself that staying in bed was impossible and that the wisest course was to sacrifice everything for even the slightest hope of being released from it. But at the same time he didn't fail to keep reminding himself that the coolest of cool deliberation was far preferable to any desperate decisions. At such moments he fixed his eyes as firmly as possible on the window, though unfortunately there was little by way of good cheer and encouragement to be gained from the sight of the morning fog, which was thick enough to obscure even the other side of the narrow street. 'Seven o'clock already,' he said to himself as the alarm-clock struck once more, 'seven o'clock already, and still such a fog.' And for a short while he lay still, breathing quietly, as if perhaps expecting from such total calm a return to normal, unquestionable reality.

But then he said to himself: 'Before it strikes a quarter past seven I must be right out of bed, without fail. Besides, by then someone from the firm will have come to inquire for me, as the premises open before seven.' And now he addressed himself to the task of rocking the whole length of his body quite evenly out of bed. If he let himself fall from the bed this way, then his head, which he intended to lift sharply on impact, would presumably escape injury. His back appeared to be hard; a fall on to the carpet was unlikely to do that much harm. His chief concern was the thought of the loud crash he was bound to make, which would probably cause anxiety behind the various doors, if not alarm. But that had to be risked.

When Gregor was already jutting halfway out from the bed—his new method was more of a game than an exertion, he only had to keep rocking away—it occurred to him how simple it would all be if someone came to help him. Two strong people—he thought of his father and the maid—would have been quite sufficient; they would only have to slide their arms under his curved back, scoop him out of bed like that, bend down with their load, and then just carefully allow him to perform his somersault on to the floor, where it was to be hoped that those little legs of his would acquire some purpose. Well, quite apart from the fact that all the doors were locked, ought he really to call for help? In spite of his predicament he was unable to suppress a smile at the thought of it.

He had already reached the stage where, if he rocked vigorously, he could scarcely keep his balance any longer, and very soon he was going to have to commit himself, for in five minutes it would be a quarter past seven—when there came a ring at the front door. 'It's someone from the firm,' he said to himself and almost froze, while his little legs only danced the faster. For a moment everything stayed quiet. 'They're not going to answer,' Gregor told himself, gripped by some insane hope. But then of course, as usual, the maid went with her heavy tread to the door and opened it. Gregor had only to hear the visitor's first word of greeting and he knew at once who it was—the chief clerk himself. Why on earth was Gregor condemned to work for a firm where the slightest lapse immediately gave rise to the gravest suspicion? Were all the employees, then, scoundrels to a man; was there not one loyal, dedicated worker among them, whom the mere failure to devote an hour or two to the firm one morning was enough to drive crazy with remorse,—so much so that he was actually incapable of getting out of bed? Would it really not have been enough to send an apprentice round to inquire—assuming all this chasing up to be necessary at all? Did the chief clerk really have to come in person, so demonstrating to the whole innocent family that the investigation of this suspicious affair could be entrusted to his wisdom alone? And more from the agitation produced by these thoughts than as the outcome of a genuine decision Gregor swung himself with all his might out of bed. There was a loud thump, though it was not really a crash. To some extent his fall was broken by the carpet, and also there was more bounce in his back than Gregor had supposed, hence the dull, relatively unobtrusive thud which resulted. The only thing was that he had failed to lift his head with sufficient care and had banged it; he twisted it and rubbed it against the carpet in pain and annoyance.

'Something's fallen down in there,' said the chief clerk in the room on the left. Gregor tried to imagine whether something like what had happened to him today might one day happen to the chief clerk himself; one really had to admit it was possible. But as if in brusque reply to this question the chief clerk took a few determined strides in the next room, making his patent leather boots creak. From the room on the right Gregor's sister whispered to him, so as to put him in the picture: 'Gregor, the chief clerk's here.' 'I know,' said Gregor to himself; but to raise his voice enough for his sister to hear him was more than he dared.

'Gregor,' his father now said from the room on the left, 'the chief clerk has arrived and wants to know why you didn't leave by the early train. We don't know what we ought to tell him. Besides, he wants to speak to you in person. So open up please. He will no doubt be good enough to excuse the untidiness of your room.' 'Good morning, Herr Samsa,' the chief clerk called out amiably meanwhile. 'He's not well,' said his mother to the chief clerk, while his father was speaking by the door, 'he's not well, believe me. Why else would Gregor have missed a train? That boy thinks of nothing but his work. It makes me almost cross the way he never goes out in the evenings; he's been here in town for the last week and every single evening he's been at home. He just sits there at the table in the living-room quietly reading the paper or studying his railway timetables. The only relaxation he gets is doing his fret-work. For instance, he spent two or three evenings making a little picture-frame; you'd be surprised how pretty it is. It's hanging there in his room; you'll see it just as soon as Gregor opens the door. I must say I'm glad you've come, sir. By ourselves we should never have persuaded Gregor to open the door; he is so obstinate. And I'm certain he's unwell, even though he said he wasn't earlier this morning.' 'I'm just coming,' said Gregor slowly and deliberately, keeping quite still so as not to miss a word of the conversation. 'I can't think of any other explanation either, madam,' said the chief clerk, 'let us hope it's nothing serious. Though I'm bound to say, on the other hand, that we businessmen are—unfortunately or fortunately, as you will—often obliged for business reasons to shrug off some mild indisposition.' 'Well then, can the chief clerk come in now?' asked his father impatiently, knocking at the door again. 'No,' said Gregor. In the room on the left an embarrassed silence fell; in the room on the right his sister began to sob.

Why didn't his sister go round to join the others? Probably she had only just got out of bed and hadn't even started to dress yet. And whatever was she crying for? Because he didn't get up and let the chief clerk in, because he was in danger of losing his job, and because the head of the firm would then start pestering his parents about those old debts? But surely those were unnecessary worries for the time being. Gregor was still here and had no intention at all of deserting his family. Admittedly at the moment he was lying on the carpet, and no one who was aware of his condition could seriously have expected him to let the chief clerk in. But this slight discourtesy, for which it should be easy to find some suitable explanation later on, could hardly mean Gregor's instant dismissal. And it seemed to Gregor that it would be much more sensible if they now left him in peace instead of disturbing him with their sobs and their entreaties. But of course it was the uncertainty that was upsetting the others and that excused their behaviour.

'Herr Samsa,' the chief clerk now called out, raising his voice, 'what's the matter with you? Here you are barricading yourself in your room, giving only yes or no for an answer, causing your parents a great deal of unnecessary anxiety, and besides—I merely mention this in passing—neglecting your duties towards the firm in a positively outrageous manner. I am speaking here in the name of your parents and your employer, and I must ask you in all seriousness to give me a clear and immediate explanation. I am astonished, astonished. I had always taken you for a quiet and reasonable young man, and now you suddenly seem bent on parading these peculiar whims. I must admit that the head of the firm did indicate to me early this morning a possible explanation for your absence—it concerned the authority to collect payments which was recently entrusted to you—but I went so far as virtually to pledge my word of honour that there could be no truth in that. But now that I am a witness to your incredible obstinacy, I find myself losing all desire to take your part in any way whatsoever. And your position in the firm is by no means assured. It was my original intention to tell you all this in private, but since you force me to waste my time here so pointlessly I see no reason why your good parents should not hear it as well. So I have to state that for some time past your work has been most unsatisfactory; this is admittedly not the best season for doing business, that we recognize, but a season for doing no business at all, Herr Samsa, such a thing does not exist, it cannot be allowed to exist.'

'But sir,' cried Gregor, beside himself and forgetting everything else in his agitation, 'I'm going to open up at once, this very moment. A slight indisposition, a dizzy spell, prevented me from getting up. I'm still lying in bed. But now I feel quite all right again. I'm just getting out of bed now. Just be patient for half a second! I'm not quite so well as I thought. But I'm all right really. How suddenly this sort of attack can take one! Only last night I felt fine, my parents can testify to that, or rather last night I did have a slight premonition. I must have shown some sign of it. Why on earth didn't I report it to the firm! But one always imagines one can get over an illness without having to stay at home. Oh sir! Spare my parents! All the accusations you're making now are quite unfounded; no one has ever mentioned a word about them to me before. Perhaps you haven't yet seen the last lot of orders I sent in. Anyway, I shall be off for my day's work by the eight o'clock train; these few hours' rest have done me good. Don't let me keep you, sir; I shall be round at the premises myself in no time, and be so kind as to pass that on and give my respects to the chief!'

And while Gregor was blurting all this out in haste, hardly aware of what he was saying, he had succeeded quite easily, perhaps owing to the practice he had already acquired in bed, in reaching the wardrobe, and was now trying to hoist himself upright against it. He meant actually to open the door, actually to show himself and speak to the chief clerk; he was eager to find out what the others, who all wanted him so badly, would say when they saw him. If they took fright, then Gregor would have no further responsibility and could rest in peace. But if they took it all calmly, then he had no reason to get excited either and he could, if he hurried, actually be at the station by eight. To begin with he slid off the polished wardrobe a few times, but at last, giving himself a final heave, he stood upright; he no longer paid attention to the pain in his lower parts, intense though it was. Now he let himself fall against the back of a nearby chair, gripping it round the edge with his little legs. And with that he had also gained control of himself, and he fell silent; for now he felt able to listen to what the chief clerk had to say.

'Did you understand a single word of that?' the chief clerk was asking his parents, 'surely he's not trying to make fools of us?' 'Oh heavens,' cried his mother, already in tears, 'perhaps he's seriously ill, and here we are tormenting him. Grete! Grete!' she then cried. 'Mother?' called his sister from the other side. They were communicating through Gregor's room. 'You must get the doctor this minute. Gregor is ill. Run for the doctor, quick. Did you hear how Gregor was speaking just then?' 'That sounded like an animal,' said the chief clerk, in a tone that was strikingly subdued compared to his mother's shrieking. 'Anna! Anna!' his father shouted through the hall to the kitchen, clapping his hands, 'fetch a locksmith at once!' And already the two girls were running with swishing skirts through the hall—how had his sister managed to dress so quickly?—and tearing open the front door. There was no sound of its slamming; presumably they had left it open, as tends to happen in homes where some great disaster has occurred.

But Gregor had grown much calmer. It was true that the words he uttered were evidently no longer intelligible, despite the fact that they had seemed clear enough to him, clearer than before, perhaps because his ear had become attuned to them. But at least the others were by now persuaded that all was not well with him and were prepared to help. He felt comforted by the confidence and the firmness with which the first instructions had been issued. He felt restored once more to human company and hoped for impressive and startling achievements from both the doctor and the locksmith, without making any precise distinction between them. In order to make his voice as clear as possible for the crucial discussions that were now imminent he coughed a little, though he took care to do it very quietly, just in case his coughing, too, might not sound quite human, a matter on which he no longer trusted his own judgement. Meanwhile in the next room complete silence had fallen. Perhaps his parents were sitting at the table with the chief clerk, whispering, perhaps they were all leaning against the door and listening.

Gregor pushed himself slowly towards the door, holding on to his chair, then he let go of it and threw himself against the door, where he propped himself up—the pads at the end of his legs were slightly adhesive—and rested for a moment from his efforts. And then he set about using his mouth to turn the key in the lock. Unhappily it seemed that he had no proper teeth—what was he to get a grip on the key with?—but to make up for that his jaws were certainly very powerful; with their help he did in fact succeed in getting the key moving and paid no attention to the fact that he was undoubtedly doing himself some damage, for a brown liquid was emerging from his mouth, flowing over the key and dripping on to the floor. 'Just listen,' said the chief clerk in the next room, 'he's turning the key.' That was a great encouragement to Gregor; but they should all have been cheering him on, his father and mother too: 'Come on, Gregor,' they should have shouted, 'keep at it, keep going at the key!' And picturing them all following his efforts with tense excitement, he clenched his jaws desperately on the key with all the strength at his command. As the key proceeded to turn, so he danced round the lock; by now he was holding himself up by his mouth alone, and either hanging on to the key or pressing it down again with the full weight of his body as the situation required. The clearer sound of the lock finally snapping back positively roused Gregor from his labours. With a sigh of relief he said to himself: 'So I didn't need the locksmith,' and he laid his head down on the handle to pull the door open.

Since he had to use this method of opening the door, it was actually open quite wide before he himself could be seen. He had first to edge his way slowly round this wing of the door, and indeed do so with the utmost care if he was not to fall flat on his back just as he was about to enter the room. He was still engaged in this difficult manoeuvre, and too busy to attend to anything else, when he heard the chief clerk utter a loud 'Oh!'—it sounded like a rushing of the wind—and now he could see him too, standing nearest to the door, as he clapped his hand to his open mouth and started slowly backing away, as if he were being driven by the steady pressure of some invisible force. His mother—in spite of the presence of the chief clerk she was standing there with her hair still let down after the night and sticking out in disarray—looked first with hands clasped at his father, then took two steps towards Gregor and sank to the floor, her skirts billowing out in circles all round her and her face buried on her breast, quite lost to view. His father clenched a fist with a menacing expression, as if he meant to beat Gregor back into his own room, then he looked uncertainly round the living-room, covered his eyes with his hands and fell into a sobbing that shook his mighty chest.

Gregor did not now enter the room at all, but leaned against the firmly bolted wing of the door, so that only one half of his body was visible, and above it his head, tilted to one side, from which he peered out at the others. Meanwhile it had grown much brighter; clearly visible now across the street was a section of the endlessly long, dark-grey building opposite—it was a hospital—with its regular row of windows starkly pitting its façade; the rain was still falling, but only in huge drops that could be seen individually and seemed almost to be flung individually to earth. The breakfast things were set out on the table in lavish abundance, for to Gregor's father breakfast was the most important meal of the day, which he would sit over for hours reading a variety of newspapers. Hanging on the wall just opposite was a photograph of Gregor from his army days, which showed him as a lieutenant, with his hand on his sword and a carefree smile, inviting respect for his bearing and his uniform. The door leading to the hall was open, and since the front door of the flat was open too, it was possible to see out to the landing and the top of the stairs going down.

'Well,' said Gregor—and he was fully aware of being the only one to have retained his composure—'now I'm going to get dressed at once, pack up my samples and be off. Are you willing, are you willing to let me go? You can see, sir, that I'm not stubborn, and I like my work; travelling is a demanding job, but I couldn't live without it. But where are you off to, sir? Back to the firm? Are you? Will you make a faithful report of all this? A man may be temporarily incapacitated for work, but that's just the right moment to remember his past achievements and to reflect that later, when the difficulty has been overcome, he will be sure to work with all the more energy and concentration. I have the greatest obligations towards the head of the firm, as you know very well. On the other hand I have my responsibilities towards my parents and my sister. I'm in a tight spot, but I shall work myself out of it again. Please don't make things harder for me than they are already. Stand up for me in the firm! Travellers aren't popular, I know. People think they make pots of money and lead a life of luxury. It's just that no one has any special reason to examine this prejudice more closely. But you, sir, have a better grasp of things than the rest of the staff, in fact—I say this in strict confidence—a better grasp than the chief himself, who in his capacity as employer can easily allow his judgement to be swayed wrongly against one of his employees. And you also well appreciate how easily the traveller, being off the premises almost all the year round, can fall prey to gossip and mishap and unfounded complaints—against which he can do nothing to defend himself, since he usually hears nothing about them, and it's not until he gets back from one of his exhausting trips that he is made to feel their consequences in his own person, by which time he can no longer discover what lies behind them. But sir, don't go off without giving me some word to show that you think I'm at least partly right!'

But at Gregor's very first words the chief clerk had already turned away, just staring back at him over his quivering shoulder with his mouth agape. And during Gregor's speech he never stood still for an instant, but without taking his eyes off him he kept moving away towards the door, though only very gradually, as if there were some secret injunction forbidding him to leave the room. But by now he had reached the hall, and to judge from the sudden movement with which he took his last step out of the living-room one might have thought that he had just scorched the sole of his foot. Once in the hall, however, he stretched out his right hand as far as he could in the direction of the staircase, as if some quite unearthly deliverance awaited him there.

Gregor recognized that he must on no account allow the chief clerk to depart in this frame of mind if his position in the firm was not to be gravely endangered. His parents did not understand the situation too well; in the course of the years they had formed the conviction that Gregor was secure in this firm for life, and besides, they were so preoccupied just now with their immediate worries that they had lost all power to look ahead. But Gregor had this power. The chief clerk had to be stopped, soothed, persuaded and finally won over; the very future of Gregor and his family depended on it! If only his sister had been there! She understood things; she had already been in tears while Gregor was still lying calmly on his back. And no doubt the chief clerk, such a one for the ladies, would have been swayed by her; she would have shut the front door and talked him out of his fright in the hall. But his sister simply wasn't there, Gregor had to act on his own. And without stopping to think that he still had no idea what his powers of locomotion were, without even considering the possibility, indeed the likelihood, that his words had once again not been understood, he let go of the door; thrust himself through the opening; tried to advance towards the chief clerk, who was by now clutching the banisters on the landing with both hands in the most ridiculous way; but then immediately, groping for support, he fell down with a little cry on to his numerous legs. No sooner had that happened than he experienced for the first time in the whole morning a sense of physical well-being; his legs had firm ground beneath them; they obeyed him perfectly, as he noted to his joy; they were even impatient to carry him off in whatever direction he chose; and he already felt sure that the final relief of all his sufferings was at hand. But at that very moment, as he lay there on the floor rocking with suppressed motion, not far away from his mother and directly opposite her, she—who had seemed so entirely self-absorbed—suddenly leapt to her feet, with her arms outstretched and her fingers splayed; cried out: 'Help, for God's sake help!'; craned her head forward as if to see Gregor better, yet quite inconsistently backed frantically away from him; had forgotten that the table with the breakfast things was behind her; sat down on it hastily, as if abstracted, when she got there; and seemed quite unaware that the big coffee-pot, overturned beside her, was pouring its contents in a steady stream on to the carpet.

'Mother, mother,' said Gregor softly, and looked up at her. For the moment the chief clerk had quite slipped from his mind; on the other hand at the sight of the flowing coffee he was unable to restrain himself from snapping his jaws in the air a few times. At that his mother let out another scream, fled from the table and fell into the arms of his father who came hurrying towards her. But just now Gregor had no time to spare for his parents; the chief clerk was already on the stairs; with his chin on the banisters he was taking a last look back. Gregor took a run to make as sure as possible of catching him; the chief clerk must have guessed something, for he leapt down several steps at one bound and disappeared; he was still yelling 'Ooh!' and it echoed through the whole staircase. Now unfortunately Gregor's father, who had kept relatively cool so far, seemed to be totally confused by this flight of the chief clerk, for instead of running after him himself, or at least not hindering Gregor in his pursuit of him, he seized with his right hand the chief clerk's walking-stick, which he had left behind on a chair together with his hat and overcoat, grabbed a large newspaper from the table with his left hand, and to the accompaniment of much stamping of the feet set about driving Gregor back into his room by flourishing the stick and the newspaper. No plea of Gregor's availed, indeed none was understood; however meekly he twisted his head his father only stamped the harder. On the other side of the room his mother had flung open a window, despite the cold weather, and was leaning right out of it with her face in her hands. A strong draught swept through from the street to the stairwell, the curtains lifted, the newspapers on the table rustled, stray pages fluttered across the floor. Relentlessly his father drove him back, making hissing noises like a savage. But Gregor still had no practice in going backwards, it really was a slow process. If only he had been allowed to turn round he would have been in his room in no time, but he was afraid of trying his father's patience with this time-consuming rotation, while at any moment that stick in his father's hand threatened to deal him a deadly blow on the back or the head. But in the end Gregor had no choice, for he found to his horror that he could not even keep his direction in reverse; and so he began, just as fast as he could, which was in fact very slowly, and constantly sending anxious side glances towards his father, to turn himself round. Perhaps his father recognized his good intentions, for he did not interfere with him in this, instead he even directed the operation now and again from afar with the point of his stick. If only it hadn't been for that intolerable hissing noise that came from his father! It made Gregor lose his head completely. He had almost completed his turn when quite preoccupied with this hissing he even made a mistake, and turned back a little the other way. But when he had at last succeeded in getting his head opposite the doorway, he discovered that his body was too wide to pass through as it was. Of course his father, in his present mood, did not even remotely consider opening the other wing of the door to provide an adequate passage for Gregor. His fixed idea was simply that Gregor must be got into his room as quickly as possible. And he would never have permitted the elaborate preparations that were necessary for Gregor to hoist himself upright and so perhaps get through the door that way. Instead he now drove Gregor on as if there were no obstacle in his path, making an exceptional amount of noise; it no longer sounded like the voice of just one single father behind him; by now things were definitely no joke any more, and Gregor thrust himself—come what might—into the doorway. One side of his body rode up, he lay at an angle in the doorway, his flank was rubbed quite raw, the white door was stained with horrid blotches, soon he was stuck fast and could by himself have moved no further, his little legs on one side hung trembling in the air, those on the other were crushed painfully against the floor—at which point his father dealt him a mighty blow from behind that came as a veritable deliverance, and he flew deep into the room, bleeding profusely. The door was slammed to with the stick, and then finally all was still.

II

It was already dusk when Gregor awoke from a deep sleep that was more like a swoon. He would certainly have woken of his own accord before long, even without being disturbed, for he felt well enough slept and rested, but he had the impression that a fleeting step and a furtive shutting of the door leading to the hall had aroused him. The light of the electric street-lamps gleamed palely here and there on the ceiling and on the upper parts of the furniture, but down below where Gregor was it was dark. Slowly, still groping awkwardly with his feelers which he was now beginning to appreciate for the first time, he pushed himself over to the door to see what had been going on there. His left side felt like one single long, unpleasantly tight scar, and he had to proceed with a regular limp on his two rows of legs. One leg, moreover, had been seriously damaged in the course of the morning's events—it was almost a miracle that only one had been damaged—and trailed uselessly behind him.

Not until he had got to the door did he discover what had actually lured him across: it was the smell of something to eat. For there stood a bowl filled with creamy milk, in which little slices of white bread were floating. He could almost have laughed for joy, for he was even hungrier now than in the morning, and he at once dipped his head almost up to his eyes in the milk. But he soon withdrew it again in disappointment; it was not just that he found eating difficult owing to the delicate state of his left side—and he could only eat if his whole gasping body was collaborating—but he did not at all care for the milk either, although milk had always been his favourite drink and that was surely why his sister had put it down for him; indeed it was almost with disgust that he turned away from the bowl and crawled back into the middle of the room.

In the living-room the gaslight was already lit, as Gregor could see through the chink of the door, but whereas normally at this hour it was his father's habit to read extracts from his evening paper, in a loud voice, to his mother and sometimes his sister as well, now there was not a sound to be heard. Well, perhaps this custom of reading aloud, which his sister was always telling him about or mentioning in her letters, had anyhow been dropped of late. But there was the same silence all round, although the flat was certainly not empty. 'What a quiet life the family's been leading,' said Gregor to himself, and as he sat there staring into the darkness he felt really proud that he had been able to provide a life of this sort in such a pleasant flat for his parents and his sister. But what if all the peace, all the comfort, all the contentment were now to come to a terrible end? Rather than lose himself in thoughts of that kind Gregor set himself in motion and crawled up and down the room.

Once during the long evening the door on one side and once the door on the other were opened a crack and quickly closed again; someone had presumably felt the urge to come in, but had then had qualms about it. Gregor now stationed himself directly by the living-room door, determined to get the hesitant visitor in somehow or at least discover who it might be; but after that the door was not opened again and Gregor waited in vain. That morning, when the doors had been locked, everybody had wanted to come in to see him; now, after he had unlocked one of the doors himself, and the others had clearly been unlocked during the day, nobody came any more, and the keys were on the outside as well.

It was well into the night before the light was put out in the living-room, and Gregor could easily tell that both his parents and his sister had stayed up until then, for all three of them could plainly be heard stealing away on tiptoe. It was now certain that no one would come in to Gregor before morning; and so he had ample time to reflect in peace and quiet on how best to reorganize his life. But the high, spacious room, in which he was obliged to lie flat on the floor, filled him with an anxiety that he could not account for—since it was after all his own room, which he had occupied for the past five years—and with an almost involuntary movement, not without a slight feeling of shame, he scuttled under the sofa, where despite the fact that his back was a little squeezed and he could no longer raise his head, he at once felt quite cosy, his only regret being that his body was too wide for the whole of it to be installed under the sofa.

There he stayed throughout the night, now in a doze from which the pangs of hunger kept rousing him with a start, now occupied with his worries and vague hopes, all of which, however, led to the same conclusion that he must for the moment keep calm and try, by exercising patience and the greatest consideration, to help his family bear the inconvenience he was bound to cause them in his present condition.

Early the next morning, it was still almost night, Gregor had the opportunity to test the strength of his new resolutions, for his sister, almost fully dressed, opened the door from the hall and peered in expectantly. She did not see him straight away, but when she spotted him under the sofa—good heavens, he had to be somewhere, he couldn't have just flown away—she was so startled that without being able to control herself she slammed the door shut again. But as though regretting her behaviour she opened it again at once, and came in on tiptoe, as if she were visiting someone who was gravely ill, or even a complete stranger. Gregor had pushed his head forward to the very edge of the sofa and was watching her. Would she notice that he had left his milk, and by no means for lack of appetite either, and would she bring in some other kind of food that suited him better? If she didn't do it of her own accord he would rather starve than draw her attention to the matter, although in fact he felt a tremendous urge to dart out from under the sofa, throw himself at his sister's feet and beg her for something good to eat. But she did at once notice, to her surprise, that the bowl was still full, except for a little milk that had been spilt round the edges; she picked it up immediately—not in fact with her bare hands but with a cloth—and carried it out. Gregor was exceptionally curious to know what she would bring him in exchange, and he indulged in all manner of speculations on the subject. But never would he have guessed what his sister, in the goodness of her heart, actually did. She brought him a whole selection, to find out what he liked, all spread out on an old newspaper. There were old, half-decayed vegetables; bones from last night's supper, covered with a solidified white sauce; a few almonds and raisins; some cheese that Gregor had declared uneatable a few days before; a slice of dry bread, a slice of bread-and-butter, and a slice of bread-and-butter with salt. In addition to all this she set down the bowl, now presumably reserved permanently for Gregor, into which she had poured some water. And out of a sense of delicacy, since she knew that Gregor would not eat in her presence, she withdrew at top speed, even turning the key in the lock to make sure Gregor realized that he was free to indulge as he pleased. Now that the meal was served his little legs went whirring off. Those wounds of his must have healed completely by now, for he no longer felt impeded at all; this astonished him, and he thought of how, a month ago, he had cut his finger slightly with his knife and how only the day before yesterday that little wound had still been painful. 'Have I perhaps grown less sensitive?' he wondered, sucking by that time greedily at the cheese, to which, more than all the other foods, he had felt immediately and forcibly attracted. In rapid succession, with tears of contentment welling in his eyes, he consumed the cheese, the vegetables and the sauce; the fresh foods, on the other hand, were not to his taste, indeed he could not even stand the smell of them, and he actually dragged the things that he did want to eat a little further off. He had long since finished his meal, and was just lying idly in the same spot, when his sister slowly began turning the key as a sign for him to retire. That made him start up at once, though he was already almost dozing off, and he scurried back under the sofa again. But it took great self-control on his part to remain under the sofa even for the short time that his sister was in the room, since his body had become somewhat bloated after the abundant meal and he could hardly breathe in the confined space down there. Between little fits of suffocation he watched with slightly bulging eyes as his unsuspecting sister took a broom and swept up not only the remains of what he had eaten, but also the foods which he had not even touched, as if these were no longer any good either, and then shovelled everything hastily into a bucket which she covered with a wooden lid and carried out of the room. Hardly had she turned her back when Gregor drew himself out from under the sofa to stretch himself and distend his belly.

Thus did Gregor now receive his food each day, once in the morning while his parents and the maid were still asleep, and a second time after the family meal at midday, for then his parents took another short nap and the maid was sent off by his sister on some errand or other. Certainly they did not want Gregor to starve any more than she did, but perhaps an indirect knowledge of his feeding arrangements was as much as they could bear, or perhaps his sister wanted to spare them anything that might have proved even mildly distressing, for indeed they were suffering enough as it was.

On what pretext the doctor and the locksmith had been got out of the flat again on that first morning Gregor was unable to discover; for since the others could not understand what he said it never occurred to them, not even his sister, that he could understand them; and so when his sister was in the room he had to content himself with her occasional sighs and invocations of the saints. It was only later, when she had begun to get used to the new situation—of course there was no question of her getting completely used to it—that Gregor sometimes caught a remark of hers which was kindly meant or could be so interpreted. 'He really liked it today,' she would say when Gregor had tucked in like a man, and when the opposite was the case, as began to happen more and more frequently, she would say almost sorrowfully: 'This time it's all been left again.'

But although Gregor was unable to get any news directly, he did overhear a certain amount from the adjoining rooms, and whenever he heard the sound of voices he would run straight to the door concerned and press his whole body against it. In the early days especially there was no conversation that did not in some way, even if only obliquely, refer to him. For two whole days there were consultations to be heard at every meal as to what should now be done; and between meals too the same topic was discussed, for there were always at least two members of the family at home, probably because no one wanted to stay in the flat alone, and to leave it quite empty was unthinkable. Also the maid had come to his mother on the very first day—it was not quite clear how much she knew of what had happened—and begged her on bended knees to be discharged forthwith, and when she took her leave a quarter of an hour later she thanked them for her discharge with tears in her eyes, as if this were the greatest favour ever bestowed on her in this household, and without any prompting she swore the most solemn oath never to say a word of the matter to anyone.

So now his sister, in conjunction with his mother, had to do the cooking as well; that was no great labour, admittedly, for the family ate practically nothing. Gregor kept hearing them vainly urging one another to eat, and never getting any answer but: 'No thanks, I've had enough' or words to that effect. They didn't seem to drink anything either. Often his sister asked his father if he wouldn't like some beer, kindly offering to fetch it herself; and when he made no reply she would say, to remove any scruples on his part, that she could always send the caretaker round for it; but then in the end his father came out with a firm 'No', and no more was said about it.

In the course of the very first day his father gave a full account, to both his mother and his sister, of the family's financial situation and prospects. Every now and then he got up from the table and brought out some receipt or notebook from the little strongbox which he had salvaged from the collapse of his business five years earlier. He could be heard undoing the complicated lock, and then securing it again after he had taken out what he was looking for. This account which his father gave, or some of it at least, was the first encouraging thing that Gregor had heard since his imprisonment. He had supposed that not a

penny remained from his father's old business, at least his father had
never said anything to the contrary, though admittedly Gregor had
never actually asked him. In those days it had been Gregor's sole concern to do his utmost to help the family forget, as quickly as possible,
the business disaster which had plunged them all into such total despair. And so he had set to work with quite exceptional energy, and
from being a junior clerk had risen almost overnight to become a
commercial traveller, as which of course he had quite different prospects and whose successes were immediately translated, by way of
commission, into hard cash that he could set down on the table before
the eyes of his astonished and delighted family. Those had been happy
times, and they had never recurred, at least not in the same splendour,
even though Gregor was later earning such good money that he could
meet the expenses of the entire family and in fact did so. They had
simply got used to it, both the family and Gregor; the money was
gratefully accepted, he provided it gladly, but it no longer gave rise to
any special warmth of feeling. It was only to his sister that Gregor remained close, and it was a secret plan of his that she, who unlike
Gregor was a keen music-lover and could play the violin most mov-
ingly, should be sent next year to the Conservatory, regardless of the
considerable expense involved, which he would have to try and meet
in some other way. During the brief periods when Gregor was based at
home the Conservatory was often mentioned in the talks he had with
his sister, though never as anything more than a beautiful dream, impossible to realize, and even these innocent allusions to the matter
were not much approved by his parents; but Gregor had set his mind
on it very definitely, and he intended to announce his plan with due
solemnity on Christmas Eve.

Such were the thoughts, futile enough in his present condition,
that passed through his mind as he clung there upright, glued to the
door, and listened. Sometimes from a general weariness he could pay
attention no longer and let his head bump carelessly against the door,
but then he held it up again at once, for even the slight noise this made
was enough to be heard next door and reduce them all to silence.
'Whatever can he be up to this time,' said his father after a pause, obviously turning towards the door, and only then would the interrupted
conversation gradually be resumed.

Gregor now had ample time to discover—for his father tended to
repeat his explanations several times, partly because it was a long time

since he had concerned himself with these matters and partly because his mother could not always grasp everything the first time—that despite the disastrous crash a certain sum, admittedly a very small one, was still intact from the old days and had increased a little in the meantime with the untouched interest. And besides that, the money which Gregor brought home every month—he only used to keep back a few odd coins for himself—had not been fully spent and had itself accumulated to form a modest capital. Gregor, behind his door, nodded his head eagerly, delighted to hear of this unexpected thrift and foresight. In fact he could have used this surplus money to pay off more of his father's debts to his chief, so bringing much nearer the day when he could have quit his present job, but as things were it was no doubt better the way his father had arranged it.

However, this money was by no means sufficient to allow the family to live on the interest, or anything of that kind; it was perhaps enough to keep the family for a year, or for two at the most, but that was all. So it was really just a sum that should not be touched, but instead put by for emergencies; as far as the money to live on went, that would have to be earned. Now his father was indeed still healthy, but he was an old man who had not worked for the past five years, and who certainly ought not to expect too much of himself; during those five years, the first period of leisure in his hardworking though unsuccessful life, he had put on a lot of fat and as a result had become distinctly slow in his movements. And as for Gregor's old mother, with her asthma, was she supposed to start earning money, when she found it a strain even to walk through the flat and spent every second day gasping for breath on the sofa by the open window? And was his sister to go out to work, who at seventeen was still no more than a child and whose mode of life it would be a crime to disturb, consisting as it did of wearing pretty clothes, sleeping late, helping in the house, indulging in a few modest amusements and above all playing the violin? Whenever the conversation turned to the necessity of earning money, Gregor always at once let go his hold on the door and threw himself down on the cool leather sofa beside it, for he felt hot all over with shame and grief.

Often he would lie there the long nights through, sleeping not a wink and just scrabbling for hours on the sofa. Or he would embark on the strenuous task of pushing an armchair over to the window and then crawling up to the sill, where propped on the chair he would lean against the window-panes, evidently inspired by some recollection of that sense of freedom that looking out of the window used to give him. For now, in fact, he found objects only a short distance away becoming daily more indistinct; he could no longer make out anything of the hospital across the street, the sight of which he used to curse because he saw it all too often; and if he hadn't known perfectly well that he lived in the peaceful, but decidedly urban Charlottenstrasse, he might have supposed that he was gazing out of his window into a wasteland in which the grey sky and the grey earth ran indistinguishably together. His observant sister only needed to notice twice that the arm-chair was standing by the window; from then on, every time she cleared up the room, she pushed the chair carefully back to the window and even began leaving the inner casement open.

If only Gregor had been able to speak to his sister and thank her for everything that she was obliged to do for him, he could have borne her attentions more easily, but as it was they oppressed him. She certainly made every effort to gloss over the unpleasantness of the whole business, and naturally in the course of time she became more adept at doing so, but equally, as time went on, it became much clearer to Gregor what was actually involved. Even the way she came in was dreadful to him. Hardly had she entered the room when, not even stopping to shut the door—for all the trouble she usually took to spare others the sight of Gregor's room—she rushed straight to the window and tore it open with impatient fingers, almost as though she were suffocating, and she would remain there for a while by the window, no matter how cold the weather, drawing in deep breaths. Twice a day she terrified Gregor with all this noise and bustle; the whole time he lay quaking under the sofa, and yet he knew very well that she would gladly have spared him this if only she had found it possible to stay in a room occupied by Gregor with the window closed.

On one occasion—perhaps a month had now elapsed since Gregor's transformation, so his sister had no special reason to be astonished by his appearance any more—she arrived a little earlier than usual and discovered him propped up at the window, motionless and at his most terrifying, gazing out. It would have been no surprise to Gregor if she had decided not to come in, since the position he occupied prevented her from opening the window at once, but not only did she not come in, she actually leapt back in alarm and shut the door; a stranger might well have thought that Gregor had been lying in wait for her and meant to bite her. Of course he immediately hid himself under the sofa, but he had to wait until midday before she came back, and she seemed much more ill-at-ease than usual. This made him realize that the sight of him was still repugnant to her and was bound to go on being repugnant, and that it probably cost her a great effort not to take to her heels at the mere sight of that small portion of his anatomy which protruded from under the sofa. In order to spare her even this sight, he one day transported a sheet to the sofa on his back—the task took him four hours—and arranged it in such a way that he was now completely covered, and his sister would not be able to see him even if she stooped down. If she had considered this sheet unnecessary, then of course she could have removed it, for it was clear enough that Gregor was hardly shutting himself off so completely for his own amusement, but she left the sheet where it was, and Gregor even fancied that he had once caught a grateful glance when he cautiously raised the sheet a little with his head to see how his sister was taking the new arrangement.

During the first two weeks his parents could not bring themselves to come in to him, and he often heard them expressing their full appreciation of his sister's present labours, whereas previously they had frequently become annoyed with her because she seemed to them a somewhat useless girl. But now both of them, his father and his mother, often waited outside Gregor's door while his sister cleared up his room, and no sooner had she emerged than she had to tell them exactly how she had found the room, what Gregor had eaten, how he had behaved this time, and whether perhaps some slight improvement was noticeable. His mother, moreover, began relatively soon to want to visit Gregor, but his father and his sister managed to dissuade her at first by employing rational arguments, to which Gregor listened most attentively and thoroughly endorsed. But later on she had to be restrained by force, and when she then cried out: 'You must let me in to Gregor, he's my own unhappy boy! Can't you see that I have to go to him?' Gregor began to think it might be a good thing after all if his mother did come in, not every day of course, but perhaps once a week; she really did understand things much better than his sister, who for all her pluck was still only a child and had perhaps, when all was said and done, only taken on such an onerous task out of childish recklessness.

Gregor's wish to see his mother was soon fulfilled. During the day-

time Gregor did not want to show himself at the window, if only out
of consideration for his parents, but his few square yards of floor-space
gave him little scope for crawling about there either; as for lying still,
he found that almost unbearable even at night, and eating had soon
ceased to afford him the slightest pleasure; so, for the sake of recre-
ation, he took up the habit of crawling all over the walls and the ceiling. In particular he enjoyed hanging from the ceiling; it was quite
different from lying on the floor; one could breathe more freely, one
felt a faint pulsation through the whole of one's body, and in Gregor's
state of almost contended distraction up there it could happen to his
own surprise that he let himself go and fell smack on the floor. But
now, of course, he had his body under much better control than before
and even when falling from such a height he did himself no damage.
His sister was quick to notice the new pastime that Gregor had discovered for himself—for he left some traces of his sticky stuff behind
here and there, simply by crawling—and she then took it into her head
to provide Gregor with the maximum crawling-space and to remove
the pieces of furniture that stood in his way, which meant above all the
wardrobe and the writing-desk. However, she could not manage this
on her own; she did not dare ask her father for help; the maid would
most certainly not have helped her, for while this young thing of six-
teen or so had been sticking it out bravely since the departure of the
previous cook, she had asked as a special favour to be allowed to keep
the kitchen door locked at all times and to open it only when expressly
summoned; so his sister had no other choice but one day, when her father was out, to fetch her mother. And indeed along she came, with
exclamations of eager delight, though at the door of Gregor's room
she fell silent. First his sister made sure, of course, that all was in order
within; only then did she let her mother enter. In great haste Gregor
had pulled down his sheet still lower and tugged it more into folds; the
whole thing really did look simply like a sheet casually thrown over
the sofa. This time Gregor also refrained from spying out from under
the sheet; he denied himself the sight of his mother on this first occasion and was just happy that she had come after all. 'Come on in, you
can't see him,' said his sister, evidently leading her mother by the
hand. Now Gregor could hear the two frail women shifting the old
wardrobe, which was really quite a weight, out from where it stood,
with his sister obstinately bearing the brunt of the labour throughout,
despite the warnings of her mother who was afraid she might strain

herself. It took a very long time. After perhaps a quarter of an hour's effort his mother declared that they had better leave the wardrobe where it was, for in the first place it was just too heavy, they would never be finished before his father came home and would have to leave it in the middle of the room, blocking Gregor's movements completely; and in the second place it was not at all certain that they were doing Gregor a favour by removing the furniture. It seemed to her that the opposite was true; she found the sight of the bare wall positively heart-rending; and why shouldn't Gregor react in the same way, since he had been used to this furniture for so long and would feel abandoned in the empty room. 'And wouldn't it look,' his mother concluded very softly—in fact she had been almost whispering the whole time, as if she were anxious that wherever Gregor's exact station might be he shouldn't even hear the sound of her voice, for of course she was convinced that he couldn't understand the words—'and wouldn't it look as if by moving the furniture we meant to show him we had given up all hope of his getting better, and were leaving him callously to his own devices? I think the best thing would be if we tried to keep the room exactly as it was before, so that when Gregor returns to us he'll find everything unchanged, and can forget what's happened in the meantime all the easier.'

At hearing these words of his mother Gregor realized that the lack of any direct human address during the course of these two months, coupled with the monotonous life within the family, must have confused his mind; otherwise he was at a loss to explain how he could seriously have wanted to have his room cleared out. Did he really want this warm room of his, so comfortably fitted with old family furniture, to be transformed into a cave, in which, no doubt, he would be free to crawl about unimpeded in all directions, but only at the price of rapidly and completely forgetting his human past at the same time? Indeed, he was on the brink of forgetting it already, and only the voice of his mother, that voice which he had not heard for so long, had brought him to his senses. Not a thing should be removed; everything must stay; the good effects of the furniture on his condition he could not do without; and if the furniture should hinder him in his senseless crawling expeditions that was no drawback, it was a great advantage.

But unfortunately his sister thought otherwise; she had become accustomed, and not without some justification, to adopt with her parents the role of a special expert whenever Gregor's affairs were being discussed; and so her mother's proposal was now sufficient reason for her to insist instead, not only on the removal of the wardrobe and the desk, which was all that she had originally intended, but on the removal of every stick of furniture in the room apart from the indispensable sofa. In demanding this she was not of course prompted merely by childish obstinacy, or by the self-confidence she had so unexpectedly and painfully acquired in recent weeks; she had also observed, as a matter of plain fact, that Gregor needed a lot of space to crawl about in, while on the other hand there was no sign that he made the slightest use of the furniture. And possibly the romantic spirit of girls of her age, which seeks an outlet at every opportunity, had played some part as well, by tempting Grete to make Gregor's plight even more horrific, so that she could perform even greater feats on his behalf. For in a room where Gregor reigned in solitary state over the bare walls it was unlikely that anyone save Grete would ever dare to set foot.

And so she refused to be swayed from her resolve by her mother, who in any case seemed unsure of herself from the sheer anxiety of being in Gregor's room; she soon grew silent and began doing what she could to help her daughter shift the wardrobe out. Well, Gregor could dispense with the wardrobe, at a pinch, but nothing more; the writing-desk must stay. And no sooner had the two women, groaning and heaving, got the wardrobe out of the room than Gregor poked his head out from under the sofa, to see how he might cautiously intervene with as much tact as possible. But as luck would have it, it was his mother who reappeared first, leaving Grete in the next room with her arms round the wardrobe, rocking it to and fro on her own without of course budging it an inch. Now his mother was not used to the sight of Gregor; it might make her ill; so Gregor hurried backwards in alarm to the other end of the sofa, though not in time to prevent the sheet at the front swaying about a little. That was enough to put his mother on the alert. She stopped short, stood still for a moment and then went back to Grete.

Although Gregor kept telling himself that nothing out of the ordinary was happening, that only a few pieces of furniture were being shunted around, all the same he soon had to confess that this coming and going of the two women, their little cries to each other, the scraping of the furniture over the floor, were affecting him like some great turmoil that was being fuelled from all sides; and no matter how much he tucked in his head and legs and cowered down with his body pressed to the floor, he was forced inescapably to the conclusion that he would not be able to put up with all this for long. They were clearing out his room; depriving him of all his dearest possessions; the wardrobe, which contained his fretsaw and other tools, was already transported; now they were working his writing-desk loose, which was almost embedded in the floor, the desk at which he had always done his homework, as a student at the commercial academy, as a grammar-school boy, yes, even back in his primary school days—and now he simply had no more time to spend weighing up the good intentions of the two women, whose very existence he had indeed almost forgotten, since by now they were working away in silence from sheer exhaustion and nothing could be heard but the sound of their laboured, faltering steps.

And so he broke out from his cover—the women were just leaning against the desk in the next room to give themselves a short breather—changed direction four times, for he really didn't know what to salvage first, then spotted the picture of the lady all swathed in furs hanging so conspicuously on what was otherwise a bare wall, crawled rapidly up to it and pressed himself against the glass, which held him fast and soothed his hot belly. This picture at least, which Gregor now covered completely, was definitely not going to be removed by anybody. He twisted his head round towards the door of the living-room so as to observe the women on their return.

They had not given themselves much of a rest and were already on their way back; Grete had put her arm round her mother and was practically carrying her. 'Well, what shall we take next?' said Grete, and glanced round. And then her eyes met Gregor's, looking down at her from the wall. Probably because her mother was there she retained her composure, brought her head down close to her mother's, to stop her eyes from wandering, and said, though rather hastily and in a trembling voice: 'Come, hadn't we better go back to the living-room for a moment?' To Gregor her intentions were plain: she wanted to get her mother to safety and then chase him down from the wall. Well, just let her try! He clung to his picture and was not going to give it up. He would rather fly in Grete's face.

But Grete's words had made her mother more anxious than ever; she stepped to one side, caught sight of the huge brown patch on the flowered wallpaper, and before it had really dawned on her that what she saw was Gregor she cried out: 'Oh God, oh God!' in a hoarse, screaming voice, collapsed across the sofa, with her arms outspread as if she were abandoning everything, and gave no further sign of life. 'You! Gregor!' cried his sister, raising her fist and glaring at him. These were the first words she had addressed to him directly since his transformation. She ran into the next room to fetch some sort of essence to revive her mother from her fainting fit; Gregor wanted to help as well—there was time enough to save his picture later on—but he was stuck fast to the glass and had to wrench himself free; then he too ran into the next room, as if he could give his sister some advice as in the old days; but once there he had to stand idly behind her; while she was rummaging among various little bottles she turned her head and gave a start of alarm; one bottle fell to the floor and broke; some kind of burning medicament splashed round him; then Grete, without further delay, grabbed as many little bottles as she could hold and ran in to her mother with them, slamming the door behind her with her foot. Now Gregor was cut off from his mother, who was perhaps nearly dying all because of him; he dared not open the door for fear of driving away his sister, who had to stay by his mother's side; there was nothing for him to do but wait; and in an agony of self-reproach and anxiety he began to crawl about, he crawled over everything, walls, furniture and ceiling, until finally, with the whole room beginning to reel around him, he dropped in despair on to the middle of the big table.

A little while elapsed; Gregor lay feebly where he was; all was quiet round about, perhaps that was a good sign. Then the doorbell rang. The maid was of course locked in her kitchen and so Grete had to go and answer. His father was back. 'What's happened?' were his first words; Grete's appearance must have told him everything. Grete replied in a muffled voice, evidently with her face pressed against her father's chest: 'Mother passed out, but she's better now. Gregor's broken loose.' 'Just what I expected,' said his father, 'just what I kept telling you, but you women won't listen.' It was clear to Gregor that his father had put the worst interpretation on Grete's all too brief account and assumed that Gregor was guilty of some act of violence. That meant he must now try and pacify his father, for he had neither the time nor the means to explain things to him. And so he fled to the door of his room and pressed himself against it, so that as soon as his father came in from the hall he should see that Gregor had the best intention of returning to his room straight away, and that there was no need to drive him back; if only the door were opened he would disappear at once.

But his father was in no mood to observe such subtleties; 'Ah!' he cried as soon as he entered, in a tone that sounded enraged and exultant at the same time. Gregor drew back his head from the door and lifted it towards his father. This was really not at all how he had pictured his father, standing there like that; admittedly he had been too preoccupied of late by his new sport of crawling to take the same interest as before in what was going on in the rest of the household, and he really ought to have been prepared to find circumstances changed. And yet, and yet, could this indeed be his father still? The same man who used to lie wearily sunk in bed whenever Gregor set out on one of his business trips; who was always reclining in the armchair in his dressing-gown, when he greeted him on his return in the evening; who was actually hardly capable of getting to his feet, but merely raised his arms to demonstrate his pleasure; and who, on the rare occasions when the whole family took a walk together, on a few Sundays each year and on high holidays, would always struggle on between Gregor and his mother, who were slow walkers anyway, even a little more slowly than they, wrapped up in his old overcoat, carefully planting his crook-handled stick before him for each step he took, and almost invariably stopping and gathering his escort round him whenever he had anything to say? Now, on the other hand, he cut a fine, upright figure, dressed in a tight-fitting blue uniform with gilt buttons, of the kind worn by bank messengers; his heavy double-chin spread out over the high stiff collar of his jacket; from under his bushy eyebrows his black eyes sent out alert and penetrating glances; his white hair, formerly so dishevelled, was combed down smooth and glistening on either side of a scrupulously exact parting. He flung his cap—which bore a gold monogram, probably that of some bank—right across the room in a wide arc to the sofa, and with his hands in his pockets, the tails of his long uniform jacket folded back, he advanced with a grimly set face on Gregor. Probably he did not know himself what he had in mind; at all events he lifted his feet unusually high; and Gregor was astonished at the gigantic size of the soles of his boots. But at this point of his reflections Gregor lingered no more; he had known from the very first day of his new life that his father considered only the sever-

est measures appropriate for dealing with him. And so he fled before
his father, pausing when his father stopped still and hurrying on again
when he made the slightest move. In this manner they circled the
room several times, without anything decisive happening, indeed
without the whole operation taking on the appearance of a chase, so
slowly did it proceed. For this reason Gregor kept to the floor for the
time being, especially since he feared that his father might regard any
flight on to the walls or the ceiling as an act of particular malevolence.
But all the same Gregor had to admit that he would not be able to
keep up even this kind of running for long; for while his father took a
single step he had to execute a whole series of movements. Signs of
breathlessness were beginning to appear, as indeed even in his former
life his lungs had never been wholly reliable. As he went staggering on
like this, hardly keeping his eyes open so as to concentrate all his powers on running; not even thinking, in his stupor, of any other means of
salvation save by running; and having almost forgotten that the walls
were at his disposal, though admittedly these walls were obstructed by
elaborately carved furniture full of sharp corners and spikes—suddenly
something came sailing past him, some object lightly tossed; it landed
on the floor and rolled away in front of him. It was an apple; a second
one came flying after it at once; Gregor stopped dead in terror; any
further running was useless, for his father had resolved to bombard
him. He had filled his pockets from the fruit bowl on the sideboard
and now he was throwing one apple after another, so far without taking careful aim. These small red apples rolled about on the floor as if
electrified, cannoning into one another. One apple, thrown without
much force, grazed Gregor's back and glanced off harmlessly. But another one that came flying immediately after it positively plunged itself into Gregor's back; Gregor attempted to drag himself on further,
as if this shocking, unbelievable pain might pass with a change of position; but he felt as if nailed to the spot, and stretched himself flat out,
in utter confusion of all his senses. With his last conscious look he saw
the door of his room being flung open and his mother rushing out
ahead of his screaming sister; in her chemise, for his sister had taken
off her dress to help her breathe when she fainted; he saw his mother
running towards his father, shedding her loosened petticoats one by
one on the floor behind her; and how she stumbled over her skirts to
fling herself upon him, and embraced him, quite united with him—but

here Gregor's sight went dim—imploring him, with her hands clasped round his father's neck, to spare Gregor's life.

III

Gregor's serious injury, which afflicted him for more than a month—the apple remained embedded in his flesh as a visible reminder, since no one had the courage to remove it—seemed to have brought home even to his father that despite his present lamentable and repugnant shape Gregor was a member of the family, who ought not to be treated as an enemy, but that on the contrary family duty required them to swallow their disgust and put up with him, simply put up with him.

And although as a result of his injury Gregor had probably suffered some permanent loss of mobility and for the present it took him long, painful minutes to traverse his room like some disabled veteran—any crawling above floor level was out of the question—, yet for this deterioration in his condition he was granted, so he felt, an entirely adequate compensation: every day towards evening the living-room door, which he used to watch intently for an hour or two beforehand, was opened; so that as he lay in the darkness of his room, invisible from the living-room, he could see the whole family at the lamp-lit table, and listen to their talk as if by general consent, not at all as he had been obliged to do previously.

It was true that these were no longer the animated conversations of earlier times, which Gregor had always thought about rather wistfully when he had had to drop wearily into his damp bed in some mean little hotel room. Now things were mostly very still. Soon after supper his father would fall asleep in his armchair; his mother and sister would caution each other to keep quiet; his mother, craning right forward under the lamp, would stitch away at her fine lingerie for a fashion store; his sister, who had taken a job as a sales-girl, was learning shorthand and French in the evenings in the hope of bettering herself later on. Sometimes his father woke up, and as if he had no idea he'd been asleep would say to his mother: 'What a lot of sewing you're doing again tonight!' and then go straight back to sleep, while the two women exchanged a tired smile.

With a kind of perverse obstinacy his father refused to take off his messenger's uniform even in the house, and while his dressing-gown hung idle on the clothes hook he slept fully dressed in his chair, as if he were permanently ready for duty and awaiting even here the call of his superior. As a result his uniform, which had not been new to start with, began to lose its smartness despite all Gregor's mother and sister could do, and Gregor often spent whole evenings gazing at this uniform jacket, all covered with stains and gleaming with its constantly polished buttons, in which the old man sat most uncomfortably but peacefully sleeping.

As soon as the clock struck ten his mother tried to rouse his father with a gentle word or two and then persuade him to go to bed, for he simply wasn't getting a proper sleep where he was, and that was what he needed most since he had to go on duty at six. But with the obstinacy that had possessed him ever since he had become a bank messenger he always insisted on staying longer at the table, although he regularly fell asleep again and after that the greatest effort was needed to get him to exchange his armchair for bed. However much Gregor's mother and sister kept urging him with their little admonishments he would go on slowly shaking his head for a full quarter of an hour, keeping his eyes shut and refusing to get up. Gregor's mother plucked at his sleeve, whispered blandishments in his ear, his sister left her homework to come and help her mother, but his father remained quite unresponsive. He only sank deeper into his armchair. Not until the two women took hold of him under the arms would he open his eyes and look alternately from one to the other with the customary remark: 'What a life this is. Such is the peace of my old age.' And leaning on the two women he rose to his feet, laboriously, as if he were himself his heaviest burden, and allowed himself to be led by the women as far as the door, where he waved them away and proceeded on his own, while Gregor's mother abandoned her sewing and his sister her pen so as to run after his father and provide further assistance.

Who in this overworked and exhausted family had time to worry about Gregor any more than was absolutely necessary? The household was reduced more and more; the maid was now sent away after all; a huge bony charwoman with an untidy mop of white hair came in the mornings and evenings to do the roughest work; everything else his mother took care of, in addition to all her sewing. It even happened that various pieces of family jewellery, which his mother and sister had worn with such delight at parties and celebrations in days gone by, were sold, as Gregor discovered one evening from hearing a general discussion of the prices obtained. But the greatest complaint was always that they were unable to leave the flat, which was far too big for their present circumstances, since it was impossible to conceive how Gregor was to be moved. But Gregor could see quite well that it was not merely consideration for him that prevented a move, for he could easily have been transported in a suitable crate with a few air-holes; the main thing which kept them from moving was rather their utter hopelessness, and the feeling that they had been struck by a misfortune quite without parallel among all their friends and relations. Everything that the world requires of impoverished people they fulfilled to the utmost; his father fetched breakfast for the minor officials at the bank, his mother sacrificed herself making underwear for strangers, his sister ran up and down behind the counter at the bidding of customers; but more than this the family had not the strength to do. And the pain in Gregor's back began to hurt again as if the wound were re-opened whenever his mother and sister returned, having got his father to bed, left their work unattended, drew their chairs close together and sat there cheek to cheek; when his mother, pointing to Gregor's room, said: 'Close that door, Grete,' and he was left once more in darkness, while in the next room the women were mingling their tears or perhaps just staring dry-eyed at the table.

Gregor spent the days and nights almost entirely without sleep. Sometimes he toyed with the idea that next time the door was opened he would take the family's affairs in hand again, just as he had done in the old days; once more, after a long interval, there appeared in his thoughts the figures of the head of his firm and the chief clerk, the salesmen and the apprentices, the exceptionally dense errand boy, two or three friends from other firms, a chambermaid in one of the provincial hotels—a sweet and fleeting memory—, a cashier in a hat shop, whose affections he had earnestly but too leisurely courted—they all appeared to him, mixed up with strangers or people he had already forgotten, but instead of helping him and his family they were all of them unapproachable, and he was glad when they vanished. Then at other times he was in no mood at all to worry about his family, he was merely filled with rage at how badly he was being looked after, and although he couldn't even imagine anything that might tempt his appetite, he would still make plans for getting access to the larder and helping himself to what was after all his ration, even if he wasn't hungry. Without any longer considering what Gregor might specially fancy, his sister now hurriedly shoved any old food into his room with her foot before she ran off to work in the morning and at midday; then in the evening, regardless of whether the food had barely been tasted or whether—as was most frequently the case—it had been left completely untouched, she swept it out with a swish of the broom. The cleaning up of his room, which she now always attended to in the evenings, could not have been done more hastily. Streaks of dirt ran the length of the walls, here and there lay balls of dust and filth. At first Gregor, when his sister came in, would station himself in some corner of the room that was particularly striking in this respect, so as to make his position there a kind of reproach to her. But he might easily have stayed there for weeks without achieving any improvement in his sister; she could see the dirt as well as he could, of course, but she had simply made up her mind to leave it. At the same time she took care, with a touchiness that was quite new to her and was indeed affecting the whole family, to see that the cleaning of Gregor's room remained her own preserve. On one occasion Gregor's mother had subjected his room to a thorough clean-out, which she had only managed to accomplish with the aid of several buckets of water—all this dampness of course was a further irritation to Gregor, who lay stolidly, grumpy and motionless, on the sofa—but his mother's punishment was not long delayed. For hardly had his sister noticed the change in Gregor's room that evening when she rushed in high dudgeon into the living-room and burst, despite her mother's imploringly raised hands, into a fit of sobbing, while both parents—his father had naturally been startled out of his armchair—looked on to begin with in helpless amazement; then they too began to get going; his father reproached his mother on the right for not leaving the cleaning of Gregor's room to his sister; screamed, however, at his sister on the left that she would never be allowed to clean Gregor's room again; meantime his mother tried to drag his father, who was beside himself with emotion, into his bedroom; his sister, shaken with sobs, hammered with her little fists on the table; and Gregor hissed loudly with rage because it never occurred to any of them to close the door and spare him this spectacle and this commotion.

But even though his sister, worn out by her regular job, had got tired of caring for Gregor as she used to, it was by no means necessary for his mother to replace her in order to ensure that Gregor was not neglected. For now the charwoman was there. This elderly widow, whose strong bony frame had no doubt helped her through the worst trials in the course of her long life, was not really repelled by Gregor. Without being in any way inquisitive she had once opened the door of his room by chance, and at the sight of Gregor—who being taken completely by surprise began running to and fro, though no one was chasing him—she had merely stood there in amazement, with her hands folded in front of her. From that time on she had never failed to open his door a crack every morning and evening and look in briefly at Gregor. At first she used to call him over to her as well, with words that were probably meant to be friendly, such as: 'Come along, then, my old dung-beetle!' or 'Look at our old dung-beetle, now!' To such forms of address Gregor made no response, but stayed motionless where he was as if the door had never been opened at all. If only this charwoman, instead of being allowed to disturb him pointlessly whenever she felt inclined, had been given orders to clean out his room daily! Once, early in the morning—heavy rain was lashing against the window-panes perhaps a sign that spring was already on the way— Gregor was so exasperated when the charwoman started off again with her little stock phrases that he turned on her, as if to attack her, though of course in a slow and feeble way. But instead of taking fright, the charwoman simply lifted a chair that was standing by the door high in the air, and as she stood there with her mouth wide open it was clear that she didn't intend to shut it again until the chair in her hand came crashing down on Gregor's back. 'Aren't you coming any closer, then?' she inquired as Gregor turned away again, and put the chair calmly back in the corner.

By now Gregor ate practically nothing. Only when he happened to go past the food set out for him would he take a bite of it just for fun, hold it in his mouth for hours, and then mostly spit it out again. At first he thought it was distress at the state of his room that was keeping him from eating, but in fact it was precisely the changes in his room to which he very soon became reconciled. It had become the custom to put into this room things for which no space could be found elsewhere, and of these there were now plenty, for one room in the flat had been rented to three lodgers. These solemn gentlemen—all three wore beards, as Gregor once observed through a crack in the door— had a passion for tidiness, not only in their own room but also, since

they were now installed here as lodgers, as far as the whole household
was concerned, which meant in particular the kitchen. Any kind of
useless junk, let alone dirty junk they could not abide. Most of their
own household equipment they had in any case brought with them. As
a result many things had become superfluous, which although not
saleable could hardly be thrown away either. All these things found
their way into Gregor's room. Likewise the ash bucket and the rubbish
bin from the kitchen. Anything that was not wanted for the time being
was simply flung by the charwoman, who was always in a great hurry,
into Gregor's room; usually Gregor was lucky enough to see no more
than the object concerned and the hand that held it. Perhaps the charwoman meant to reclaim the things as time and opportunity offered,
or else to throw the whole lot out at once, but in fact they just remained lying wherever they had first landed, except when Gregor
pushed his way through the junk-heap and set it moving, at first from
necessity, because there was no other space free for crawling, but later
with increasing enjoyment, although after such excursions he would
lie motionless for hours, dead-tired and miserable.

Since the lodgers often had their supper at home as well, in the
communal living-room, on certain evenings the living-room door
stayed closed; yet Gregor found it no hardship to forego the opening
of the door; indeed, several times already when it had been opened in
the evening he had failed to take advantage of it and had lain, without
the family's noticing, in the darkest corner of his room. But on one occasion the door to the living-room had been left slightly ajar by the
charwoman, and thus it had remained even when the lodgers came
along in the evening and the lamp was lit. They seated themselves at
the top end of the table, where in the old days his father and mother
and Gregor had sat, unfolded their napkins, and picked up their knives
and forks. At once his mother appeared in the doorway with a dish of
meat, and close behind her his sister, bearing a dish piled high with
potatoes. Thick clouds of steam rose from the food. The lodgers bent
over the dishes that were set in front of them, as if they wished to examine them before eating, and in fact the one sitting in the middle,
who seemed to be regarded as an authority by the other two, sliced
into a piece of meat while it was still on the dish, evidently to deter-
mine whether it was sufficiently tender or whether perhaps it should
be returned to the kitchen. He was satisfied, and both mother and sis-

ter, who had been watching anxiously, breathed again freely and began to smile.

The family itself ate in the kitchen. None the less, before going into the kitchen his father came into the living-room and with a great bow made a round of the table, cap in hand. The lodgers rose as one man and mumbled something into their beards. When they were alone again, they ate in almost complete silence. It seemed strange to Gregor that among all the various noises of the meal he could constantly pick out the sound of their champing teeth, as if to demonstrate to Gregor that for eating teeth were needed, and that even with the finest toothless jaws one could accomplish nothing. 'I've got appetite enough,' said Gregor sadly to himself, 'but not for things of that kind. How these lodgers feed themselves up, while I waste away!'

On that very evening—during the whole of this time Gregor couldn't remember having once heard the violin—the sound of violin-playing came floating across from the kitchen. The lodgers had already finished their supper, the one in the middle had brought out a newspaper and given the other two a page apiece, and now they were leaning back in their chairs, reading and smoking. When the violin began to play they pricked up their ears, got to their feet, and tiptoed to the hall doorway where they stood together in a little bunch. They must have been heard from the kitchen for his father called out: 'Is the music disturbing you at all, gentlemen? It can be stopped at once.' 'On the contrary,' said the middle lodger, 'wouldn't the young lady care to come in to us and play here, where it's so much more relaxed and comfortable?' 'Oh, with pleasure,' cried his father, as if he were the violinist. The lodgers went back into the room and waited. Presently along came his father with the music-stand, his mother with the music and his sister with the violin. Calmly his sister got everything ready to play; his parents—who had never let rooms before and so treated the lodgers with excessive politeness—did not even dare to sit down in their own chairs; his father leaned against the door, in his buttoned-up livery jacket, with his right hand thrust between two of the buttons; his mother, however, was offered a chair by one of the gentlemen, and she sat down on it just where he had happened to put it, tucked away in a corner.

His sister began to play; his father and mother, from either side of her, attentively followed the movements of her hands. Gregor, attracted by the playing, had ventured a little further forward and already had his head inside the living-room. It hardly struck him as odd that he had recently begun to show so little consideration for the others; previously such thoughtfulness had been his pride. And yet it was now more than ever that he had reason to stay hidden, since owing to all the dust which lay thick in his room and flew about at the slightest movement, he too was quite coated in dust; on his back and trailing from his sides he carried fluff, hairs and remnants of food about with him; his indifference to everything was far too great for him to have lain on his back and scoured himself against the carpet, as once he had done several times a day. And in spite of his condition he felt no shame in edging forward a little over the spotless living-room floor.

To be sure, no one paid any attention to him. The family was completely absorbed by the violin-playing; the lodgers, however, who had first stationed themselves, with their hands in their pockets, much too close behind his sister's music-stand—so close that they could all have read the music, which must surely have bothered his sister—soon withdrew to the window, muttering among themselves with their heads down, and there they remained while his father anxiously watched them. Indeed it now seemed only too obvious that they had been disappointed in their hopes of hearing good or entertaining violin-playing, that they had had enough of the whole performance and were putting up with the further disturbance of their peace out of mere politeness. In particular, the way they all sent their puffs of cigar smoke through nose and mouth towards the ceiling suggested a high degree of irritability. And yet how beautifully was his sister playing. Her face was inclined to one side, with a searching and sorrowful look her eyes followed the notes of the music. Gregor crawled a little further forward, keeping his head close to the floor so that it might be possible for their eyes to meet. Was he an animal, that music could move him so? It seemed to him as if the way were opening towards the unknown nourishment he craved. He was determined to press on until he reached his sister, to pluck at her skirt, and thus to indicate to her that she should come into his room with her violin, for here there was no one worthy of her playing as he would be worthy of it. He would never let her out of his room again, at least not for so long as he lived; his terrible shape would be of service to him for the first time; at every door of his room he would stand guard at once, hissing and spitting at all intruders; his sister, however, should not be forced to stay with him, but should do so freely; she should sit beside him on the sofa, bend down her ear to him, and then he would confide to her that he had the firm intention of sending her to the Conservatory, and that if the misfortune had not intervened he would have announced this to everybody last Christmas—surely Christmas must be past by now?—without paying attention to any objections. After this declaration his sister would be so moved that she would burst into tears, and Gregor would raise himself up to her shoulder and kiss her on the neck, which now that she went out to work was no longer covered with ribbon or collar.

'Herr Samsa!' cried the middle lodger to Gregor's father, and without wasting another word pointed with his forefinger at the slowly advancing Gregor. The violin fell silent, the middle lodger first smiled to his friends with a shake of his head and then looked at Gregor again. His father seemed to consider it more urgent to pacify the lodgers than to drive Gregor out, although they were not at all agitated and Gregor appeared to be entertaining them more than the violin-playing. He hurried over to them, trying to urge them back into their own room with his outstretched arms and simultaneously to block their view of Gregor with his body. Now they really did become a trifle angry—it was not clear whether his father's behaviour was responsible, or whether it was the realization, now dawning on them, that they had unwittingly had such a next-door neighbour as Gregor. They demanded explanations of his father, raising their arms in their turn; they tugged uneasily at their beards, and only with reluctance backed towards their room. Meanwhile his sister had emerged from the state of abstraction into which she had fallen after her playing had been so rudely interrupted; after holding her violin and bow for a while slack in her hanging hands and continuing to gaze at the music as if she were still playing, she had suddenly pulled herself together, laid her instrument down on her mother's lap—she was still sitting in her chair with her lungs heaving, struggling for breath—and had run into the lodgers' room, on which they were now converging more rapidly under pressure from his father. One could see the covers and pillows on the beds obeying his sister's practised hands as they flew in the air and arranged themselves in order. Before the lodgers had even reached their room she had finished making the beds and slipped out. Once again his father seemed so possessed by his obstinacy that he was forgetting every scrap of respect that was after all due to his tenants. He just kept pressing and pressing until, in the very door of the bedroom, the middle lodger gave a thunderous stamp of his foot and so brought him to a halt. 'I declare herewith,' said he, raising his hand and casting his eyes around for Gregor's mother and sister too, 'that in view of the revolting conditions prevailing in this household and family'—here he spat promptly on the floor—'I give immediate notice. Naturally I shall not be paying a penny for the period I have already spent here; on the contrary, I shall be considering whether to lodge some claim for damages against you, which will—I assure you—be very easy to substantiate.' He stopped and stared straight ahead of him, as if expecting something. And sure enough his two friends at once chimed in with the words: 'And we, too, give immediate notice.' Thereupon he seized the door-handle and shut the door with a bang.

Gregor's father staggered with groping hands to his armchair and collapsed into it; it looked as if he were stretching himself out for his usual evening nap, but the violent nodding of his head, as if it were quite out of control, showed that he was anything but asleep. All this time Gregor had lain motionless on the spot where the lodgers had caught sight of him. His disappointment at the failure of his plan, and perhaps also the weakness caused by prolonged lack of food, made it impossible for him to move. He feared with a fair degree of certainty that in the very next moment everything would collapse over his head in some general disintegration, and he waited. He was not even stirred when the violin slipped from his mother's trembling fingers and fell from her lap with a reverberating clang.

'Dear parents,' said his sister, slapping her hand on the table by way of introduction, 'things can't go on like this. Perhaps you don't realize that but I do. I refuse to utter my brother's name in the presence of this monster, and so all I say is: we must try and get rid of it. We've done everything humanly possible to look after it and put up with it, I don't believe anyone can reproach us in the slightest.'

'She's right ten times over,' said his father to himself. His mother, who was still gasping for breath, a wild look in her eyes, began to cough into her hand with a hollow sound.

His sister rushed over to his mother and put a hand on her forehead. His father's thoughts seemed to have become clearer as a result of his sister's words; he had sat up straight and was playing with his uniform cap among the plates that still lay on the table from the lodgers' supper; from time to time he glanced at the inert form of Gregor.

'We must try to get rid of it,' said his sister, now addressing her father only, since her mother couldn't hear a word for her coughing, 'it will be the death of both of you, I can see that coming. When one has to work as hard as we all do, how can one stand this constant torment at home as well. At least I can't face it any more.' And she burst into such violent sobbing that her tears flooded down on to her mother's face, where she wiped them away mechanically.

'My child,' said her father pityingly, and with evident understanding, 'but what are we to do?'

Gregor's sister just shrugged her shoulders, to show the helplessness that had now come over her during her fit of weeping, in contrast to her previous assurance.

'If he could understand what we said,' said her father, half questioningly; Gregor's sister, still sobbing, waved her hand vehemently to show how unthinkable that was.

'If he could understand what we said,' repeated the old man, and by closing his eyes absorbed his daughter's conviction that this was impossible, 'then perhaps we might be able to come to some arrangement with him. But as things are—'

'He's got to go,' cried his sister, 'that's the only solution, father. You must just try to get rid of the idea that it's Gregor. That's our real disaster, the fact that we've believed it for so long. But how can it be Gregor? If it were Gregor, he would have realized long since that it isn't possible for human beings to live together with a creature like that, and he would have gone away of his own accord. Then we wouldn't have a brother, but we'd be able to go on living and honour his memory. But as it is, this creature persecutes us, drives away our lodgers, obviously wants to occupy the whole flat and let us sleep out in the street. Just look, father,' she suddenly shrieked, 'he's at it again!' And in a state of panic that was quite incomprehensible to Gregor his sister abandoned her mother, positively shoving herself off from her chair as if she would rather sacrifice her mother than stay near Gregor, and dashed behind her father, who from sheer alarm at her behaviour got to his feet as well, and half raised his arms in front of her as though to protect her.

But Gregor had not the slightest intention of frightening anybody,

least of all his sister. He had merely begun to turn himself round so as
to travel back to his room, and that did admittedly look spectacular,
since because of his infirm condition he had to use his head to assist
him in this difficult manoeuvre, by raising it several times and then
knocking it against the floor. He paused and looked about him. His
good intentions appeared to have been recognized; the alarm had only
been a momentary one. Now they were all silently and sorrowfully
watching him. His mother lay back in her armchair with her legs outstretched and pressed together, her eye-lids almost dropping with fa-
tigue; his father and sister sat side by side, his sister had put her arm
round her father's neck.

'Now perhaps I'm allowed to turn round,' thought Gregor, and began his labours again. He couldn't suppress the wheezing caused by his
exertions, and from time to time he had to rest. Nor did anyone harass
him, it was all left entirely to him. When he had completed the turn
he at once set off on his journey in a straight line. He was amazed at
the distance separating him from his room, and failed to understand
how in his weak state he had recently covered the same stretch almost
without realizing it. So intent was he on just crawling fast, he barely
noticed that not a word, not a single exclamation from his family was
disturbing his progress. Only when he was already in the doorway did
he turn his head; not completely, for he felt his neck growing stiff; but
enough to see that nothing behind him had changed except that his
sister had risen to her feet. His last glimpse was of his mother, who
was by now sound asleep.

Hardly was he inside his room when the door was pushed to with
all speed, bolted and locked. The sudden noise at his back startled
Gregor so much that his legs gave way under him. It was his sister who
had shown such haste. She had been standing there ready and waiting,
then she had sprung lightly forward, Gregor had not heard her coming at all; and she cried out 'At last!' to her parents as she turned the
key in the lock.

'And now?' Gregor asked himself, looking round him in the darkness. Soon he made the discovery that he was by now quite unable to
move. This caused him no surprise; he was more inclined to think it
strange that he had, until now, managed to propel himself at all on
those thin little legs. Otherwise he felt relatively comfortable. It was
true that he felt pains all over his body, but it seemed to him that these
were growing fainter and fainter and would finally pass away alto-

gether. The rotting apple in his back and the inflamed area round it, all covered with soft dust, hardly troubled him any longer. His thoughts went back to his family with tenderness and love. His own opinion that he must disappear was if anything even firmer than his sister's. In this state of vacant and peaceful reflection he remained until the tower clock struck three in the morning. He was still just conscious of the first signs of the general brightening outside his window. Then his head sank fully down, of its own accord, and his last faint breath ebbed out from his nostrils.

When the charwoman arrived early in the morning—from sheer energy and impatience she always slammed all the doors, no matter how often she had been asked not to, so hard that no peaceful sleep in the flat was possible after she'd come—she noticed nothing unusual, to begin with, on her normal brief visit to Gregor. She thought he was lying so still there on purpose, making a show of hurt feelings; she credited him with all kinds of cunning. Since she happened to have the long broom in her hand she tried to tickle Gregor with it from the door. When that had no effect either she became annoyed and jabbed into Gregor a little, and it was only when she had shoved him out of position without meeting any resistance that she began to take notice. Having soon grasped the facts of the matter, she opened her eyes wide and gave a low whistle; then without wasting time she tore open the bedroom door and yelled at the top of her voice into the darkness: 'Just come and look, the creature's done for; it's lying there dead and done for!'

The Samsa parents sat up in the parental bed, and first had to overcome the shock the charwoman had given them before they could take in her message. Then, however, Herr and Frau Samsa climbed rapidly out of bed, one from each side; Herr Samsa threw the blanket round his shoulders, Frau Samsa came forth in nothing but her nightgown; thus arrayed they stepped into Gregor's room. Meanwhile the door of the living-room had opened too, where Grete had been sleeping since the lodgers had moved in; she was fully dressed, as if she hadn't slept at all, and her pale face seemed to confirm the fact. 'Dead?' said Frau Samsa and looked up inquiringly at the charwoman, though she could well have checked for herself and could see plainly enough without doing so. 'I'll say so,' said the charwoman, and to prove it she pushed Gregor's corpse well to one side with her broom. Frau Samsa made a move as if to hold back the broom, but then stopped. 'Well,' said Herr Samsa, 'now thanks be to God.' He crossed himself, and the three women followed his example. Grete, whose eyes never left the corpse, said: 'Just look how thin he was. It's such a long time since he's eaten anything. The food came out again just as it was brought in.' Indeed, Gregor's body was completely flat and dry; this could really be seen for the first time now that the little legs no longer supported it and there was nothing else to distract the eye.

'Come in with us for a little, Grete,' said Frau Samsa with a sad smile, and Grete followed her parents into their bedroom, not without a glance back at the corpse. The charwoman shut the door and opened the window wide. Despite the early hour the cool air had a certain mildness in it. After all, it was already the end of March.

The three lodgers emerged from their room and looked round in astonishment for their breakfast; they had been forgotten. 'Where's our breakfast?' the middle lodger demanded gruffly of the char-woman. But she put her finger to her lips and without a word hastily beckoned them into Gregor's room. In they went and there, where it was by now fully light, they stood in a circle round Gregor's corpse, with their hands in the pockets of their somewhat shabby jackets.

Thereupon the door of the Samsas' bedroom opened and Herr Samsa appeared in his uniform, his wife on one arm, his daughter on the other. They all looked a little tearful; from time to time Grete pressed her face against her father's sleeve.

'Leave my house this instant!' said Herr Samsa, and pointed to the door without letting go of the women. 'How do you mean?' said the middle lodger, slightly taken aback, with a sugary smile. The other two held their hands behind their backs and kept rubbing them to-gether, as if in gleeful anticipation of a real set-to from which they were bound to emerge victorious. 'I mean exactly what I say,' replied Herr Samsa, and in line abreast with the two women he advanced upon the lodger. At first that gentleman stood quite still, with his eyes on the ground, as if things were forming a new pattern in his mind. 'So I think we'll be off,' he then said, and looked up at Herr Samsa as though, in a sudden access of humility, he were even seeking fresh ap-proval for this decision. Herr Samsa merely gave him a series of brief nods, staring at him hard. At that the lodger really did set off for the hall, with long strides; his two friends, who had been all attention for some while and had quite stopped rubbing their hands, now went pos-itively hopping after him, as if they feared Herr Samsa might get into the hall before them and cut them off from their leader. In the hall they all three took their hats from the coat-rack, drew their sticks out from the umbrella stand, bowed in silence, and quitted the flat. Herr Samsa, with what proved to be quite unfounded mistrust, followed them with the two women out on to the landing; leaning against the banisters they watched the three gentlemen slowly but surely descending the long flight of stairs, vanishing from sight on each floor at a certain turn of the stairway and after a few moments reappearing again; the lower they got, the more the Samsa family's interest in them dwindled; and when a butcher's boy with his tray on his head climbed proudly up towards them, and then swung on past them, Herr Samsa and the women withdrew from the banisters, and they all returned as if relieved into the flat.

They decided to spend this day resting and going for a walk; they had not only earned such a respite from work, they absolutely needed it. And so they sat down at the table and wrote three letters of apology, Herr Samsa to the bank manager, Frau Samsa to the man who sent her needlework, and Grete to the proprietor of her shop. While they were writing the charwoman came in to say that she was off, for she had finished her morning's work. The three letter writers at first simply nodded without looking up, but when the charwoman kept hanging about they raised their eyes in annoyance. 'Well?' asked Herr Samsa. The charwoman stood smiling in the doorway, as if she had some great good news for the family but was not going to pass it on unless she were properly questioned. The little ostrich feather in her hat, which stuck up almost straight and had irritated Herr Samsa the whole time she had been with them, swayed gently in all directions. 'What is it you want, then?' asked Frau Samsa, for whom the charwoman had more respect than for the others. 'Yes, well,' the charwoman replied, amid so much good-humoured laughter that she couldn't continue for a while, 'it's about the business of getting rid of that thing next door, well, you don't have to worry about it. It's all been seen to.' Frau Samsa and Grete bent forward over their letters, as if they intended to go on writing; Herr Samsa, who perceived that the charwoman was now eager to begin describing everything in detail, checked her firmly with an outstretched hand. But since she was not to be allowed to tell her story, she recalled the great hurry she was in; obviously offended, she called out 'Goodbye all,' whirled round violently, and departed from the flat with a terrible slamming of doors.

'She'll get her notice tonight,' said Herr Samsa, but he received no answer either from his wife or his daughter, for the charwoman seemed to have shattered the peace of mind that they had barely won. They rose, went to the window, and remained there clasping each other tight. Herr Samsa turned round in his chair towards them and watched them quietly for a while. Then he called out: 'Come along, come along now. Let these old troubles rest at last. And have a little thought for me as well.' The two women complied at once, hastened over to him, fondled him and quickly finished their letters.

Then they all three left the flat in company, something they had not done for months, and took a tram into the open country on the outskirts of the city. Their tramcar, in which they were the only passengers, was quite filled with warm sunshine. Leaning comfortably back in their seats they discussed their prospects for the time ahead, and it appeared on closer inspection that these were by no means bad, for all three of them had jobs which—though they had never really asked one another about this in any detail—were entirely satisfactory and especially promising for the future. The greatest immediate improvement in their situation would of course come about easily through a change of residence; they would now take a smaller and cheaper, but also a better placed and altogether more manageable flat than their present one, which Gregor had picked for them. While they were thus conversing, it struck the two Samsa parents almost at the same moment, as they observed their daughter's increasing liveliness, that despite all the labours which had turned her cheeks pale she had recently blossomed into a pretty and shapely girl. Growing quieter now, and coming almost unconsciously to agreement by an exchange of glances, they reflected that the time was also ripe to find her a good husband. And it was like a confirmation of their new dreams and good intentions when at the end of the journey their daughter was the first to rise to her feet and stretch her young body.

IN THE PENAL COLONY

'IT'S A PECULIAR KIND of apparatus,' said the officer to the voyager, and he surveyed the apparatus, which was after all quite familiar to him, with a certain admiration. It seemed to have been no more than politeness that had prompted the voyager to accept the invitation of the commandant, who had suggested that he witness the execution of a soldier who had been condemned for insubordination and insulting a superior officer. Probably there was no great interest in this execution in the penal colony itself. At all events, the only persons present apart from the officer and the voyager, in this deep sandy little valley enclosed by barren slopes all round, were the condemned man, a dull-witted wide-mouthed creature of dishevelled aspect, and a soldier, who held the heavy chain controlling the smaller chains which were fastened to the condemned man's ankles, wrists and neck, chains which were themselves linked together. In fact, the condemned man wore an air of such hangdog subservience that it looked as if he might be allowed to run free on the slopes and would simply have to be whistled for when the execution was due to begin.

The voyager was not much taken with the apparatus, and he walked up and down behind the condemned man with almost visible indifference while the officer made the final preparations, now crawling underneath the apparatus, which was sunk deep in the ground, now climbing a ladder to inspect its upper parts. These were tasks that might really have been left to a mechanic, but the officer performed them with great enthusiasm, whether because he was a particular devotee of this apparatus or because for some other reasons the work could be entrusted to no one else. 'Everything's ready now!' he called out at last and climbed down from the ladder. He was utterly exhausted, breathing with his mouth wide open, and had tucked two delicate ladies' handkerchiefs under the collar of his uniform. 'Surely these uniforms are too heavy for the tropics,' said the voyager, instead of inquiring about the apparatus as the officer had expected. 'Of course,' said the officer, as he washed the oil and grease from his hands in a bucket of water that was standing ready, 'but they mean home to us; we don't want to lose touch with the homeland.—But now just have a look at this apparatus,' he added at once, drying his hands with a towel and indicating the apparatus at the same time. 'Up to this point I've had to do some of the tasks by hand, but from now on the apparatus works entirely by itself.' The voyager nodded and followed the officer. The latter was anxious to cover himself against all eventualities and added: 'Of course faults do sometimes occur; I hope we shall get none today, but one has to allow for the possibility. After all, the apparatus has to operate for twelve hours without a break. But even if faults do occur they are only quite minor ones and can be rectified at once.'

'Won't you take a seat?' he asked finally, pulling out a cane chair from a pile of them and offering it to the voyager; he was unable to refuse. He now found himself sitting at the edge of a pit, into which he cast a fleeting glance. It was not very deep. On one side of the pit the excavated earth had been heaped up to form an embankment; on the other side of it stood the apparatus. 'I don't know,' said the officer, 'whether the commandant has already explained the apparatus to you.' The voyager made a vague sort of gesture; the officer asked for nothing better for now he could explain the apparatus himself. 'This apparatus,' he said, taking hold of a connecting-rod and leaning on it, 'is an invention of our former commandant. I took part myself in the very first experiments and I was also involved in every stage of the work up to its completion. However, the credit for the invention belongs to him alone. Have you ever heard of our former commandant? No? Well, I'm not exaggerating when I say that the organization of the whole penal colony is his work. We, his friends, were already aware when he died that the colony forms such a self-contained whole that his successor, even if his head was bursting with new schemes, would find it impossible to alter any part of the old system, at least for many years to come. And what we foretold has come to pass; the new commandant has had to admit as much. A pity you never knew the former commandant!—But,' the officer interrupted himself, 'I go chattering on, while his apparatus stands here before us. It consists, as you see, of three parts. In the course of time each of these three parts has acquired a sort of popular name. The lower part is called the bed, the upper one is called the designer, and this middle one here, which is suspended between them, is called the harrow.' 'The harrow?' asked the voyager. He had not been listening with much attention; the sun was beating down so fiercely into this shadeless valley; it was hard to collect one's thoughts. All the more did he admire the officer, who in his tight full-dress uniform, weighed down by its epaulettes and hung about with braiding, was expounding his subject with such zeal and for good measure, while still in full flow, giving the odd turn to some screw with his screwdriver. As for the soldier, he seemed to be in much the same state as the voyager. He had wound the condemned man's chain round both his wrists, and with one hand propped on his rifle and his head lolling back was paying no attention to anything. This did not surprise the voyager, for the officer was speaking French, and French was certainly not a language that either the soldier or the condemned man could understand. It was however all the more remarkable that the condemned man was trying his best, despite this, to follow the officer's explanations. With a kind of sleepy persistence he kept directing his gaze wherever the officer pointed, and when the voyager now broke in with his question he imitated the officer by switching his eyes to the voyager.

'Yes, the harrow,' said the officer, 'it's a good name for it. The needles are set in rather like the teeth of a harrow, and the whole thing operates like a harrow, except that it stays in one place and performs with far greater artistry. In any case you'll soon get the hang of it. Here, on the bed, is where the condemned man is laid.—You see, what I want to do is describe the apparatus first, and only then set the actual programme going. Then you'll be able to follow it better. Besides, one of the cogwheels in the designer is badly worn; it grates horribly when it's turning; then you can hardly hear yourself speak; spare parts are unfortunately hard to come by here.—So here is the bed, as I was saying. It's completely covered with a layer of cotton-wool; the purpose of that will become clear to you later on. On this cotton-wool the condemned man is laid face down, quite naked of course; here are straps for the hands, here for the feet, and here for the neck, to fasten him down. Here at the head of the bed, where as I've said the man lies with his face down to begin with, is this little stub of felt, which can be easily adjusted to push straight into the man's mouth. Its object is to prevent screaming and biting of the tongue. The man is bound to take the felt, of course, since otherwise his neck would be broken by the neck strap.' 'That's cotton-wool?' asked the voyager, leaning forward. 'Yes indeed,' said the officer with a smile, 'feel for yourself.' He took the voyager's hand and drew it over the surface of the bed. 'It's a specially treated cotton-wool, that's why it looks so unrecognizable; I'll come to its purpose in a moment.' By now the voyager was beginning to feel some stirring of interest in the apparatus; with one hand raised to protect himself against the sun he gazed up at it. It was a large structure. The bed and the designer were of the same size and looked like two dark chests. The designer was mounted some two metres above the bed; both were joined at the corners by four brass rods that almost flashed in the sunlight. Between the two chests, suspended on a steel belt, was the harrow.

The officer had scarcely noticed the voyager's previous indifference, but clearly he now sensed his awakening interest; so he paused in his explanations to give the voyager time to survey undisturbed. The condemned man imitated the voyager; since he was unable to lift a hand to cover his eyes he blinked up unprotected into the glare.

'All right, so there lies our man,' said the voyager, leaning back in his chair and crossing his legs.

'Yes,' said the officer, pushing his cap back a little and passing a hand over his sweltering face, 'now listen! Both the bed and the designer have their own electric battery; the bed needs one for itself and the designer one for the harrow. As soon as the man is strapped down, the bed is set in motion. It quivers, with the smallest and most rapid of vibrations, both from side to side and up and down. You will have seen similar devices in sanatoria; but in the case of our bed all the movements are precisely calculated; the point is that they must correspond with the most painstaking exactness to the movements of the harrow. But it is to the harrow that the actual carrying out of the sentence belongs.'

'And what in fact is the sentence?' asked the voyager. 'You don't even know that?' said the officer in astonishment, biting his lips: 'Forgive me if my explanations may appear disorderly, I do beg your pardon. The truth is that it used to be the commandant himself who gave the explanations, but the new commandant has absolved himself from this duty; all the same, that he should not even have told such an eminent visitor'—the voyager attempted to wave away this honour with both hands but the officer insisted on the expression—'not even have told such an eminent visitor of the form that our sentencing takes, that's yet a further innovation on his part which—,' here he had an oath on his lips, but recovered himself and said merely: 'I was not informed of this; the fault is not mine. In any case I am indeed the one best equipped to explain our kind of sentence, for I have with me here'—he patted his breast pocket—'the relevant drawings in our former commandant's own hand.'

'The commandant's own drawings?' asked the voyager: 'Did he then combine everything in his own person? Was he soldier, judge, engineer, chemist, draughtsman?'

'Yes, indeed,' said the officer, nodding his head with a glassy, meditative look. Then he inspected his hands; they did not seem to him clean enough to touch the drawings; so he went over to the bucket and washed them once again. Then he drew out a small leather folder and said: 'Our sentence does not sound severe. The condemned man has the commandment that he has transgressed inscribed on his body with the harrow. This condemned man, for instance'—the officer indicated the man—'will have inscribed on his body: Honour thy superiors!'

The voyager cast a quick glance at the man; he was standing with bowed head as the officer pointed to him, apparently straining all his powers of hearing to make something out. But the movement of his closed and bulging lips showed clearly that he understood not a word. The voyager had a number of questions in mind, but at the sight of the man he asked only: 'Does he know his sentence?' 'No,' said the officer and was about to continue with his explanations, but the voyager cut him short: 'He doesn't know his own sentence?' 'No,' said the officer again, and he paused for a moment as if expecting the voyager to give some reason for his question, then he said: 'There would be no point in announcing it to him. You see, he gets to know it in the flesh.' The voyager would have said no more, but he became aware of the condemned man's gaze turned upon him; it seemed to be asking if he could approve the procedure described. So having already leant back in his chair the voyager bent forward again and put another question: 'But at least he knows that sentence has been passed on him?' 'Nor

that either,' said the officer, smiling at the voyager as if expecting to
hear further strange communications from him. 'But surely,' said the
voyager, wiping his brow, 'do you mean that the man still doesn't
know how his defence was received?' 'He has had no opportunity to
defend himself,' said the officer, looking in another direction, as if he
were talking to himself and wished to spare the voyager the embarrassment of being told such self-evident things. 'But he must have had
the opportunity to defend himself,' said the voyager, and rose from his
seat.

The officer perceived that he was in danger of being held up for a
long time in his explanation of the apparatus; he therefore went over
to the voyager, linked arms with him and pointed to the condemned
man, who stood stiffly to attention now that he had so obviously become the centre of interest—the soldier also gave a tug to the chain—
and said: 'The situation is as follows. Here in the penal colony I have
been appointed as judge. Despite my youth. For I was the former
commandant's assistant in all penal matters and I also know the apparatus better than anyone else. The principle on which I base my decisions is this: guilt is always beyond question. Other courts cannot
follow this principle since they are composed of more than one member, and furthermore they have higher courts above them. Here that is
not the case, or at least it was not so in the time of our former commandant. Admittedly the new one has shown signs of wishing to interfere with my judgements, but hitherto I have succeeded in warding
him off and I shall continue to do so.—You wanted to have this particular case explained; it is quite simple, as they all are. A captain reported to me this morning that this man, who is assigned to him as a
servant and sleeps outside his door, had been asleep on duty. It is his
duty, you see, to get up every time the hour strikes and salute the captain's door. Certainly no onerous duty, and a necessary one, for he
must remain alert both to guard and to wait on his master. Last night
the captain wished to ascertain whether the servant was performing
his duty. On the stroke of two he opened the door and found him
curled up asleep. He fetched his horsewhip and struck him across the
face. Instead of then getting up and begging for pardon, the man
seized his master by the legs, shook him and yelled: "Throw away that
whip or I'll gobble you up."—Those are the facts of the case. The captain came to me an hour ago; I wrote down his statement and at once
appended the sentence. Then I had the man put in chains. That was

all very simple. If I had first summoned the man and interrogated him it would only have led to confusion. He would have lied; if I had succeeded in refuting these lies he would have replaced them with fresh lies, and so forth. But as it is I've got him and I won't let him go.—Is everything now clear? But time's getting on, the execution ought to be starting and I still haven't finished explaining the apparatus.' Pressing the voyager to resume his seat, he went back to the apparatus and began: 'As you can see, the shape of the harrow corresponds to the human form; here is the harrow for the trunk, here are the harrows for the legs. Reserved for the head is just this one small engraver. Is that clear to you now?' He bent forward amiably towards the voyager, willing to provide the most comprehensive explanations.

The voyager studied the harrow with a frown. The information about the judicial process had failed to satisfy him. All the same, he had to remind himself that this was a penal colony, that special measures were necessary here, and that military procedures had to be adhered to throughout. But he also placed some measure of hope in the new commandant, who evidently intended to introduce, however slowly, a new kind of process that went beyond this officer's limited understanding. Pursuing this line of thought the voyager asked: 'Will the commandant attend the execution?' 'It is not certain,' said the officer, put out by the abrupt question, and his friendly expression became contorted: 'That is just why we must lose no time. I shall even have to curtail my explanations, much as I regret it. But of course tomorrow, when the apparatus has been cleaned up—its only drawback is that it becomes so messy—I could easily add the more detailed points. For the present, then, just the essentials.—When the man is lying on the bed, and this has been set vibrating, the harrow is lowered on to his body. It adjusts itself automatically so that the tips of the needles just touch the body; once the adjustment is completed this steel belt tautens immediately to form a rigid bar. And now the performance begins. The uninitiated onlooker notices no external difference in the punishments. The harrow appears to do its work in a uniform manner. As it quivers, its points pierce the body, which is also quivering from the vibration of the bed. So as to enable anyone to scrutinize the carrying out of the sentence, the harrow is made of glass. Getting the needles mounted in the glass presented certain technical problems, but after numerous experiments we managed it. No effort was spared, you understand. And now anyone can observe through the glass how the inscription on the body takes place. Wouldn't you like to come and take a closer look at the needles?'

The voyager got slowly to his feet, walked across and bent over the harrow. 'You notice,' said the officer, 'two kinds of needles in a variety of patterns. Each long needle has a short one beside it. It is the long one that writes, and the short one squirts out water to wash away the blood and keep the script clear at all times. The mixture of blood and water is then led here into small channels and finally it flows into this main channel which has a drainpipe into the pit.' The officer traced with his finger the exact course that the fluid had to take. When he then, in order to make the picture as vivid as possible, cupped his hands at the mouth of the pipe as if to catch the outflow, the voyager lifted his head, and groping behind him with one hand began to back away towards his chair. He saw then to his horror that the condemned man had also followed the officer's invitation to inspect the harrow at close quarters. He had pulled the sleepy soldier a little way forward on the chain and was bending over the glass too. One could see him searching with a puzzled look for what the two gentlemen had just been examining, and in the absence of any explanation being quite unable to find it. He bent over this way and that. Repeatedly he ran his eyes over the glass. The voyager wanted to drive him away, for what he was doing was probably a punishable offence. But the officer took a firm hold of the voyager with one hand and with the other grabbed a clod of earth from the embankment and threw it at the soldier. The latter looked up with a start, saw what the condemned man had dared to do, dropped his rifle, dug his heels into the ground and tugged his charge backwards so violently that he collapsed; then he stood looking down at him as he writhed about and rattled his chains. 'Stand him up!' shouted the officer, for he realized that the voyager's attention was being seriously distracted by the condemned man. The voyager was even leaning across the harrow without taking any notice of it and was only concerned with seeing what was happening to the man. 'Be careful with him!' shouted the officer again. He ran round the apparatus, grasped the condemned man under the armpits with his own hands, and with the help of the soldier he got him on to his feet after much slipping and sliding.

'Now I know everything about it,' said the voyager when the officer came back to him. 'Except the most important thing,' said he, seizing the voyager's arm and pointing upwards: 'Up there in the designer is the machinery which controls the movements of the harrow, and this machinery is set according to the drawing which represents the sentence passed. I am still using the drawings of the former commandant. Here they are'—he pulled several sheets out of the leather folder—'though I'm afraid I can't let you handle them, they're my most precious possession. Just sit down and I'll show you them from here, then you'll be able to see everything easily.' He held up the first sheet. The voyager would have been happy to say something complimentary, but all he could see was a maze of criss-cross lines which covered the paper so closely that it was difficult to make out the blank spaces between them. 'Read it,' said the officer. 'I can't,' said the voyager. 'But it's quite clear,' said the officer. 'It's very artistic,' said the voyager evasively, 'but I can't decipher it.' 'Yes,' said the officer with a laugh, putting the folder away again, 'it's no copy-book lettering for school children. It needs to be perused for a long time. But I'm sure you'd understand it too in the end. Of course it can't be any simple script; you see, it's not supposed to kill straight away, but only after a period of twelve hours on average; the turning-point is calculated to come at the sixth hour. So the actual lettering has to be surrounded with many, many decorations; the text itself forms only a narrow band running round the body; the rest of the body is set aside for the embellishments. Are you now able to appreciate the work of the harrow and of the whole apparatus?—Well just watch, then!' He bounded up the ladder, set a wheel turning, called down: 'Look out, stand aside!' and everything started up. If it had not been for the grating wheel, it would have been magnificent. As if this offending wheel had come as a surprise to him, the officer threatened it with his fist, then spread his arms in apology towards the voyager and came hurrying down to observe the working of the apparatus from below. There was still something not quite right, something that he alone could detect; he climbed up once more, reached inside the designer with both hands, and then to get down faster, instead of using the ladder, slid down one of the poles and began yelling as loud as he could in the voyager's ear, so as to make himself heard above the din: 'Can you follow the sequence? The harrow begins to write; as soon as it has completed the first draft of the inscription on the man's back, the layer of cotton-wool rolls and turns the body slowly on to its side, to give the harrow a fresh area to work on. Meanwhile the raw parts already inscribed come to rest against the cotton-wool, which being specially prepared immediately staunches the bleeding and makes all ready for a new deepening of the script. Then as the body is turned further round these teeth here at the edge of the harrow tear the cotton-wool away from the wounds, fling it into the pit, and the harrow can set to work again. So it goes on writing, deeper and deeper, for the whole twelve hours. For the first six hours the condemned man survives almost as before, he merely suffers pain. After two hours the felt stub is removed, for the man no longer has the strength to scream. Here in this electrically heated bowl at the head of the bed we put warm rice porridge, of which the man can, if he feels inclined, take as much as his tongue can reach. Not one of them misses the opportunity. I am aware of none, and my experience is considerable. Not until the sixth hour does the man lose his pleasure in eating. At that point I usually kneel down here and observe this phenomenon. The man rarely swallows the last morsel; he simply rolls it round in his mouth and spits it into the pit. I have to duck then, or he would spit it in my face. But how still the man grows at the sixth hour! Enlightenment dawns on the dullest. It begins around the eyes. From there it spreads out. A spectacle that might tempt one to lay oneself down under the harrow beside him. Nothing further happens, the man simply begins to decipher the script, he purses his lips as if he were listening. You've seen that it isn't easy to decipher the script with one's eyes; but our man deciphers it with his wounds. It is a hard task, to be sure; he needs six hours to accomplish it. But then the harrow impales him completely and throws him into the pit, where he splashes down on the watery blood and the cotton-wool. With that the judgement is done, and we, the soldier and I, shovel some earth over him.'

The voyager, inclining an ear to the officer, was watching the machine at work with his hands in his pockets. The condemned man was watching likewise, but uncomprehendingly. He was bending forward a little with his eye on the waving needles when the soldier, at a sign from the officer, slashed through his shirt and trousers from behind with a knife, so that they slipped off him; he tried to catch at them as they fell to cover his nakedness, but the soldier hoisted him in the air and shook the last rags from his body. The officer stopped the machine, and in the silence that followed the condemned man was laid under the harrow. The chains were loosed, and in their place the straps were fastened; in the first moment this seemed almost a relief to the condemned man. And now the harrow lowered itself a little further, for he was a thin man. When the needle-points touched him a shudder ran over his skin; while the soldier was busy with his right hand, he stretched out his left hand in some unknown direction; but it was towards the spot where the voyager was standing. The officer was constantly looking sideways at the voyager, as if trying to read from his face how the execution, which he had by now at least superficially explained, was impressing him.

The strap that was intended for the wrist tore apart; presumably the soldier had pulled it too tight. The officer's help was needed, the soldier showed him the broken piece of strap. So the officer went across to him and said, with his face turned to the voyager: 'The machine is so very complex, something is bound to rip or break here and there; but one mustn't allow that to cloud one's overall judgement. In any case, we can find a replacement for the strap without delay; I shall use a chain; admittedly that's bound to affect the delicacy of the vibrations as far as the right arm is concerned.' And while he was fastening the chain he added: 'The resources for maintaining the machine are now severely limited. Under the former commandant I had free access to a special fund set aside for the purpose. There used to be a store here which kept spare parts of every possible kind. I confess that I was almost extravagant in that respect; in the past I mean, not now, as the new commandant claims, but then everything merely serves him as an excuse to attack the old arrangements. Now he has the machine fund under his personal control, and if I send for a new strap the old broken one is required as evidence, the new one takes ten days to arrive and when it comes it's of inferior quality and hardly fit for anything. But how I'm supposed to operate the machine without a strap in the meantime, that's something nobody cares about.'

The voyager reflected: It's always a serious business to intervene decisively in other people's affairs. He was neither a citizen of the penal colony nor a citizen of the state to which it belonged. If he wished to condemn this execution, or even to prevent it, they could say to him: You are a stranger, hold your peace. To that he could make no answer, but simply add that in this instance he was a mystery to himself, for he was voyaging as an observer only, and by no means with any intention of changing other people's judicial systems. But here the circumstances were indeed extremely tempting. The injustice of the procedure and the inhumanity of the execution were beyond all doubt. No one could presume any kind of self-interest on the voyager's part,

for the condemned man was unknown to him, was no fellow country-
man, and by no means a person who inspired sympathy. The voyager
himself had recommendations from people in high places, had been
received here with great courtesy, and the fact that he had been invited
to attend this execution even seemed to suggest that his opinion of the
judicial system was being sought. And this was all the more likely since
the commandant, as he had just heard in the plainest possible terms,
was no supporter of this procedure and adopted an almost hostile attitude towards the officer.

At that moment the voyager heard a scream of rage from the officer. He had just succeeded, not without difficulty, in thrusting the felt
stub into the condemned man's mouth when the man, in an uncontrollable fit of nausea, closed his eyes and vomited. Hastily the officer
pulled him away from the felt and tried to turn his head towards the
pit; but it was too late, the filth was already running down the machine. 'It's all the fault of the commandant!' screamed the officer, shaking the nearest brass rods in a blind fury, 'my machine's being befouled
like a pigsty.' He showed the voyager what had happened with trembling hands. 'Haven't I spent hours trying to make clear to the commandant that for one whole day before the execution no food must be
given. But the new moderate tendency has other ideas. The commandant's ladies stuff the man full of sweetmeats before he's led away. All
his life he's lived on stinking fish and now he has to eat sweets! All
right, one might let that pass, I wouldn't object, but why don't they get
me a new felt stub, which I've been begging for these last three
months. How can one not be sickened to take a piece of felt in one's
mouth which more than a hundred men have sucked and gnawed at as
they died?'

The condemned man had laid his head down and was looking
peaceful, the soldier was busy cleaning the machine with the condemned man's shirt. The officer went up to the voyager, who in some
vague disquiet took a step backwards, but the officer took him by the
hand and drew him aside. 'I should like to have a few words with you
in confidence,' he said, 'if you'll allow me.' 'Of course,' said the voyager, and listened with downcast eyes.

'This procedure and this form of execution, which you now have
the opportunity of admiring, have at present no open supporters left
in our colony. I am their sole defender, and at the same time the sole
defender of the legacy of our former commandant. I can no longer

contemplate any further development of the system; all my energy is consumed in preserving what we have. When the old commandant was alive, the colony was full of his supporters; the old commandant's strength of conviction I do have in some measure, but I have none of his power; as a result his supporters have melted away, there are still plenty of them about but no one will admit it. If you went into the tea-house today, that's to say on an execution day, and listened to what people were saying you'd probably hear nothing but ambiguous remarks. They'd all of them be supporters, but under the present commandant and given his present beliefs they're completely useless as far as I am concerned. And now I ask you: Is the work of a lifetime'—he indicated the machine—'to be ruined because of this commandant and the women who influence him? Can one allow that to happen? Even if one may only have come to our island for a few days as a stranger? But there's no time to lose, there are plans afoot to contest my jurisdiction; meetings are already taking place in the commandant's headquarters from which I am excluded; even your own visit here today seems to me a sign of the times; they are cowardly and send you, a stranger, out in advance.—How different an execution used to be in the old days! The day before the performance the entire valley was already crammed with people; everyone came along just to watch it; early in the morning the commandant appeared with his ladies; fanfares roused the whole camp; I reported that everything was ready; the important persons—every high official was required to attend—arranged themselves round the machine; this pile of cane chairs is a pathetic survival from those days. The machine was freshly cleaned and glittering, I used to fit new spare parts for almost every execution. Before hundreds of pairs of eyes—all the spectators standing on tiptoe right up to the top of the slopes—the condemned man was laid under the harrow by the commandant himself. The tasks that a common soldier is allowed to do today then fell to me, the presiding judge, and I counted it an honour. And then the execution began! No jarring sound disturbed the working of the machine. Many even ceased to watch and lay with their eyes closed in the sand; all of them knew: Now justice is taking its course. In the silence nothing could be heard but the moaning of the condemned man, half muffled by the felt. Nowadays the machine cannot wring from the man any groans that are too loud for the felt to stifle; but in those days a corrosive fluid that we are no longer permitted to use dripped from the inscribing needles. Yes, and then came the sixth hour! It was impossible to grant every request to watch from close up. The commandant in his wisdom decreed that the children should be given priority; of course I myself, by virtue of my office, could always be close at hand; often I would be squatting there with a small child in either arm. How we all drank in the transfigured look on the tortured face, how we bathed our cheeks in the glow of this justice, finally achieved and soon fading! O comrade, what times those were!' The officer had obviously forgotten who it was he was addressing; he had embraced the voyager and laid his head on his shoulder. The voyager was in great embarrassment, he looked around impatiently over the officer's head. The soldier had by now finished his cleaning up and had just tipped some rice porridge into the bowl from a tin. No sooner had the condemned man noticed this when he began, apparently now fully recovered, to reach out for the porridge with his tongue. The soldier kept pushing him away, since the porridge was no doubt meant for later, but it was certainly just as improper that the soldier should stick his dirty hands into it and devour some of it before the condemned man's ravenous eyes.

The officer quickly pulled himself together. 'I wasn't trying to play on your feelings,' he said, 'I know how impossible it is to make those times comprehensible today. In any case, the machine still operates and it is effective on its own. It is effective even if it stands all alone in this valley. And the corpse still falls at the last with the same unfathomable smoothness into the pit, even if there are not, as there used to be, hundreds gathered like flies around it. In those days we had to install a stout railing round the pit; it has long since been torn down.'

The voyager wanted to avert his face from the officer and looked aimlessly about him. The officer thought he was contemplating the desolate state of the valley; he therefore seized him by the hands, moved round to look him in the eyes and asked: 'Can't you just see the shame of it?'

But the voyager said nothing. The officer left him alone for a little while; with his legs apart, hands on hips, he stood still, looking down at the ground. Then he smiled at the voyager in an encouraging way and said: 'I was quite close to you yesterday when the commandant invited you. I overheard the invitation. I know our commandant. I realized at once what he was aiming at. Although he has power enough to proceed against me he doesn't yet dare, but what he does mean to do is to expose me to your judgement, the judgement of a respected foreigner. He has calculated it all carefully; this is only your second day on the island, you did not know the old commandant and his ideas, you are conditioned by European ways of thought, perhaps you object on principle to capital punishment in general and to this mechanical kind of execution in particular, furthermore you are bound to see that the execution is a sad affair, taking place without public sympathy on a machine that is already worn—all these things considered, might it not well be (so thinks the commandant) that you should disapprove of my methods? And if you do disapprove (I'm still speaking from the commandant's point of view) then you won't conceal the fact, for after all you surely have confidence in your own well-tried convictions. On the other hand, you have seen and learnt to respect many peculiarities of many different peoples, so perhaps you may not speak out with full force against our procedures, as you might do in your own country. But the commandant has no need of that. One passing, one merely unguarded remark will be enough. It doesn't even need to express your true opinion so long as it seems to fit his own purpose. He will question you with the greatest cunning, of that I'm quite sure. And his ladies will sit round in a circle and prick up their ears; you might say, for example: "We have a different kind of judicial process," or "In our country the accused is granted a hearing before he is sentenced", or "With us the condemned man is informed of his sentence," or "We have other sentences besides the death penalty," or "We only used torture in the Middle Ages." All these statements are as true as they seem to you self-evident, innocent remarks that in no way impugn my procedure. But how will the commandant react to them? I can see him, our good commandant, pushing his chair aside and rushing out on to the balcony, I can see his ladies streaming out after him, I can hear his voice—the ladies call it a voice of thunder—and what he now says goes like this: "A famous researcher from the West, given the task of examining the judicial system in all the countries of the world, has just said that our own procedure, based on ancient custom, is inhumane. Given this verdict from such a distinguished person, I naturally cannot tolerate this procedure any longer. With effect from today I therefore ordain—etc." You wish to remonstrate, you never said what he is asserting, you have never called my procedure inhumane, on the contrary you regard it, thanks to your deep insight, as the most humane and the most worthy of humanity, you also admire this machinery—but it is all too late; you never find your way on to the balcony, which is by now filled with ladies; you want to draw attention to yourself; you want to cry out; but a lady's hand covers your mouth—and both I and the work of the old commandant are done for.'

The voyager had to suppress a smile; so easy, then, was the task he had supposed would be so difficult. He said evasively: 'You overesti-mate my influence; the commandant has read my letters of recom-mendation, he knows well that I am no expert in legal procedures. If I were to express an opinion it would be the opinion of a private indi-vidual, carrying no more weight than that of anyone else and certainly far less than the opinion of the commandant, who has, I think I'm right in saying, very extensive powers in this penal colony. If his opin-ion of this procedure is as clear-cut as you believe, then I'm afraid the end of the procedure has indeed come, without the need for any mod-est assistance on my part.'

Had the officer understood by now? No, he had still not under-stood. He shook his head vigorously, glanced briefly round at the con-demned man and the soldier, who both abandoned their porridge with a jerk, came up close to the voyager and said in a lower voice, not looking him in the eye but at somewhere on his coat: 'You don't know the commandant; the position in which you stand towards him and the rest of us is—if you'll forgive the expression—so to speak an innocu-ous one; your influence, believe me, cannot be rated too highly. I was delighted when I heard that you were to be the only one to attend the execution. This directive of the commandant was aimed at me, but now I shall turn it to my advantage. Without being distracted by any false whisperings and scornful looks—which would have been in-evitable given a larger attendance—you have listened to my explana-tions, have seen the machine, and are now on the point of watching the execution. No doubt your judgement is already firm; should any trifling doubts still remain, the sight of the execution will remove them. And now I appeal to you: give me your help against the com-mandant!'

The voyager let him go no further. 'But how could I do that,' he cried, 'that's quite impossible. I can no more help you than I can dam-age your interests.'

'You can,' said the officer. The voyager noticed with some alarm that the officer was clenching his fists. 'You can,' repeated the officer with even greater insistence. 'I have a plan that is bound to succeed. You believe the influence you have is not enough. I know that it is. But even granted you are right, surely it is necessary to try all means, even possibly inadequate ones, in order to preserve the old system? So let me tell you my plan. If it is to succeed, the most important thing is for you to say as little as possible about your verdict on the procedure in the colony today. Unless you are asked directly you should on no account express an opinion; but what you do say must be brief and non-committal; it should appear that you find it hard to discuss the matter, that you feel embittered, that if you were to speak openly you would almost start cursing and swearing. I'm not asking you to tell lies; not at all; you should simply give brief answers, such as: "Yes, I witnessed the execution," or "Yes, I heard all the explanations." Just that, nothing more. Your bitterness, which we want them to recognize, is of course amply justified, but not in the way the commandant imagines. He will naturally misunderstand it completely and interpret it to suit his own book. That's what my plan depends on. Tomorrow there's to be a great meeting of all the high administrative officials at the commandant's headquarters, with the commandant himself presiding. Of course the commandant has succeeded in turning all such meetings into public spectacles. He has had a gallery built that is always packed with spectators. I am forced to take part in the discussions although they make me shudder with disgust. Now at all events you are sure to be invited to this meeting; if you act today according to my plan the invitation will become an urgent request. But if for some mysterious reason you aren't invited, you'll have to ask for an invitation; there'll be no doubt about your getting one then. So there you are tomorrow, sitting in the commandant's box with the ladies. He keeps looking up to make sure you're there. After various unimportant, ridiculous items brought in merely to impress the audience—it's mostly some matter of harbour works, they always keep talking about harbour works!—the question of our judicial procedure comes up for discussion. If it's not brought up by the commandant, or not soon enough, I'll see to it that it happens. I'll stand up and report today's execution. Quite briefly, just the statement that it has taken place. Such a statement is not in fact usual there, but I shall make it all the same. The commandant thanks me, as is his custom, with an amiable smile, and then he can't restrain himself, he seizes his opportunity. "We have just heard," he will say, or words to that effect, "the report of an execution. To that I should merely like to add that this particular execution was witnessed by the famous researcher who, as you all know, has done our colony the exceptional honour of his visit. Our meeting today is also given greater importance by his presence among us. Should we not now ask the famous researcher how he judges our traditional mode of execution and the procedure that leads up to it?" Applause on all sides, of course; general approval, with no one more vociferous than I am. The commandant bows to you and says: "Then in the name of us all I put that question to you." And now you step forward to the parapet. Be sure to place your hands where everyone can see them, or the ladies will take hold of them and play with your fingers.—And now at last you speak out. I don't know how I shall endure the tension of the hours waiting for that moment. In your speech you must set yourself no limits, let the truth ring out, lean out over the parapet and bawl, yes indeed, bawl out your conclusions, your unshakeable conclusions to the commandant. But perhaps you don't wish to do that, it's not in keeping with your character, perhaps in your country people behave differently in such situations, very well then, that too will be quite sufficient, don't even stand up, just say a few words, whisper them just loud enough to reach the ears of the officials below, that will suffice, you don't even need to mention the lack of public interest in the execution, the grating wheel, the broken strap, the revolting felt, all the rest you can leave to me, and believe me, if my speech doesn't drive him out of the hall, it will force him to his knees, so that he has to confess: Old commandant, to your power I bow.—That is my plan; are you willing to help me carry it out? But of course you are willing, more than that, you must.' And the officer seized the voyager by both arms and looked him in the face with heaving breast. He had shouted his closing words so loud that even the soldier and the condemned man had begun to take notice; though they could understand nothing they stopped eating for a moment and looked across, chewing, at the voyager.

The answer that he must give had been clear to the voyager from the very beginning; he had experienced too much in his lifetime for him to falter here; he was fundamentally honourable and without fear. All the same he did now hesitate, at the sight of the soldier and the condemned man, for a fleeting moment. But then he said, as he had to: 'No.' The officer blinked several times but kept his eyes fixed upon him. 'Do you want me to explain?' asked the voyager. The officer nodded silently. 'I am an opponent of this procedure,' the voyager now said, 'even before you took me into your confidence—a confidence that I shall of course in no circumstances abuse—I had already been considering whether I should be justified in taking a stand against this procedure, and whether an intervention on my part would have even the remotest chance of success. It was clear to me who I must turn to in the first place: it was the commandant, of course. You made this even clearer, which is not to say that you helped to strengthen my resolve; on the contrary I can sympathize with your sincere conviction, even though it cannot influence my judgement.'

The officer remained silent, turned towards the machine, grasped one of the brass rods and then, leaning back a little, looked up at the designer as if to check that all was in order. The soldier and the condemned man seemed to have struck up a friendship; the condemned man was making signs to the soldier, difficult though this was because of the tightness of the straps; the soldier was bending down to him; the condemned man whispered something to him and the soldier nodded.

The voyager followed the officer and said: 'You don't yet know what I intend to do. I am certainly going to tell the commandant what I think of the procedure, but I shall do so privately, not at a public meeting; nor shall I be staying here long enough to be called into any meeting; I'm sailing early tomorrow morning or at least going aboard my ship.'

It did not look as if the officer had been listening. 'So the procedure hasn't convinced you?' he murmured, smiling as an old man smiles at the nonsense of a child and pursues his own real thoughts behind that smile.

'Then the time has come,' he said at last, and looked suddenly at the voyager with a light in his eyes that seemed to hold a kind of summons, some call to participate.

'The time for what?' asked the voyager uneasily, but he got no answer.

'You are free,' said the officer to the condemned man in his native tongue. The man did not believe it at first. 'You're free, I tell you,' said the officer. For the first time the face of the condemned man came fully to life. Was it the truth? Was it just a whim of the officer's that might pass? Had the foreign visitor secured his pardon? What could it be? So his face seemed to be asking. But not for long. Whatever it might be, he intended to be really free if he could, and he began to shake himself about as far as the harrow allowed.

'You'll tear my straps,' shouted the officer, 'keep still! We're going to undo them.' He gave a sign to the soldier and they both set to work. The condemned man chuckled quietly to himself without uttering a word, turning his face now to the officer on his left, now to the soldier on his right, and not forgetting the voyager either.

'Pull him out,' the officer ordered the soldier. A certain amount of care was needed in doing so because of the harrow. The condemned man already had a number of minor lacerations on his back as a result of his impatience.

But from now on the officer hardly paid any further attention to him. He went up to the voyager, took out his little leather folder again, leafed through it and eventually found the sheet he was looking for, which he showed to the voyager. 'Read it,' he said. 'I can't,' said the voyager, 'I've already told you I can't read those scripts.' 'Just look at it carefully,' said the officer, coming to the voyager's side so as to read with him. When that proved of no use either he began tracing in the air with his little finger, which he held well above the paper as if this must on no account be touched, trying in this way to make it easier for the voyager to read. And the voyager did make every effort, for he wanted to please the officer in this respect at least, but he found it impossible. Now the officer began to spell out the writing letter by letter and then he read it out again as a whole. ' "Be just!"—that's what it says,' he declared, 'surely you can read it now.' The voyager bent down so close over the paper that the officer moved it further away for fear of his touching it; the voyager said nothing more, but it was obvious that he had still been unable to read it. ' "Be just!"—that's what it says,' the officer repeated. 'Maybe,' said the voyager, 'I'm prepared to believe you.' 'Very good, then,' said the officer, at least partly satisfied, and climbed up the ladder with the sheet; with great care he inserted the sheet in the designer and then he appeared to be rearranging the entire machinery; it was a most laborious business, evidently involving the very smallest of the wheels, at times the officer's head disappeared completely inside the designer so closely did he have to examine the mechanism.

The voyager kept a constant watch on this operation from down below, his neck grew stiff and his eyes ached from the sunlight that flooded the sky. The soldier and the condemned man were occupied only with each other. The condemned man's shirt and trousers, which were already lying in the pit, were fished out by the soldier on the point of his bayonet. The shirt was indescribably filthy, and the condemned man washed it in the bucket of water. When he then put on his shirt and trousers both the soldier and the condemned man had to burst out laughing, for of course they had been slit up the back. Perhaps the condemned man thought it was his duty to amuse the soldier, he whirled round and round in front of him in his slashed clothes, while the soldier squatted on the ground and slapped his knees with laughter. However, they did still control themselves to some extent in view of the presence of the gentlemen.

When the officer had at last completed his work up above, he once more surveyed the whole thing in all its parts with a smile, this time slamming down the lid of the designer, which had stayed open till now, climbed down, looked into the pit and then at the condemned man, observed with satisfaction that he had extracted his clothes, went over then to the bucket of water to wash his hands, noticed too late the revolting filth, was sad that he was now quite unable to wash them, plunged them finally—this alternative did not satisfy him, but he had to accept it—into the sand, whereupon he stood up and began to unbutton the coat of his uniform. As he did so, there at once fell into his hands the two ladies' handkerchiefs that he had stuffed under his collar. 'Here you are, your handkerchiefs,' he said, and tossed them over to the condemned man. And to the voyager he said in explanation: 'Presents from the ladies.'

Despite the evident haste with which he took off his uniform coat and then undressed completely, he nevertheless handled each piece of clothing with the greatest care, even running his fingers specially over the silver braid of his tunic and shaking a tassel into place. But all this care was hardly in keeping with the fact that no sooner was he finished with each piece of clothing when he flung it at once, with an indignant jerk, into the pit. The last thing that was left to him was his short sword with its belt. He drew it out of its scabbard, broke it in pieces, then gathered everything together, the bits of sword, the scabbard and the belt, and hurled them all from him so violently that they clanged together in the pit below.

Now he stood there naked. The voyager bit his lips and said nothing. He knew what was going to happen, but he had no right to hinder the officer in any way. If the judicial procedure that was so dear to the officer's heart was really on the point of being abolished—possibly as a

result of the voyager's own intervention, to which he felt himself committed—then the officer was now acting perfectly rightly; the voyager
would have acted no differently in his place.

The soldier and the condemned man understood nothing at first,
to begin with they were not even watching. The condemned man was
filled with glee at getting his handkerchiefs back, but he was not allowed to enjoy them for long, for the soldier snatched them away from
him with a quick, unforeseeable swoop. Now the condemned man in
turn tried to pull the handkerchiefs out from under the soldier's belt
where the latter had tucked them away for safety, but the soldier was
on his guard. And so they struggled with each other, half in fun. Not
until the officer was quite naked did they begin to take notice. The
condemned man in particular seemed to have been struck with the
sense of some drastic reversal. What had been happening to him was
now happening to the officer. Perhaps it would go on like that to the
bitter end. Presumably the foreign visitor had given the order. This
was vengeance, then. Without himself having suffered to the end, he
was going to be revenged to the end. A broad, silent grin appeared on
his face now, and there it stayed.

The officer, however, had turned to the machine. It had been clear
enough earlier that he understood the machine well, but now it was almost staggering to see how he handled it and how it obeyed him. He
only had to stretch out a hand towards the harrow for it to raise and
lower itself several times, until it reached the right position to receive
him; he merely gripped the edge of the bed and it began at once to vi-
brate; the felt stub came to meet his mouth, one could see that the
officer did not actually want it, but his hesitation lasted only for a moment, he quickly submitted and accepted it. All was now ready, only
the straps were still hanging down at the sides, but these were clearly
unnecessary, the officer had no need to be fastened down. But then the
condemned man noticed the loose straps, in his opinion the execution
was not complete unless the straps were fastened, he beckoned vigorously to the soldier and they both ran across to strap the officer down.
The latter had already stretched out a foot to kick the crank that
would set the designer in motion; then he saw that the two men had
arrived; so he withdrew his foot and allowed himself to be strapped
down. But now of course the crank was no longer within his reach;
neither the soldier nor the condemned man would be able to find it,
and the voyager was determined not to lift a finger. It was not neces-

sary; hardly were the straps in place when the machine began to operate; the bed vibrated, the needles danced over the skin, the harrow moved gently up and down. The voyager had been staring at it for some time before it occurred to him that a wheel in the designer should have been grating; and yet all was still, not even the faintest whirring could be heard.

As a result of this silent working the machine positively escaped attention. The voyager looked across to the soldier and the condemned man. The condemned man was the livelier of the two, everything about the machine interested him, now he was bending down, now reaching up, always with his forefinger outstretched to point something out to the soldier. The voyager found this offensive. He was determined to stay here to the end, but he could not have borne the sight of these two for long. 'Go home,' he said. The soldier might have been prepared to do so, but the condemned man felt the order almost as a punishment. He implored with his hands clasped to be allowed to stay, and when the voyager shook his head and would not relent he even went down on his knees. The voyager saw that giving orders was useless, he was about to go over and chase the pair away. At that moment he heard a noise above him in the designer. He looked up. Was that cogwheel giving trouble after all? But it was something else. Slowly the lid of the designer lifted until it fell open completely. The teeth of a cogwheel came into view and rose up, soon the whole wheel appeared, it was as if some mighty force were compressing the designer so that there was no more room for this wheel, the wheel turned until it reached the edge of the designer, fell to the ground, and then rolled along upright in the sand for a little way before it toppled over. But up aloft a second wheel was already emerging, followed by many others, big ones and little ones and ones that were hard to distinguish, with all of them the same thing happened; one kept thinking, surely at least by now the designer must be empty, but then a new, particularly numerous group appeared, rose up, fell to the ground, rolled along the sand and toppled over. Engrossed in this spectacle, the condemned man quite forgot the voyager's command, the cogwheels completely fascinated him, he kept trying to catch one and urging the soldier to help him as he did so, but each time he drew back his hand in alarm, for another wheel would immediately follow it and give him a fright, at least as it started to roll.

The voyager, on the other hand, was deeply disturbed; the machine was obviously disintegrating; its peaceful action was an illusion; he had the feeling that it was now his duty to protect the officer, since he was no longer able to take care of himself. But while the falling cogwheels had been absorbing his whole attention he had omitted to keep an eye on the rest of the machine; now, however, once the last cogwheel had left the designer and he bent over the harrow he had a new and still more disagreeable surprise. The harrow was not writing, it was just stabbing, and the bed was not rolling the body over but just heaving it up quivering into the needles. The voyager wanted to intervene, if possible to bring the whole thing to a standstill, for this was no torture such as the officer had wished to achieve, this was just plain murder. He stretched out his hands. But at that moment the harrow rose with the body spitted on it and swung to the side, as it otherwise did only when the twelfth hour had come. Blood flowed in a hundred streams, unmixed with water, the water-jets too had failed this time. And now the very last stage failed as well, the body refused to free itself from the long needles, it poured out its blood yet it hung there over the pit without falling. The harrow began to move back to its old position, but as if noticing that it was not yet free of its burden it stayed above the pit where it was. 'Come and help!' yelled the voyager to the soldier and the condemned man, and himself seized the officer's feet. He meant to push against the feet from his end while the two took hold of the officer's head from the other so that he might be slowly detached from the needles. But the other two could not make up their minds to come; the condemned man actually turned away; the voyager had to go over to them and compel them to take up their place at the officer's head. In doing so he caught sight, almost against his will, of the face of the corpse. It was as it had been in life; no sign of the promised deliverance could be detected; what all the others had found in the machine, the officer had not found; his lips were pressed firmly together, his eyes were open and had the expression of life, their look was calm and convinced, through his forehead went the point of the great iron spike.

As the voyager, with the soldier and the condemned man behind him, reached the first houses of the colony the soldier pointed to one of them and said: 'Here is the tea-house.'

On the ground floor of this house was a deep, low, cavernous room, its walls and ceiling blackened with smoke. It was open to the street along the whole of its width. There was little to distinguish the tea-house from the other houses of the colony, which apart from the palatial buildings of the commandant's headquarters were all very dilapidated, and yet the effect it had on the voyager was that of a historical reminder and he felt the power of earlier times. He approached it and made his way, followed by his companions, between the empty tables that stood in front of the tea-house in the street; then he breathed in the cool, musty air that came from the interior. 'The old man is buried here,' said the soldier, 'the priest wouldn't allow him a place in the graveyard. For a time they couldn't decide where to bury him, in the end they buried him here. The officer won't have told you anything about it because of course that was what he was most ashamed of. He even tried a few times at night to dig the old man up, but he was always chased away.' 'Where is the grave?' asked the voyager, who was unable to believe the soldier. At once the two of them, the soldier and the condemned man, ran ahead and pointed with outstretched hands to where the grave was. They led the voyager through to the rear wall, where there were customers sitting at a few of the tables. These were apparently dockers, powerfully built men with short black glittering beards. All were in shirt-sleeves and their shirts were ragged; they were poor, humiliated folk. As the voyager approached a few of them got up, backed against the wall and stared at him. 'It's a stranger,' so the whisper went round, 'he wants to look at the grave.' They pushed one of the tables aside, and under it there really was a grave-stone. It was a simple stone, low enough to be hidden beneath a table. It bore an inscription in very small letters, the voyager had to kneel down to read it. It read: 'Here lies the old commandant. His followers, who must now be nameless, have dug him this grave and placed this stone. It is prophesied that after a given number of years the commandant will rise again, and will lead out his followers from this house to reconquer the colony. Have faith and watch!' When the voyager had read this and risen to his feet he saw the men standing round him smiling, as if they had read the inscription with him, had found it laughable, and were inviting him to share their opinion. The voyager pretended not to notice, distributed a few coins among them, waited until the table had been pushed over the grave, left the tea-house and made his way to the harbour.

The soldier and the condemned man had found some acquaintances in the tea-house who detained them. But they must soon have torn themselves away, for the voyager had only got halfway down the long flight of steps that led to the boats when they came running after him. Probably they wanted to force the voyager at the last minute to take them with him. While he was negotiating down below with a ferryman to take him out to the steamer, the pair of them came racing down the steps, in silence, for they did not dare to shout. But by the time they reached the foot of the steps the voyager was already in the boat and the ferryman was just casting off. They could still have managed to leap into the boat, but the voyager picked up a heavy knotted rope from the deck, threatened them with it and so held them at bay.

A COUNTRY DOCTOR

Little Tales

The New Advocate

W E HAVE A NEW ADVOCATE, Dr Bucephalus. In his outward appearance there is little to recall the time when he was
still the war-horse of Alexander of Macedon. Anyone who is familiar
with the circumstances will notice a thing or two, of course. But the
other day, on the forecourt steps, I even saw a quite simple usher lost
in admiration as he watched the advocate, with the expert eye of the
regular racegoer, climbing up with a high-stepping tread that made
each of his steps ring out on the marble.

On the whole the admission of Bucephalus meets with the approval of the Bar. With remarkable insight people tell themselves that
Bucephalus is, given the present order of society, in a difficult position,
and that he deserves for that reason, as well as on account of his historical importance, at least a sympathetic reception. Today—it cannot
be denied—there is no Alexander the Great. There are indeed plenty
of those who know how to murder; even the skill required to spear a
friend across the banqueting table is not lacking; and many find Mace-
donia too constricting, so that they curse Philip the father—but no
one, no one can lead the way to India. Even in those days the gates of
India were beyond reach, but the royal sword pointed to where they
stood. Today the gates have been carried off to some quite other, re-
moter and loftier places; no one shows the direction; many hold

swords in their hands, but only to brandish them, and the eye that tries to follow them grows confused.

So perhaps it really is best to do what Bucephalus has done, and immerse oneself in the books of the law. Free, his flanks unconstrained by the grip of his rider, in the still light of the lamp, far from the din of the Battle of Issus, he reads and turns the pages of our ancient books.

A Country Doctor

I WAS IN GREAT DIFFICULTY; a seriously ill patient was awaiting me in a village ten miles away; thick driving snow filled the
wide expanse between us; I had a carriage, a light one with large
wheels, just the right thing for our country roads; wrapped up in my
fur coat, my bag of instruments in my hand, I stood in the yard all
ready to go; but the horse was missing, the horse. My own horse had
succumbed the night before to its over-exertions in this icy winter;
now my servant-girl was running round the village trying to borrow a
horse; but it was hopeless, I knew it, and here was I standing aimlessly
about, more and more deeply covered in snow, more and more unable
to move. The girl appeared on her own in the gateway, waving her
lantern; of course, whoever would lend out his horse just now for a
journey like this? I trudged across the yard once more; I could find no
solution; absently, in my distress, I kicked at the rotten door of the
pigsty which had not been used for years. The door opened and
clapped to and fro on its hinges. Warmth emerged, and a smell as of
horses. A dim stable lantern was swinging from a rope within. A man,
crouching down in the low-pitched shed, raised his open blue-eyed
face. 'Shall I harness the horses up?' he asked, crawling out on all
fours. I was at a loss for something to say and merely bent down to see
what else there was in the sty. The servant-girl was standing at my
side. 'You never know what you're going to find in your own house,'
said she, and we both laughed. 'Hey brother, hey sister!' cried the
groom and two horses, mighty creatures with powerful flanks, pro-
pelled themselves forward one behind the other by the sheer force of
their twisting bodies, with their legs tucked in and dipping their
shapely heads like camels, out through the door-hole which they filled
completely. But the next moment up they stood, high on their long
legs, their coats giving off a dense cloud of steam. 'Give him a hand,' I
said, and the willing girl made haste to pass the harness to the groom.

But hardly is she near him when the groom flings his arms round her and claps his face to hers. She screams out and comes running to me; imprinted on her cheek are the red marks of two rows of teeth. 'You brute,' I shout in fury, 'do you want the whip?' but then recollect at once that he is a stranger; that I don't know where he comes from, and that he is helping me of his own free will when all others fail. As if he knows what I am thinking he takes no offence at my threat, but just turns round to me once, still busy with the horses. 'Get in,' he says then and sure enough: all is ready. Never before, so I note, have I ridden behind such a splendid pair and I climb gaily in. 'I shall drive, though, you don't know the way,' say I. 'Of course,' says he, 'I shan't be coming at all, I'm staying with Rose.' 'No,' shrieks Rose, and rightly foreseeing her inevitable fate she flees into the house; I hear the door-chain rattle as she puts it up; I hear the lock spring to; I can even see how she puts out the lights in the hall, and then chasing through the rooms all the lights in them as well, so as to escape detection. 'You're coming with me,' I tell the groom, 'or I abandon the journey, urgent though it is. I don't intend to sacrifice the girl to you as payment for the ride.' 'Away you go!' he cries; claps his hands; the carriage is whirled away like a stick in the current; I just have time to hear the door of my house burst and splinter under the groom's assault, then my eyes and ears are filled with a mighty rushing that pervades all my senses. But that too is no more than a moment, for as though my patient's yard opened out directly beyond my gate, I am already there; the horses are standing quietly; the snow has stopped falling; moonlight all around; my patient's parents come hurrying out of the house; his sister behind them; I am almost lifted out of the carriage; from their confused talk I can gather nothing; in the sick-room the air is almost unbreathable; smoke is rising from the neglected stove; I shall have to push open the window; but first of all I must look at the patient. Gaunt, with no fever, neither cold nor hot, with empty eyes, without a shirt, the young lad raises himself out of the bed-clothes, puts his arms round my neck and whispers in my ear: 'Doctor, let me die.' I glance around me; no one has heard; the parents are leaning forward in silence and awaiting my verdict; the sister has brought up a chair for my bag. I open the bag and search among my instruments; the boy keeps reaching out for me from his bed to remind me of his request; I pick up a forceps, examine it in the candle-light and put it back again. 'Yes,' I reflect profanely, 'in cases like this the gods help out, send along the missing horse, add a second one in view of the urgency, and for good measure provide the groom—' Only now do I remember Rose again; what am I to do, how can I save her, how can I drag her out from under that groom, ten miles away from her, uncontrollable horses before my carriage? These horses, who have now somehow loosened their straps; push open the windows, I know not how, from the outside; poke their heads in, one through each window, and unperturbed by the family's cries are contemplating the patient. 'I'll be on my way back at once,' I say to myself, as if the horses were summoning me to start the journey, yet I allow the sister, who thinks I am overcome by the heat, to help me out of my fur coat. A glass of rum is set before me, the old man pats me on the shoulder, the sacrifice of this treasure of his justifies the familiarity. I shake my head; the narrow circle of the old man's thoughts would repel me; only for that reason do I decline the drink. The mother stands by the bed-side and beckons me over; I obey, and while one of the horses neighs loudly up at the ceiling I lay my head against the boy's chest, my wet beard making him shiver. I confirm what I already knew: the boy is in good health; somewhat feeble circulation, saturated with coffee by his anxious mother, but in good health and best kicked out of bed at once. Changing the world is not my affair, so I let him lie. I am employed by the district and do my duty to the limit, if not indeed beyond it. Though badly paid I am open-handed and always willing to assist the poor. It still remains for Rose to be taken care of; but then the boy may have his way, as far as I'm concerned, and I shall be ready to die as well. What am I doing here in this endless winter! My horse has per-ished, and there is no one in the village who will lend me theirs. I have to haul my pair out of the pigsty; if they didn't happen to be horses I should have to drive sows. That's how it is. And I nod to the family. They know nothing about it, and if they did know they wouldn't be-lieve it. Writing prescriptions is easy, but communicating with folk otherwise is hard. Well, that's about the end of my visit, I suppose; once again I've been troubled unnecessarily; I'm used to it, with the help of my night-bell the whole district torments me; but that I should this time have had to abandon Rose as well, that fair young girl who has lived in my house for years, almost without my noticing her—this sacrifice is too great, and I shall have to try, by some subtle means or other, to get it all worked out in my head so that I don't let fly at this family, who with the best will in the world cannot restore Rose to me.

But then, as I close my bag and make a sign for my fur coat, and the family stands there together in a group, the father sniffing at the glass of rum in his hand, the mother, probably disappointed in me—well, what do people expect?—tearfully biting her lips, and the sister flourishing a blood-soaked handkerchief, I almost do feel prepared to admit the possibility that the boy may perhaps be sick after all. I go over to him, he smiles at me as if I might be bringing him the best of all nourishing broths—ah, now both horses are neighing; no doubt the noise is ordained from above to facilitate the examination—and now I discover: yes, the boy is sick. On his right side, in the region of the hip, a wound has opened up as big as the palm of my hand. Rose-red, in various shades, dark in the depths, paler towards the edges, finely grained, with blood welling unevenly, open like a mine at the surface. Thus from the distance. A closer look reveals a further complication. Who can set his eyes on that without whistling softly? Worms, as thick and as long as my little finger, rose-red themselves and blood-spattered in addition, held fast in the depths of the wound, are wriggling with their little white heads and their numerous legs towards the light. Poor boy, you are past helping. I have found your great wound, this flower in your side is destroying you. The family is happy, they see me occupied; the sister tells the mother, the mother tells the father, and the father tells some visitors who come tiptoeing in, with their arms outstretched for balance, through the moonlight of the open door. 'Will you save me?' the boy whispers with a sob, quite blinded by the life in his wound. That's what people are like in my district. Always asking the impossible of their doctor. They have lost their old faith; the priest sits at home and picks his vestments to pieces, one by one; but the doctor is expected to accomplish everything with his sensitive surgical hand. Well, just as you please: I have not volunteered my services; if you misuse me for sacred ends I'll put up with that too; what more can I hope for, I, an old country doctor, robbed of his servant-girl! And they come, the family and the village-elders come, and they take off my clothes; a choir of schoolchildren with the teacher at its head stands outside the door and sings this verse to the simplest of tunes:

> Strip his clothes off, then he'll heal us,
> If he doesn't, strike him dead!
> He's only a doctor, a doctor after all.

There I stand stripped of my clothes, regarding the people calmly with my head bowed and my fingers in my beard. I am perfectly composed and superior to them all, and so I remain, though it doesn't help me, for now they take me up by the head and the feet and carry me over to the bed. They lay me down against the wall, on the side of the wound. Then all leave the room; the door is closed; the singing stops; clouds cover the moon; the bedclothes lie warm around me; the horses' heads in the open windows sway to and fro like shadows. 'You know,' says a voice in my ear, 'I have very little faith in you. You're just another one who's been wafted in from somewhere, you didn't get here on your own two feet. Instead of helping you're cramping me on my death-bed. What I'd like best is to scratch your eyes out.' 'You are right,' say I, 'it's a disgrace. But then I'm a doctor. What am I to do? Believe me, it isn't easy for me either.'

'Am I supposed to be content with that excuse? Oh, I suppose I must. I always have to be content. I came into the world with a beautiful wound; that's all I was endowed with.' 'Young friend,' I say to him, 'your trouble is: you don't see things in the round. I have been in all the sick-rooms, far and wide, and I can tell you this: your wound is none so bad. Made with two slanting blows of the axe. Many there are who proffer their side and can hardly hear the axe in the forest, let alone that it's coming closer.' 'Is that really so, or are you deluding me in my fever?' 'It is really so, you can take a medical officer's word for it on your way.' And he took it and was still. But now it was time to think of my own escape. The horses were still standing faithfully in their places. Clothes, fur coat and bag were swiftly gathered up; I wasn't going to waste any time getting dressed; if the horses sped back as fast as they had come, I should almost leap straight from this bed into mine. One horse obediently withdrew from the window; I flung my bundle into the carriage; the fur coat flew too far, just one of its sleeves was caught up on a hook. Good enough. I swung myself on to the horse's back. The straps trailing loose, one horse barely attached to the other, the carriage wandering about behind, the fur coat last of all in the snow. 'Look lively!' I cried, but it had no effect; slowly, like old men, we crawled through the waste of snow; for a long time we could hear behind us the children's new but erroneous song:

> Now patients all, be joyful,
> The doctor's been laid to your side!

Never shall I reach home like this; my flourishing practice is done for; a successor is stealing what I have, but in vain since he cannot replace me; in my house the loathsome groom is raging; Rose is his victim; I refuse to reflect on it. Naked, exposed to the frost of this unhappiest of ages, with an earthly carriage, unearthly horses, old man that I am, I go drifting around. My fur coat is hanging from the back of the carriage, but I cannot reach it, and not one of my busy pack of patients lifts a finger. Betrayed! Betrayed! If you once respond to a faulty ring on the night-bell—it can never be made good.

Up in the Gallery

IF SOME FRAIL, consumptive equestrienne on a shaky circus-horse were to be driven round and round before an indefatigable audience for months on end without respite by a merciless, whip-flourishing ringmaster, whirled along on her horse, throwing kisses, swaying from the waist, and if this performance were to stretch out to the incessant blare of the orchestra and the ventilators into the ever-unfolding grey of the future, accompanied by the fading and renewed swelling of applause from the clapping hands which are really steam-hammers—then, perhaps, might a young visitor up in the gallery come racing down the long flight of steps, through row after row, burst into the ring, and cry out his 'Halt!' through the fanfares of the ever-obedient orchestra.

But since that is not so; a lovely lady, pink and white, comes floating in, through the curtains which are proudly opened for her by the liveried attendants; the manager, humbly trying to catch her eye, breathes at her in an attitude of animal devotion; tenderly lifts her up on the dapple-grey, as if she were his own most precious granddaughter setting out on a dangerous journey; cannot make up his mind to give the signal with his whip; finally prevails on himself and gives it with a crack; runs along, open-mouthed, at the horse's side; keeps a sharp-eyed watch on each of the rider's leaps; is hardly able to grasp the extent of her skill; shouts attempted warnings to her, using the English terms; furiously exhorts the grooms who are holding the hoops to take the most painstaking care; before the great somersault implores the orchestra to be silent with his hands upraised; at last lifts the little one down from her trembling horse, kisses her on both cheeks, and considers no ovation from the audience sufficient; while she herself, supported by him, high on tiptoe, in a swirl of dust, with outstretched arms, little head thrown back, wants the whole circus to share in her happiness—since this is so, the visitor up in the gallery lays his face on the parapet, and sinking into the closing march as if into a deep dream, he weeps without knowing it.

A Leaf from an Old Manuscript

IT WOULD SEEM that much has been neglected in the defence of our fatherland. We have not worried our heads about this until recently and have continued with our work as usual; but the events of the latter days have been causing us concern.

I have a cobbler's workshop in the square in front of the imperial palace. Scarcely have I opened my shop at daybreak when I see armed men already posted at the end of every street leading into the square. These are not our soldiers, however, but evidently nomads from the north. By some means that is incomprehensible to me they have penetrated as far as the capital, although this is a very long way from the frontier. At all events, there they are; it seems that every morning there are more of them.

As lies in their nature they camp in the open, for houses they cannot abide. They occupy themselves with sharpening swords, whittling arrows, practising their horsemanship. They have transformed this quiet square, which has always been kept scrupulously clean, into a veritable pigsty. We do sometimes attempt to dash out of our shops and dispose of the worst of the filth at least, but this happens less and less often, for the effort is useless; besides, it involves the risk of our being trampled by the horses or cut by the whips.

Converse with the nomads is impossible. They do not know our language, indeed they barely have one of their own. They communicate with one another much as jackdaws do. This screeching of jackdaws is constantly in our ears. Our way of life, our institutions, they neither understand nor wish to understand. As a result they show no interest in any kind of sign language either. You may dislocate your jaw and twist your wrists out of joint, they have still not understood you nor will they ever understand. They often make grimaces; then they show the whites of their eyes and foam at the mouth, but they intend to convey nothing by it, not even a threat; they just do it because that is how they are made. Whatever they need, they take. It cannot be said that they use force. When they make a grab for something you stand aside and abandon it all to them. They have taken their fair share from my stock, as well. But I can hardly complain when I observe, for example, how it fares with the butcher across the way. No sooner has he brought in his supplies when they are all snatched away from him and the nomads are devouring them. Even their horses eat meat; often a horseman and his horse will be lying alongside each other, both feeding off the same piece, one from either end. The butcher is apprehensive and does not dare to stop his meat deliveries. We can understand this, however, and we collect money to support him. If the nomads were to get no meat, who knows what might occur to them; who knows, for that matter, what will occur to them even if they do get their daily meat.

The other day the butcher had the idea that he might at least save himself the trouble of slaughtering, and next morning he brought out a live ox. He must not be allowed to do this again. For perhaps an hour I was lying flat on the floor at the very back of my workshop, and had piled all my clothes and my blankets and bolsters on top of me, just so as not to hear the bellowing of that ox which the nomads were leaping on from all sides to tear out pieces of its warm flesh with their teeth. All had been long since quiet before I ventured out again; like drunkards round a wine-barrel they lay exhausted round the remains of the ox.

It was just then that I thought I had caught sight of the emperor himself at one of the windows of his palace; never does he emerge otherwise into these outlying apartments, always he keeps only to his innermost garden; but this time he was standing, or so at least it seemed to me, at one of his windows, looking down with his head bowed at the turmoil before his gates.

'What will happen now?' we all ask ourselves. 'How long can we endure this burden and torment? The imperial palace has drawn the nomads to it, but it does not know how to drive them away. The gate remains closed; the guards, who were once always marching ceremoniously in and out, keep inside behind barred windows. It is to us artisans and tradesmen that the salvation of the fatherland is entrusted; but we are not equal to such a task; never, indeed, have we claimed that we were capable of performing it. It is a misunderstanding; and it is proving our ruin.'

Before the Law

BEFORE THE LAW stands a doorkeeper. To this doorkeeper there comes a man from the country and asks to be admitted to the law. But the doorkeeper says that he cannot at present grant him admittance. The man considers, and then asks whether that means he may be admitted later on. 'It is possible,' says the doorkeeper, 'but not at present.' Since the gate leading to the law stands open as always and the doorkeeper steps aside, the man bends down to look through the gateway into the interior. When the doorkeeper sees this he laughs and says: 'If it tempts you so, then try entering despite my prohibition. But mark: I am powerful. And I am only the lowest doorkeeper. In hall after hall stand other doorkeepers, each more powerful than the last. The mere sight of the third is more than even I can bear.' The man from the country has not expected such difficulties; the law, he thinks, should be accessible to everyone and at all times; but as he now takes a closer look at the doorkeeper in his fur coat, at his large pointed nose, his long, sparse, black Tartar beard, he decides that it is better, after all, to wait until he receives permission to enter. The doorkeeper gives him a stool and lets him sit down to one side of the door. There he sits for days and years. He makes many attempts to be admitted and wearies the doorkeeper with his entreaties. The doorkeeper often conducts little examinations with him, questioning him about his home and about much else; but they are impersonal questions such as dignitaries ask, and he always concludes by repeating once again that he cannot yet admit him. The man, who has equipped himself well for his journey, uses up all that he has, however valuable it is, in order to bribe the doorkeeper. The latter always accepts everything, but saying as he does so: 'I only accept so you won't feel there's anything you haven't tried.' Throughout the many years the man observes the doorkeeper almost without interruption. He forgets the other doorkeepers, and this first one seems to him the sole obstacle barring his admission to the law. He curses his misfortune, fiercely and loudly in the early years; later, as he grows old, he merely grumbles away to himself. He becomes childish, and since during his long study of the doorkeeper he has even discovered the fleas in his fur collar, he begs the fleas as well to help him and change the doorkeeper's mind. Finally his sight begins to fail and he does not know whether it is really growing darker around him or whether his eyes are just deceiving him. But he can indeed perceive in the darkness a radiance that streams out unquenchably from the doorway of the law. Now he has not much longer to live. Before his death all the experiences of the long years assemble in his mind to form a question which he has never yet asked the doorkeeper. He beckons to him since he can no longer raise his stiffening body. The doorkeeper has to bend down to him, for the difference in height has changed very much to the man's disadvantage. 'What is it that you still want to know?' asks the doorkeeper, 'you are insatiable.' 'Surely everyone strives to reach the law,' says the man, 'how does it happen that for all these many years no one except me has ever asked for admittance?' The doorkeeper recognizes that the man is at his end, and in order to reach his failing ears he raises his voice and bellows at him: 'No one else could ever have been admitted here, since this entrance was intended for you alone. Now I am going to close it.'

Jackals and Arabs

WE WERE ENCAMPED in the oasis. My companions were asleep. An Arab, a tall figure in white, strode past; he had been seeing to the camels and was going to his sleeping place.

I flung myself on my back in the grass; I wanted to sleep; I could not; the wailing howl of a jackal in the distance; I sat up again. And what had been so far off was suddenly close at hand. A seething mass of jackals around me; dull golden eyes gleaming out and fading away; lean bodies in orderly and nimble motion, as if controlled by a whip.

One came up from behind me, pushed through under my arm, pressing against me as if he needed my warmth; then he stepped almost eye to eye in front of me and spoke:

'I am the oldest jackal, far and wide. I am glad I'm still able to welcome you here. I'd almost given up hope, for we've been awaiting you for countless ages; my mother waited and her mother and every mother as far back as the first mother of all the jackals. Believe me!'

'I am surprised,' I said, forgetting to light the pile of firewood lying ready to keep the jackals off with its smoke, 'I'm very much surprised to hear it. I've only come down from the far north by chance, and I'm making a short journey. What is it you want then, jackals?'

And as if these words, perhaps all too friendly, had given them courage, they drew their circle closer round me; they were all breathing fast with a snarl in their throats.

'We are aware,' began the eldest, 'that you come from the north; that is just what we build our hopes on. People up there understand things that aren't understood by the Arabs down here. From their cold arrogance, I can tell you, no spark of understanding can be struck. They kill animals in order to eat them, and carrion flesh they despise.'

'Don't talk so loud,' said I, 'there are Arabs sleeping near.'

'You really must be a stranger here,' said the jackal, 'or you'd know that never in all history has a jackal been afraid of an Arab. Why, do you think we should be afraid of them? Is it not misfortune enough to be banished among such creatures?'

'Perhaps, perhaps,' said I, 'I don't presume to judge things so remote from my concerns; it seems to be a most ancient feud; so it probably runs in the blood; so maybe blood will be needed to end it.'

'You are very wise,' said the old jackal; and they all breathed even faster; their lungs straining, although they were standing still; a sour smell came from their gaping mouths which at times I had to grit my teeth to bear, 'you are very wise; what you say accords with our ancient teachings. So what we shall do is take their blood, and the feud is ended.'

'Oh!' I exclaimed, more vehemently than I meant to, 'they'll defend themselves; they'll shoot you down in packs with their muskets.'

'You misunderstand us,' said he, 'after human fashion, which seems to persist in the far north as well. Killing them is not at all what we have in mind. All the waters of the Nile would never suffice to wash us clean. The mere sight of their living flesh is enough to send us running off, out into a purer air, out into the desert which is therefore our home.'

And all the jackals standing round me, their number now increased by many others come up from afar, lowered their heads between their forelegs and polished them with their paws; it was as if they were trying to conceal their revulsion, a revulsion so terrible it made me want to leap clean out of their circle.

'What do you propose to do, then?' I asked, trying to get to my feet; but I was unable to do so; two young beasts behind me had fastened their teeth in my coat and my shirt; I had to remain seated. 'They are carrying your train,' explained the old jackal gravely, 'it's a token of respect.' 'They must let me go!' I cried, turning now to the old jackal, now to the youngsters. 'Of course they will,' said the old one, 'if you so wish. But it will take a little time, because as custom requires they have bitten in deep and first they must gradually loosen their jaws. Meanwhile, pray hear what we ask.' 'Your behaviour hasn't put me in a very receptive frame of mind,' I said. 'Don't hold our clumsiness against us,' said he, and now he began to make use of his natural wailing tone, 'we are only poor creatures, we have nothing but our teeth; we depend for all that we want to do, the good and the bad, on our teeth alone.' 'What is it that you want, then?' I said, only slightly appeased.

'Master,' he cried, and every jackal set up a howl; the howling from the furthest distance seemed to reach my ears like a melody. 'Master, you are to end the strife that is dividing the world. You are exactly the man our ancients described as the one to accomplish it. We must be granted peace from the Arabs; air that we can breathe; the whole round of the horizon purified of their presence; never again the piteous cry of a sheep slaughtered with an Arab knife; every manner of beast must die in peace; we must be left undisturbed to drink them empty and cleanse them to the bone. Purity, purity is our sole desire'—and now all of them were crying and sobbing—'how can you endure it in this world, you noble heart and sweet entrails? Filth is their white; filth is their black; a thing of loathing is their beard; the corner of their eye is enough to make you spit; and when they lift an arm, all hell gapes in their armpit. Therefore, O master, therefore, beloved master, with the help of your all-powerful hands, with the help of your all-powerful hands, take up these scissors and cut their throats!' And in obedience to a jerk of his head a jackal came trotting up, from one of whose corner-teeth there dangled a small pair of sewing scissors, covered in ancient rust.

'Right, so we've come to the scissors at last, and that's enough of it!' cried the Arab leader of our caravan, who had been creeping up to us against the wind and now cracked his gigantic whip.

All the jackals ran off in haste, but some distance off they stopped, cowering close together; the many beasts so stiff and tight-packed that it looked like a narrow hurdle, wreathed in flickering will-o'-the-wisps.

'And so, master, now you too have seen and heard this spectacle,' said the Arab, laughing as heartily as the reserve of his race allowed. 'So you know what the creatures are after?' I asked. 'Of course, master,' said he, 'that's common knowledge; for so long as there have been Arabs these scissors have wandered the desert, and they will go on wandering with us until the end of time. Every European is offered the scissors to perform the great work; they imagine that every European is the very one called to perform it. They have an insane hope, these animals; they are fools, veritable fools. And we love them for it; they are our dogs; more beautiful ones than yours are. Now look, a camel has died in the night, I have had it brought along.'

Four bearers arrived and threw the heavy carcass down in front of us. Hardly had it touched the ground when the jackals raised their voices. As if they were drawn, each one, on a cord, irresistibly, they came hesitatingly forward, their bellies to the ground. They had forgotten the Arabs, forgotten their hatred; all else was obliterated by the presence of the reeking carcass that held them in its spell. One jackal was already hanging at the camel's throat and his first bite found the artery. Each muscle of his body twitched and jerked in its place, like a frenzied little pump that is utterly and hopelessly committed to the quenching of a raging fire. And by now they all lay piled up high on the carcass, each one labouring away.

Then out lashed the leader with his biting whip, fiercely to and fro across their backs. They raised their heads; still half numb in their ecstasy and stupor; saw the Arabs standing before them; now they were made to feel the whip on their muzzles; they sprang back and retreated a little. But already the blood of the camel was lying in pools, steaming high; in many places its body was torn wide open. They could not resist; back they came once more; once more the leader raised his whip; I caught hold of his arm.

'You are right, master,' he said, 'we will leave them to their task; besides, it's time to break camp. Now you have seen them. Wonderful creatures, aren't they? And how they do hate us!'

A Visit to the Mine

TODAY THE CHIEF ENGINEERS came to see us down below. The management has issued some directive or other about the boring of new tunnels, and along came these engineers to undertake the preliminary survey. How young these people are and yet how much they differ from one another already! They have developed independently, and even at such an early age the clearly marked character of each is openly displayed.

One, black-haired and vivacious, lets his eye wander about everywhere.

A second with notepad in hand makes jottings as he goes, looking around him, comparing, noting down.

A third, with his hands thrust into his coat pockets so that everything about him is taut, holds himself erect, preserves his dignity; only by an incessant biting of the lips does he reveal his impatient, irrepressible youth.

A fourth keeps giving the third explanations that he has not asked for; smaller than the other and trotting at his side like a seducer, he seems with his raised finger to be expatiating on the subject of everything within sight.

A fifth, perhaps the highest in rank, allows no one to accompany him; he is now at the front, now at the rear; the whole group takes its step from him; he is wan and frail; responsibility has hollowed out his eyes; often he presses his hand to his forehead in thought.

The sixth and the seventh are walking arm in arm, stooping a little, heads close together, in intimate conversation; if this were not so obviously our coal-mine and our place of work in the deepest tunnel, one might suppose these bony, beardless gentlemen with the bulbous noses were young clerics. One of them is mostly laughing to himself with a cat-like purring sound; the other, also smiling, conducts the conversation and beats some kind of time to it with his free hand. How sure of their position these two gentlemen must be, indeed how well they must have already served our mine despite their youth, for them to be allowed on such an important occasion, under the eyes of their chief, to occupy themselves so unswervingly with their own affairs, or at least with affairs that are unconnected with the immediate task in hand. Or could it be possible that despite all their laughing and their lack of attention nothing really important escapes them? One hardly dares express a definite opinion about such gentlemen as these.

But on the other hand there can be no question that the eighth, for example, is incomparably much more on the spot than they are, more so indeed than all the other gentlemen. Everywhere he has to be touching something, and tapping it with a little hammer which he is forever taking out of his pocket and tucking away there again. He often goes down on his knees in the dirt, despite his elegant attire, and taps the ground, then again he taps the walls or the roof overhead as he goes along. Once he stretched himself out at full length and lay still; we were beginning to think an accident had occurred; but then with a little jerk of his slim body he sprang to his feet again. So it was just another investigation he had been making. We reckon that we know our mine and its kinds of rock, but what this engineer is constantly exploring in this fashion is beyond us.

A ninth is pushing a sort of baby-carriage which contains the measuring apparatus. Extremely expensive instruments, embedded deep in the finest cotton-wool. It should really be the attendant's job to push this carriage, but he has not been entrusted with it. An engineer has had to step in and one can see that he is glad to do it. He is probably the youngest of them, perhaps he doesn't understand all the instruments yet, but he keeps his eye fixed on them constantly; at times this almost brings him into danger of running the carriage into one of the walls.

But there is another engineer on hand who is walking alongside the carriage and prevents this from happening. This man evidently knows the instruments inside out and seems to be the one who is actually in charge of them. From time to time, without stopping the carriage, he takes out some component or other, peers through it, screws it open or shut, shakes it and taps it, holds it to his ear and listens; and finally, while the man pushing the carriage usually brings it to a halt, he places the small object, which is barely visible from a distance, back in its place with all possible care. This engineer is a trifle domineering, but he is so only on behalf of the instruments. As much as ten paces ahead of the carriage we are expected to make way for it, at a silent wave of his finger, even where there is no room to step aside.

Behind these two gentlemen goes the unoccupied attendant. While all the gentlemen, as can be taken for granted in view of their great knowledge, have long since shed any trace of arrogance, the attendant seems to have accumulated it all in his own person. With one hand tucked behind his back and the other in front stroking his gilt buttons or the fine cloth of his uniform, he gives frequent nods to right and to left, as if he assumes that he has received some salutation from us but is unable to verify the fact from his exalted position. Needless to say we do him no such honour, although to look at him one might almost think there was something astonishing about being the office attendant in our mining company. Of course, we laugh at him behind his back, but since not even a thunderclap could induce him to turn round he somehow remains as an incomprehensible figure in our estimation.

There will be little more work done today; the interruption has been too protracted; a visit of this kind sweeps all thoughts of work away with it. It is all too tempting to stand gazing after the gentlemen into the darkness of the pilot tunnel down which they have disappeared. Besides, our shift will soon be coming to an end; we shall no longer be here to witness their return.

The Next Village

MY GRANDFATHER USED TO SAY: 'Life is astonishingly short. When I look back now it is all so condensed in my memory that I can hardly understand, for example, how a young man can decide to ride over to the next village, without his being afraid—quite apart from unfortunate accidents—that the whole span of a normal happy life is far from being adequate for such a ride.'

A Message from the Emperor

THE EMPEROR—so it is told—has sent to you, his solitary wretch of a subject, the minute shadow that has fled from the imperial sun into the furthermost distance, expressly to you has the emperor sent a message from his deathbed. He made the messenger kneel by his bedside and whispered the message to him; so much store did he set by it that he made him repeat it in his ear. With a nod of his head he confirmed the accuracy of the words. And before all the spectators of his death—every obstructing wall has been knocked away and on the towering open stairways there stand round him in a ring all the dignitaries of the empire—before all these has he dispatched his messenger. At once the messenger set out on his way; a strong, an indefatigable man; striking out now with one arm, now the other, he cleaves a path through the throng; if he meets with resistance he points to his breast, which bears the sign of the sun; and he forges ahead with an ease that none could match. But the throng is so vast; there is no end to their dwellings; if he could reach open country how fast would he fly, and soon you would surely hear the majestic pounding of his fists on your door. But instead of that, how vain are his efforts; he is still only forcing his way through the chambers of the innermost palace, never will he get to the end of them; and if he succeeded in that, nothing would be gained; down the stairs he would have to fight his way; and if he succeeded in that, nothing would be gained; the courtyards would have to be traversed, and after the courtyards the second, outer palace; and again stairs and courtyards; and again a palace; and so on for thousands of years; and if at last he should burst through the outermost gate—but never, never can that happen—the royal capital would still lie before him, the centre of the world, piled high with all its dregs. No one can force his way through here, least of all with a message from a dead man.—But you sit at your window and dream up that message when evening falls.

A Problem for the Father of the Family

THERE ARE SOME who say that the word Odradek is of Slavonic origin, and they try to account for its formation on that basis. Others again believe that it derives from the German and is merely influenced by Slavonic. The uncertainty of both interpretations, however, probably justifies the conclusion that neither is correct, especially since neither permits one to attach a meaning to the word.

No one, of course, would occupy himself with such studies if a creature called Odradek did not in fact exist. At first glance it looks like a flat, star-shaped spool for thread, and indeed it does actually seem to be wound with thread; or rather, with what appear to be just odds and ends of old thread, of the most various kinds and colours, all knotted together and even tangled up with one another. But it is not simply a spool, for projecting from the middle of the star is a small wooden crossbar, and to this another little bar is attached at a right angle. By means of this latter bar on one side and one of the points of the star on the other, the whole thing is able to stand upright as if on two legs.

One might be tempted to suppose that this object had once been designed for some purpose or other and was now merely broken. But this does not seem to be the case; at least there are no indications of it; nowhere are there stumps or fractures visible that might suggest anything of the kind; the whole thing certainly appears senseless, and yet in its own way complete. It is not possible to state anything more definite on the matter since Odradek is exceptionally mobile and refuses to be caught.

He resides by turns in the attic, on the stairs, in the corridors, in the entrance hall. Sometimes he is not to be seen for months; so presumably he has moved into other houses; but then he invariably comes back to our own house again. Sometimes when one comes out of one's room and he happens to be propping himself up against the banisters down below, one feels inclined to speak to him. Naturally one doesn't ask him any difficult questions, one treats him—his diminutive size is itself sufficient encouragement to do so—like a child. 'What's your name?' one asks him. 'Odradek,' he says. 'And where do you live?' 'No fixed abode,' he says, and laughs; but it is only the sort of laughter that can be produced without lungs. It sounds something like the rustling of fallen leaves. That is usually the end of the conversation. Even these answers, by the way, are not always forthcoming; often he remains dumb for a long time, like the wood he appears to consist of.

It is in vain that I ask myself what is likely to become of him. Is he capable of dying? Everything that dies has previously had some kind of goal, some kind of activity, and at this activity it has worn itself away; in the case of Odradek that does not apply. Can it be, then, that he might one day still be rolling down the stairs, with ends of thread trailing after him, before the feet of my children and my children's children? He obviously does no harm to anyone; but the idea that he might also outlive me I find almost painful.

Eleven Sons

I HAVE ELEVEN SONS.

The first is nothing much to look at, but he is serious and intelligent; all the same I do not rate him very highly, though of course I love him as my child like all the others. His thinking seems to me too simple. He looks neither to right nor left, nor can he see very far; he keeps running round and round his limited range of ideas, or rather he rotates within it.

The second is good-looking, slim, well-proportioned; it is a delight to see him in his stance as a fencer. He, too, is intelligent, but he is also a man of the world; he has seen a great deal, so that even our native heath seems to tell him more secrets than it reveals to those who have stayed at home. Yet he by no means owes this asset solely, or even primarily, to his travels; it belongs rather to this child's inimitable natural talent, a talent that is acknowledged, for example, by anyone who attempts to copy that spectacular high-dive which he performs, involving a whole series of somersaults and yet kept under such passionately firm control. The courage and desire to follow his example remain strong right up to the end of the springboard, but then, instead of diving, the imitator suddenly sits down and raises his arms in apology.—And despite all that (I ought really to be overjoyed at having such a child) my feelings towards him are not altogether unclouded. His left eye is slightly smaller than his right and blinks a good deal; only a small fault, to be sure, which lends him an even more rakish aspect than he would otherwise have, and no one faced with the unapproachably aloof and finished quality of his whole being would spot that smaller, blinking eye as an imperfection. I, his father, do so. Of course it is not the physical flaw itself that distresses me, but a slight irregularity of the spirit that somehow corresponds to it, some kind of stray poison in the blood, a certain inability to round off that pattern of his life which is visible to me alone. On the other hand, it must be confessed, that is precisely what makes him a true son of mine, for this flaw of his is at the same time the flaw of our whole family and merely all too apparent in this son.

The third son is similarly good-looking, but he has not the kind of good looks that I admire. His is the beauty of the singer: the curving lips; the dreamy eye; the head that asks for a background of drapery to achieve its effect; the exaggerated swell of the chest; the hands that swiftly flutter up and far too swiftly fall; the legs that move in a mincing way because they have not the strength to carry. And what is more: the tone of his voice is lacking in fullness; it deceives momentarily; makes the connoisseur prick up his ears; but trails away soon after.— While on the whole there is every temptation to show off this son I prefer to keep him in the background; he does not push himself forward, though this is not because he is aware of his shortcomings, it is out of innocence. Moreover, he does not feel at home in the present time; as though he did not belong just to my family, but to another one as well, one long lost to him, he is often melancholy and nothing can raise his spirits.

My fourth son is perhaps the most sociable of them all. A true child of his age, he is comprehensible to everyone, he stands on ground that is common to all and everybody feels inclined to give him a passing nod. Possibly this universal approval lends a certain lightness to his character, a certain liberty to his movements, a certain nonchalance to his judgements. Some of his remarks bear frequent repetition, but admittedly only some of them, for all in all he does suffer, to say it again, from an excessive facility. He is like someone who makes a splendid take-off from the ground, cleaves the air like a swallow, but then comes sadly to grief in the barren dust, a mere nothing. Such reflections destroy all my pleasure at the sight of this child.

The fifth son is kind and good; promised far less than he fulfilled; was so insignificant that one positively felt alone in his presence; but has none the less achieved a certain standing. If I were to be asked how that has happened I would scarcely know how to reply. Maybe it is innocence that can best find a passage through the raging elements of this world, and innocent he is. Perhaps all too innocent. Friendly to everyone. Perhaps all too friendly. I must admit: I do not feel happy when people sing his praises to me. It really seems to make praise a little too easy if one bestows it on someone so obviously praiseworthy as this son of mine.

My sixth son appears, at first sight anyhow, to be the most profound of all. He is given to hanging his head, yet at the same time he is a great talker. So it is not easy to deal with him. If he is about to be worsted, he falls into invincible melancholy; if he gains the upper hand then he maintains it by his chatter. Yet I cannot deny that he is capable of a certain kind of passionate absorption; often, in broad daylight, he fights his way through his thoughts as though immersed in a dream. Without being ill—on the contrary he enjoys excellent health—he staggers sometimes, particularly in the twilight, yet he needs no assistance, he never falls. Perhaps his physical development is to blame for this phenomenon, he is far too tall for his age. This means that his appearance as a whole lacks grace, despite conspicuously graceful details, for instance the hands and the feet. He also has an unattractive forehead; both the skin and the bone structure have a sort of shrunken quality.

The seventh son belongs to me perhaps more than all the others. The world cannot appreciate him; it does not understand his peculiar brand of wit. I do not overrate him; I know he is insignificant enough; if the world's only fault were not to appreciate him it would still remain spotless. But inside the family circle I should not like to be without this son. He contributes both a restlessness and a respect for tradition, and he combines the two, at least according to my own feeling, to form an incontestable whole. It is true that he has not, himself, any idea what to make of this combination; he will not be the one to set the wheel of the future turning; but his disposition is so stimulating, so rich in hope; I could wish that he might have children, and that these might have others in their turn. Unfortunately this wish shows no sign of being fulfilled. With a self-satisfaction that I can understand, though I must equally deplore it, and which certainly stands in the most dazzling contrast to the opinion of those around him, he drifts about on his own, pays no attention to girls, and yet will always retain his good humour.

My eighth son is my child of sorrow, and I do not really know why. He looks at me like a stranger, though for my part I feel a close paternal attachment to him. Time has healed a great deal; but once the mere thought of him made me shiver. He goes his own way; has broken off all contact with me; and with his thick skull and his small athletic body—only his legs were very weak when he was a boy, but that may have corrected itself in the meantime—he is sure to get through well enough wherever he pleases. Often I have felt like calling him

back and asking him how things were going, why he cut himself off so
from his father and what he was basically after, but by now he is so remote and so much time has passed, now things had better just stay as
they are. I hear he is the only one of my sons to have grown a beard;
of course that can hardly look well on a man as short as he is.

My ninth son is very elegant, and has that melting look that is designed specially for women. So melting is it that it can even seduce me
on occasion, though I well know that a wet sponge would be literally
enough to wipe away all that celestial lustre. But the strange thing
about this boy is that he does not in the least aim to seduce; he would
be content to spend his whole life lying on the sofa, wasting his
charming gaze on the ceiling, or for preference even letting it rest beneath his eyelids. When he has adopted this favourite position of his,
he is fond of talking and talks quite well; concisely and vividly; but still
only within narrow limits; once he oversteps these, as their narrowness
makes inevitable, his talk becomes quite empty. One would give him a
sign to stop if one had any hope that those sleep-laden eyes were capable of noticing it.

My tenth son has the reputation of being an insincere character.
This I do not wish wholly to deny, nor wholly to confirm. What is certain is that anyone who sees him approaching, with an air of solemnity
far beyond his years, in a frock coat always tightly buttoned, an old but
meticulously brushed black hat, with an expressionless face, somewhat
protruding chin, eyelids bulging weightily over his eyes, an occasional
two fingers raised to his lips—anyone who sees him thus will think:
the man is a boundless hypocrite. But now, just listen to him speaking!
With understanding; with deliberation; briefly and to the point; inter-
cepting questions with wicked acuteness; in astonishing, self-evident
and cheerful accord with the whole scheme of things; an accord that of
necessity tautens the neck and lifts up the whole body. Many who
think themselves very wise and who, for this reason as they would have
it, have felt repelled by his outward appearance have been powerfully
attracted by what he has to say. Then again, there are people who are
indifferent to his appearance but consider his words hypocritical. I, as
his father, will not attempt to decide the matter here, though I must
admit that those of the latter opinion are at all events to be taken more
seriously than those of the former.

My eleventh son is delicate, probably the weakest among my sons;
but his weakness is deceptive; he can in fact be strong and resolute at

times, though admittedly even then it is his weakness that is somehow fundamental. Yet this is no weakness to be ashamed of, it is rather something that appears as weakness only in this world of ours. Is not, for example, even readiness for flight a kind of weakness, since it is, after all, only swaying and uncertainty and fluttering? Something like that is what my son displays. Such qualities are not of course pleasing to a father; for they tend evidently towards the destruction of the family. Sometimes he looks at me as if to say: 'I will take you with me, father.' Then I think: 'You are the last person I would trust myself to.' And again his look seems to say: 'Then at least let me be the last.'

Those are the eleven sons.

A Fratricide

IT HAS BEEN ESTABLISHED that the murder took place in the following manner:

Towards nine in the evening, one clear moonlit night, Schmar, the murderer, took up his station at the corner where Wese, the victim, must turn out from the street where his office was into the street where he lived.

Cold night air, enough to chill one to the bone. But Schmar wore only a thin blue suit; he even had his jacket unbuttoned. He did not feel the cold; besides, he kept on the move. The murder weapon, half bayonet, half kitchen knife, was held firmly in his grip and fully exposed to view. He examined it by the moonlight; the blade glittered; not enough for Schmar; he struck it against the bricks of the pavement to make the sparks fly; regretted that, perhaps; and to repair the damage drew it across the sole of his boot like a violin bow; as he stood there on one leg, bending forward, he listened to the sound of the knife against his boot, and at the same time he cocked an ear for any sound from the fateful side-street.

Why did Pallas, man of private means, permit all this to happen, as he watched from close by at his window on the second floor? Try to fathom human nature! With his collar turned up, dressing-gown wrapped round his ample body, he gazed down at the scene, shaking his head.

And five houses further on, diagonally across the street, with a fox-fur over her nightgown, Frau Wese was looking out for her husband who was unusually late home today.

At last the door-bell of Wese's office clangs, too loud for a door-bell, across the town, up to the heavens; and Wese, the industrious night-worker, as yet invisible from this street, as yet only heralded by the sound of the bell, sallies forth from his building; at once the pavement begins to number his tranquil steps.

Pallas leans far out of his window; he must not miss a thing. Frau

Wese, reassured by the bell, shuts her window with a clatter. Schmar, however, kneels down; he presses, having no other parts exposed, only his face and hands against the brickwork; where all are freezing, Schmar is aglow.

On the very line that divides the two streets Wese comes to a halt, just propping himself in the street beyond with his walking-stick. A whim. The night sky has attracted him, with its dark blue and its gold. Unsuspecting, he contemplates it; unsuspecting, he smoothes back his hair beneath his lifted hat; no pattern is taking shape up there to announce the immediate future to him; everything stays in its pointless, inscrutable place. Quite reasonable, on the face of it, that Wese should walk on, but he walks into the knife of Schmar.

'Wese!' cries Schmar, standing on tiptoe, his arm stretched up, the knife pointing sharply down, 'Wese! Julia waits in vain!' And into the throat from the right and into the throat from the left and thirdly deep into the belly strikes Schmar. Water-rats, slit open, produce a similar sound to that produced by Wese.

'Done,' says Schmar, and he flings the knife, superfluous blood-stained ballast, against the nearest house-front. 'O bliss of murder! The release, the soaring excitement of shedding another man's blood! Wese, you old night-bird, friend, drinking companion, you are seeping away in the darkness below the street. Why aren't you simply a bladderful of blood, for me to squash you and make you disappear completely. Not all has been fulfilled, not every blossoming dream matured, the weight of your solid remains still lies here, impervious now to every kick. What can the wordless question mean that you ask by it?'

The double-doors of Pallas's house burst open; he stands on the threshold, choking down all the surging venom in his body. 'Schmar! Schmar! All's been noted, nothing missed.' Pallas and Schmar inspect each other. Pallas is satisfied, Schmar comes to no conclusion.

Frau Wese comes running up, a crowd on either side of her, her face quite aged with terror. Her fur coat falls open, she throws herself on Wese; her body in its nightgown belongs to him, the fur coat, closing over the pair like turf over a grave, belongs to the crowd.

Schmar, suppressing his remaining feelings of nausea with an effort, rests his mouth against the shoulder of the policeman who, with a light step, leads him away.

A Dream

JOSEF K. WAS DREAMING:
It was a fine day and K. felt like going for a walk. But hardly had he taken a couple of steps before he was in the cemetery. There he found strangely contrived paths, impracticably winding, but he glided along one such path as if he were floating in the air, with unshakeable poise, above a torrential stream. From some distance away he fixed his eye on a grave-mound that had been freshly thrown up, where he wanted to stop. He found something almost fascinating about this mound and it seemed to him that he could not reach it fast enough. But at times he could hardly see it, his view of it was obscured by flags, furling and unfurling and flapping against one another with great force; those who carried these flags were invisible, but there appeared to be some great celebration in progress.

While he was still gazing into the distance, he suddenly caught sight of the same grave-mound by the path beside him, indeed he had almost passed it. He quickly leapt into the grass. Since the path went rushing on under his foot as he jumped, he lost his balance and fell on his knees just in front of the mound. Two men were standing behind the grave and were holding a grave-stone in the air between them; hardly had K. appeared when they thrust the stone into the earth, where it stood as if built into the ground. At once a third man emerged from some bushes, whom K. recognized immediately as an artist. He was clad only in trousers and a carelessly buttoned shirt; on his head he wore a velvet cap; in his hand he held an ordinary pencil with which he was describing figures in the air even as he approached.

He now proceeded to apply this pencil to the top part of the grave-stone; it was a very tall stone, he had no need to bend down at all; though he did have to crane forward, for the grave-mound, which he wanted to avoid stepping on, lay between him and the stone. So he stood on tiptoe and supported himself with his left hand against the flat of the stone. By some particular turn of skill he succeeded in producing, with his ordinary pencil, gold lettering; he wrote: 'Here lies—' Each letter appeared clear and beautiful, deeply incised and of the most perfect gold. When he had written these two words he looked back at K.; K., who was most eager to see how the inscription would go on, hardly paid any attention to the man but just kept his eyes on the stone. And sure enough, the man prepared to resume his writing, but he could not do it, there was something stopping him, he let his pencil sink and turned round to K. once more. This time K. looked at him in return, and he saw that the artist was in great embarrassment, yet unable to explain why. All his former liveliness had vanished. This made K. embarrassed, too; they exchanged helpless glances; there was some dreadful misunderstanding between them which neither could resolve. And at this untimely moment a little bell began to toll from the cemetery chapel, but the artist gesticulated with his raised hand and the bell stopped. After a little while it began again; this time quite softly, and breaking off again without special request; it was as if it just wanted to test its sound. K. was inconsolable at the artist's predicament, he began to weep, and sobbed for a long time with his face in his hands. The artist waited until K. had calmed down, and then decided, since he could find no other solution, to continue writing after all. The first little stroke that he made was a deliverance for K., but the artist obviously only accomplished it with the utmost reluctance; nor was the script any longer so beautiful, above all it seemed to be lacking in gold, the line dragged on pale and unsteady, the letter merely came out very large. It was a J, by now it was almost finished, when the artist furiously stamped one of his feet into the mound so that the earth all round flew high in the air. K. understood him at last; there was no time left for him to apologize; with all his fingers he dug away at the earth, which hardly resisted; everything seemed to be prepared in advance; a thin layer of earth had been raised just for show; immediately beneath it a great hole with steep walls opened out, and into this, as some gentle current turned him over on to his back, K. sank down. But while he then, with his head still raised, was already being received into the impenetrable depths below, up above his name went racing with mighty flourishes across the stone.

Enraptured by this sight, he awoke.

A Report to an Academy

ESTEEMED GENTLEMEN of the academy!
You have done me the honour of asking me to present a report to
the academy concerning my past life as an ape.

I regret to say that I find myself unable to comply with your request as thus formulated. Almost five years now separate me from apehood, a short period, perhaps, as reckoned by the calendar, but an
eternity to have to gallop through as I have done, accompanied along
stretches of the course by excellent people, advice, applause and or-
chestral music, and yet essentially alone, since all such company
remained—to pursue the metaphor—well on the far side of the rails.
This achievement would have been impossible had I sought to cling
wilfully to my origins, to the memories of my youth. It was precisely
the renunciation of all self-will that I had laid upon myself as my first
commandment; I, a free ape, submitted myself to this yoke. But as a
result these memories, for their part, closed themselves off from me
more and more. If initially a way of return lay open for me—had men
so wished—through the whole great archway of the heavens that span
the earth, this grew ever lower and narrower behind me as I was
driven forward through the successive stages of my development; I felt
ever more comfortable and secluded in the world of men; the storm
sweeping after me from my past abated; today it is no more than a
draught that cools my heels; and the distant hole through which it
comes, and through which I once came, has become so small, that
even if I had the strength and the will to run back so far, I should have
to scrape the hide from my body to get through it. To speak plainly,
much as I like using images for these things; to speak plainly: your
own apehood, gentlemen, in so far as you have something of the sort
behind you, cannot be further removed from you than mine is from
me. Yet everyone who walks this earth feels a tickling at his heel: from
the little chimpanzee to the great Achilles.

In the narrowest sense, however, I can perhaps make some reply to your inquiry after all, and indeed it gives me great pleasure to do so. The first thing I learnt was: how to shake hands; a handshake betokens frankness; allow me therefore today, as I stand at the summit of my career, to supplement that first frank handshake with the frankness of my present words. What I have to tell the academy will not amount to anything essentially new, and it will fall far short of what has been asked of me and what with the best will in the world I am unable to communicate—all the same, it should at least indicate the guideline that an erstwhile ape has followed, as he penetrated into the human world and established himself there. Yet I should certainly have no right to say even the little that follows unless I were entirely sure of myself, and if I had not achieved a position that is by now unassailable on all the great variety stages of the civilized world:

I come from the Gold Coast. For the account of my capture I have to depend on the reports of others. A hunting expedition from the firm of Hagenbeck—with whose leader, by the way, I have since consumed many a bottle of good red wine—was lying in wait in the scrub by the river bank when I came down to drink one evening, in the midst of a company. They fired at us; I was the only one that was hit; they got me twice.

Once in the check; that was a slight wound; but it left a large, bald, red scar, which earned me the repulsive and utterly inappropriate name of Red Peter—a positively apish invention, as if to suggest that the only thing distinguishing me from that performing ape Peter, a creature with some small reputation who met his end the other day, was this red mark on my cheek. But that is by the way.

The second shot got me below the hip; that was a bad wound; it is responsible for the fact that I still limp a little to this day. Recently I read an article, written by one of those ten thousand wind-bags who expatiate about me in the press, claiming that my ape nature was not yet wholly suppressed; the proof being that when visitors come to see me I am particularly inclined to take off my trousers so as to show them the spot where the bullet entered. That fellow ought to have each single finger of his scribbling hand shot away, one by one. I am permitted, I presume, to remove my trousers before anyone I please; nothing will be found there save a well-groomed coat of fur and the scar made—let us choose for this particular purpose a particular word, which should not however be misunderstood—the scar made by a heinous shot. Everything is open and above board; there is nothing to conceal; where the truth is at stake, every high-minded person will cast the refinements of behaviour aside. On the other hand if the writer of that article were to take off his trousers when visitors come, things would certainly appear in a different light, and I will let it stand to his credit that he does not. But in that case let him spare me in return with his delicacy!

After those shots I awoke—and this is where my own memories gradually begin—in a cage between decks aboard the Hagenbeck company steamer. It was no ordinary barred cage with four sides; instead it had three sides fastened to a crate; so the crate made the fourth side of the cage. The whole thing was too low to stand up in and too narrow to sit down. So I had to squat, with bent and constantly trembling knees, and furthermore—since at first I probably wished to see nobody, but just stay in the dark all the time—with my face turned towards the crate, while the bars of the cage cut into my flesh behind. Such a method of confining wild beasts is considered advantageous during the initial period, and today, after my own experience, I cannot deny that from the human point of view this is indeed the case.

But I did not think about that at the time. I had, for the first time in my life, no way out; certainly there was none straight ahead; straight ahead was the crate, plank fixed firmly to plank. Admittedly there was one gap running between them, which I greeted, when I first discovered it, with a howl of foolish rapture; but this gap was nowhere near big enough even to stick one's tail through, and no amount of an ape's strength could widen it.

Apparently, so I was told later, I made exceptionally little noise, from which they concluded that I was either on the point of extinction or that I would, supposing I managed to survive the first critical period, prove most amenable to training. I survived that period. Muffled sobbing, painful flea-hunting, weary licking of a coconut, beating my skull against the side of the crate, sticking out my tongue at anyone who came near—such were the first occupations of my new existence. But in all this just the one, single feeling: no way out. Of course what I then felt, in ape fashion, I can now only represent in human terms, and misrepresent it therefore; but even if I can no longer reach back to the old ape-truth, this does at least lie in the direction I have indicated, of that there is no doubt.

Up to now I had always had so many ways out, and now I had none. I was stuck fast. I would have had no less freedom of movement if they had nailed me down. And why was this so? Scratch yourself raw between the toes and you won't find the reason. Shove yourself back against the bar until it nearly cuts you in two and you won't find the reason. I had no way out; but I had to make one for myself, for I could not live without it. Always up against this crate—that would inevitably have been the end of me. But up against the crate is where apes belong with Hagenbeck—very well, then, I would cease to be an ape. A clear, a beautiful line of thought, one which I must have somehow hatched out in my belly, for that is the way apes think.

I fear that it may not be understood precisely what I mean by a way out. I use the term in its most ordinary and its fullest sense. I deliberately do not say freedom. I do not mean that grandiose feeling of freedom in all directions. Perhaps I may have known that as an ape, and I have come across men who yearn for it. But for my part it was not freedom that I sought, either then or now. Let me say in passing: freedom is all too often self-deception among men. And if freedom counts as one of the most sublime of feelings, equally sublime is the deception that corresponds to it. Many a time in variety theatres, waiting for my turn to come on, have I watched some pair of acrobats high up in the roof, performing on their trapezes. They swung, they rocked, they leapt, they floated into each other's arms, one carried the other in his teeth by the hair. 'This, too, is human freedom,' I thought, 'arbitrary movement.' What a mockery of mother nature! No building could withstand the laughter of the assembled apes at a sight like that.

No, freedom was not what I wanted. Only a way out; to right, to left, no matter where; I made no other demand; even if the way out should prove deceptive as well; the demand was small, the deception could be no greater. Onwards, onwards! Anything but stay still, with arms upraised, crushed against the side of a crate.

Today I can see it all clearly: without the profoundest inward calm I should never have got away. And indeed, perhaps I owe all that I have become to the calm that came over me after the first few days aboard ship. And for that calm, I might also well say, I had the members of the crew to thank.

They are a decent lot of people, when all is said and done. I can still recall with pleasure the sound of their heavy footsteps which used to echo through my head when I was half asleep. It was their habit to set about everything they did immensely slowly. If one of them wanted to rub his eyes, he would lift his hand like a dead weight. Their jokes were coarse but hearty. Their laughter always had a gruffness in it that sounded dangerous but meant nothing. They always complained that my fleas jumped over on to them; yet they were never seriously angry with me on that account; they knew, after all, that fleas flourish in my fur and that fleas are jumpers; so they came to terms with it. Sometimes when they were off duty a few would sit down in a semi-circle round me; hardly speaking, but making cooing grunts to one another; smoking their pipes, stretched out against the crates; slapping their knees as soon as I made the slightest movement; and now and then one of them would take a stick and tickle me where I liked being tickled. If I were invited today to make a voyage on that ship, I should certainly decline the invitation; but it is equally certain that not all the memories I might muse on between decks would be repellent ones.

Above all, the calmness that I acquired from the company of these folk prevented me from making any attempt to escape. When I now look back, it seems to me that I must have already had some inkling that I had to find a way out if I wanted to survive, but also that the way out was not to run away. I cannot tell any more whether flight was in fact possible, though I believe it was; flight should always be possible for an ape. With my teeth in their present state I have to be careful just cracking an ordinary nut, but then I should probably have managed in time to bite my way through the padlock on the door. I did not do it. What good would it have done me? As soon as I had poked my head out I would have been recaptured, and locked away in some even worse cage; or I might have slipped unnoticed among some other animals, perhaps the boa constrictors opposite, and breathed my last in their arms; or I might even have succeeded in creeping up on deck and jumping overboard, in which case I would have been rocked for a little on the deep and then drowned. Desperate remedies. I did not work things out in such a human way, but under the influence of my surroundings I behaved as if I had.

I did not work things out; but I did observe everything with complete calm. I watched these men walking up and down, always the same faces, the same movements, often it seemed to me they were one and the same man. So this man or these men were moving about unmolested. A lofty goal began to dawn upon me. No one made me any promise that if I became like them the bars of my cage would be lifted. Such promises, for things that seem incapable of fulfilment, are not given. But make good the fulfilments and the promises will duly appear afterwards, just where you had earlier looked for them in vain. Now there was nothing about these men in themselves that particularly attracted me. Had I been a devotee of that freedom just mentioned, I would surely have preferred the ocean to the way out that I saw reflected in these men's dreary gaze. But anyhow I had been observing them for a long time before such things occurred to me, indeed it was only the accumulated weight of my observations that pushed me in the right direction.

It was so easy to imitate these people. I could spit after only a few days. Then we used to spit in one another's faces; the only difference was that I licked my face clean afterwards, they did not. I could soon smoke a pipe like an old hand; and if I also pressed my thumb down the bowl of the pipe, a roar of approval went up from the whole crew; only the difference between an empty pipe and a full one was something that took me a long time to understand.

What gave me the most trouble was the gin-bottle. The smell was a torture to me; I forced myself as best I could; but it took weeks for me to conquer my aversion. Strangely enough, the men took these inner struggles of mine more seriously than anything else. I cannot differentiate between these people even when I recollect, but there was one of them who came again and again, alone or with friends, by day, by night, at all kinds of hours; he would set himself down in front of me with the bottle and give me instruction. He could not make sense of me, he wanted to solve the riddle of my being. He would slowly uncork the bottle and then look at me to see whether I had understood him; I confess, I was always watching him with the wildest, the most precipitate attention; no such human pupil could any teacher hope to find on the whole surface of the earth; after the bottle was uncorked he would lift it to his mouth; I following him with my eyes right into his gullet; he nods, pleased with me, and puts the bottle to his lips; I, in an ecstasy of dawning enlightenment, scratch myself, amid squeals, here, there and everywhere at random; he is delighted, tips the bottle and takes a swig; I, impatient and desperate to emulate him, befoul myself in my cage, which again gives him great satisfaction; whereupon he, holding out the bottle at arm's length in front of him and returning it with a flourish to his lips, leans back with exaggerated pedantry and empties it at a single draught. I then, worn out by my ex-

cessive ambition, can follow him no longer and cling limply to the
bars, while he completes the theoretical part of the lesson by stroking
his belly and grinning.

And only now does the practical exercise begin. Am I not already
all too exhausted by the theory? Indeed I am, all too exhausted. That
is a part of my destiny. All the same I reach, as best I can, for the bottle that is held out for me; uncork it, trembling; with this success I feel
my strength gradually returning; I lift the bottle, which by now I can
hardly distinguish from the original; put it to my lips and—and fling it
down with loathing, with loathing, although it is empty and contains
nothing but the smell, fling it down with loathing to the floor. To the
sorrow of my teacher, to the even greater sorrow of myself; nor do I
succeed in placating either of us by the fact that I do not forget, even
after throwing the bottle away, to stroke my belly in the most exemplary fashion and produce the accompanying grin.

All too frequently the lesson took this course. And to the credit of
my teacher: he was not angry with me; sometimes, indeed, he may
have held his burning pipe against my fur, until it began to smoulder
in some place that I found hard to reach, but then he always extinguished it again himself with his massive, gentle hand; he was not angry with me, he recognized that we were both fighting on the same
side against the nature of apes and that I had the harder task.

What a triumph it was then, both for him and for me, when one
evening before a large audience—perhaps it was some kind of party, a
gramophone was playing, an officer was strolling about among the
crew—when on this evening, just when no one happened to be looking, I seized a gin-bottle that had been left inadvertently in front of my
cage, uncorked it in the approved manner, with the attention of the assembled company gradually mounting, put it to my lips, and without
hesitation, without grimacing, like a professional drinker, with eyes
rolling and throat gurgling, really and truly drank it dry; then threw
the bottle from me, not in despair this time but with artistic skill; forgot, indeed, to stroke my belly; but instead, because I could not help
myself, because I felt compelled, because all my senses were reeling,
cried out a short, sharp 'Hallo!,' broke into human speech, sprang
with this cry into the community of men, and felt their echoing cry:
'Listen, he's speaking!' like a caress over the whole of my sweat-
drenched body.

I repeat: I felt no desire to imitate men; I imitated them because I was seeking a way out, and for no other reason. Nor did that first triumph take me far. My speaking voice failed again at once; it did not come back for months; my aversion to the gin-bottle returned even more strongly than before. But all the same, my course was now set for me, once and for all.

When I was handed over to my first trainer, in Hamburg, I soon grasped the two possibilities that were open to me: the Zoological Gardens or the variety stage. I did not hesitate. I told myself: do all in your power to get into variety; there lies the way out; the zoo is only another barred cage; if you land there you are lost.

And I began to learn, gentlemen. Oh yes, one learns when one has to; one learns if one wants a way out; one learns relentlessly. One watches over oneself with a whip; one flays oneself at the slightest sign of resistance. My ape nature went racing out of me, head over heels and away, so that my first teacher became himself almost apish in consequence; he soon had to abandon my instruction and be removed to a mental hospital. Fortunately he was soon discharged.

But I used up a great many teachers, indeed even several at once. When I had become more confident of my abilities, with the public already following my progress and my future beginning to look bright, I engaged instructors on my own account, established them in five communicating rooms and learned from them all simultaneously, by leaping continually from one room to the other.

The progress I made! Those rays of knowledge penetrating from every side into my awakening brain! I will not deny it: it gladdened my heart. But I must also admit: I did not overrate it, not even then, and how much the less do I do so today. By dint of exertions as yet unequalled upon this earth I have attained the cultural level of an average European. In itself that might be nothing to speak of, yet it is something, indeed, in so far as it has helped me out of my cage and provided me with this special kind of way out, the human way. There is an excellent idiom in German: to slip off into the undergrowth; that is what I did, I slipped off into the undergrowth. I had no other way to go, always provided that freedom was not to be my choice.

If I consider my development and the goal it has so far reached, I can neither complain nor can I feel satisfied. With my hands in my trouser pockets, my bottle of wine on the table, I half lie, half sit in my rocking-chair and look out of the window. If a visitor comes, I receive him politely. My manager sits in the ante-room; when I ring he comes in and listens to what I have to say. In the evening there is almost always a performance, and the success I enjoy would probably be hard to surpass. When I come home late at night from banquets, from scientific receptions, from informal gatherings with friends, a little half-trained chimpanzee is awaiting me and I enjoy her company after the fashion of apes. By day I have no wish to see her; for she has that wild, confused look of the trained animal in her eye; no one but me can recognize it, and it is more than I can bear.

On the whole I have at least achieved what I set out to achieve. Let it not be said that it was not worth the effort. In any case, I am not seeking anyone's judgement, I wish only to spread knowledge, I am only reporting; to you, too, esteemed gentlemen of the academy, I have only made a report.

THE COAL-SCUTTLE RIDER

ALL THE COAL USED UP; the coal-scuttle empty; the shovel now meaningless; the stove breathing out cold; the room inflated with frosty air; trees beyond the window rigid with rime; the sky a silver shield against anyone looking for help from there. I must have coal; I can't be allowed to freeze to death; behind me is that pitiless stove, before me the equally pitiless sky, as a result I must ride out at all speed between them and seek help from the coal-merchant in the middle. However, his senses have already become dull to my usual appeals; I shall have to prove to him in detail that I have no single grain of coal-dust left, and thus what he means to me is the very sun in the firmament. I must come like the beggar who appears on the doorstep with a death-rattle in his throat, and proposes to expire there, so that the cook in the grand house makes up her mind to give him the dregs of the last coffee-pot; just so must the coal-merchant, furious, yet touched by some gleam of the commandment 'Thou shalt not kill', fling a shovelful into my scuttle.

My manner of approach must decide the matter; so I ride off on my coal-scuttle. As a coal-scuttle rider, with my hands up on the handle, the simplest kind of bridle, I steer myself with some difficulty down the stairs; but once below, my scuttle rises up, superbly, superbly; camels, couched low on the ground, cannot rise up more proudly, shaking themselves under the stick of their driver. Off we go through the icy streets at a steady trot; often I am lifted as high as the first storey of the houses; never do I sink to the level of the front doors. And then at an exceptional height I hover outside the cellar of the coal-merchant, where he crouches far below over his little table, writing; so as to let out the excessive heat he has opened the door.

'Coal-merchant!' I cry, in a voice burned hollow by the frost, wreathed in the clouds of my breath, 'please, coal-merchant, give me a little coal. My scuttle is now so empty that I can ride on it. Be so good. I'll pay for it as soon as I can.'

The coal-merchant puts his hand to his ear. 'Do I hear aright?' he asks his wife over his shoulder, as she sits knitting on her seat against the stove. 'Do I hear aright? A customer.'

'I can't hear a thing,' says his wife, breathing serenely out and in over her knitting-needles, her back agreeably warmed.

'But yes,' I cry, 'it's me; an old customer; faithful and true; just temporarily out of funds.'

'Wife,' says the merchant, 'it is someone, it is; I can't be so wholly deceived; it must be an old, a very old customer for him to speak to my heart like this.'

'What's wrong with you, man?' asks his wife, pausing for a moment and pressing her knitting to her breast, 'it's no one, the street's empty, all our customers are supplied; we could shut up the shop for days and take a rest.'

'But I'm sitting up here on my coal-scuttle,' I cry, and my eyes become blurred with unfeeling tears of cold, 'please do just look up here; you'll spot me at once; I beg you for a shovelful; and if you give me two I'll be more than delighted. All the other customers are supplied, are they not? Oh, if only I could hear it clattering into my scuttle this moment!'

'I'm coming,' says the merchant, and off he sets on his short legs to climb the cellar steps, but his wife is already at his side, holds him by the arm and says: 'You stay here. If you must be so obstinate I'll go up myself. Remember that bad fit of coughing you had last night. But for the sake of a little business, even if it's only imaginary, you're prepared to forget your wife and child and sacrifice your lungs. I'll go.' 'Then be sure to tell him all the kinds we have in stock; I'll call the prices after you.' 'Right,' says his wife, and climbs up to the street. Naturally she sees me at once.

'Madam coal-merchant,' I cry, 'your humble servant; just one shovelful of coal; straight into this scuttle; I'll transport it home myself; one shovelful of your worst quality. I'll pay you in full, of course, but not just now, not just now.' How like a knell sound those words 'not just now', and how confusingly they mingle with the evening chimes from the church tower nearby!

'What does he want, then?' calls the merchant. 'Nothing,' his wife calls back, 'there's nothing here; I see nothing, I hear nothing; only six o'clock striking and it's time to close. The cold is terrible; tomorrow we'll probably have a lot more work.'

She sees nothing and hears nothing; but all the same she loosens her apron-strings and tries with her apron to waft me away. Alas, she succeeds. All the virtues of a good mount my coal-scuttle has, but re-sistance it lacks; it is too light, a woman's apron sweeps its legs from under it.

'You wicked woman,' I cry out as I depart, while she, turning back to the shop, waves a hand in the air, half in contempt, half in satisfac-tion, 'you wicked woman! I asked for a shovelful of the worst quality, and you wouldn't give it me.' And with that I ascend into the regions of the glaciers and disappear for good.

A FASTING-ARTIST

Four Stories

First Sorrow

A TRAPEZE ARTIST—this art, practised high in the domes of the great variety theatres, is acknowledged to be one of the most difficult within men's reach—had arranged his life, at first simply out of perfectionism, but later also from the force of a habit which had grown tyrannical, in such a way that he remained, for the whole period of each engagement, day and night on his trapeze. All his needs, which were indeed very modest ones, were supplied by relays of attendants who kept watch below, hauling up and down everything that was required on high in specially constructed containers. This mode of life gave rise to no particular difficulties as far as the general public was concerned; it was merely somewhat distracting that he should have stayed aloft, as was impossible to conceal, while the other acts were in progress, and that although he mostly kept still at such times he would attract an occasional stray glance from the audience. The management forgave him this, however, because he was an exceptional, an irreplaceable artist. And of course they appreciated that he did not live like this out of mischief, and that this was in fact the only way he could keep in constant practice.

But it was also healthy up there as well, and when during the warmer months the side windows all round the dome were thrown open, and with the fresh air the sun came flooding into the gloom of the interior, it was even beautiful. It is true that his social intercourse was limited; it was only rarely that a fellow-acrobat clambered up the rope-ladder to join him, and then they would sit together on the trapeze, leaning out to right and left on the safety-ropes and gossiping; or there might be workmen mending the roof who would exchange a few words with him through an open window; or the fire officer, inspecting the emergency lighting on the topmost balcony, would call across to him with some respectful but almost unintelligible remark. Otherwise all around him was still; just occasionally some stage hand, having perhaps wandered into the empty theatre of an afternoon, might gaze thoughtfully up into the almost impenetrable heights, where the trapeze artist, with no means of knowing that he was observed, was practising his skills or resting.

The trapeze artist might have been able to go on living like this undisturbed had it not been for the inevitable travelling from place to place, which he found exceedingly painful. Of course his business manager saw to it that the trapeze artist was spared any unnecessary protraction of his sufferings: in the case of local moves within the same town racing cars were used, and they tore, preferably at night or in the early hours of the morning, through the deserted streets at breakneck speed, though always too slowly for the trapeze artist's consuming impatience; for railway travel a whole compartment was reserved, in which the trapeze artist could find some kind of substitute, however wretched, for his normal way of life by spending the journey up on the luggage-rack; in the next town to be visited on their circuit the trapeze was in its place in the theatre long before the arrival of the trapeze artist, and in addition every door leading to the auditorium had been flung open, every gangway cleared—yet even so the happiest moments of the manager's life were always those when the trapeze artist ultimately set his foot on the rope-ladder, and in a flash, at long last, was hanging once more above from his trapeze.

Despite the number of journeys that the manager had already brought to a successful conclusion, each fresh one was still a trial to him, for these journeys, apart from anything else, were clearly playing havoc with the trapeze artist's nerves.

So it happened one day when they were again on the move together, the trapeze artist lying on the luggage-rack dreaming, the manager leaning back in the window seat opposite reading a book, that the trapeze artist suddenly addressed him in a low voice. The manager was instantly at his service. The trapeze artist said, biting his lips, that from now on he must always have for his performance, instead of just the one trapeze as hitherto, two trapezes, two trapezes facing each other. The manager at once consented. But the trapeze artist, as if to show that in this case the manager's approval was as irrelevant as, for example, his opposition would have been, declared that henceforth he would never again, in no circumstances whatever, perform on just a single trapeze. The very idea that such a thing might happen seemed to make him shudder. The manager, hesitant and watchful, once more emphasized his complete agreement, two trapezes were better than one, and besides, the new arrangement would have the further advantage of adding variety to the production. Thereupon the trapeze artist suddenly burst into tears. Deeply alarmed, the manager jumped up and asked what the matter was, and getting no answer he climbed on to the seat, stroked him and laid his cheek against him, so that he too was bathed in the trapeze artist's tears. But it was only after much questioning and many soothing words that the trapeze artist sobbed: 'Only this one single bar in my hands—how can I survive like that!' Now it was somewhat easier for the manager to comfort him; he promised to send a telegram from the very next station to the next town on their circuit about a second trapeze; reproached himself for having let the trapeze artist work for so long on just one trapeze and thanked him and praised him warmly for having at last brought this error to his attention. And in this way the manager succeeded in slowly pacifying the trapeze artist, and he could return to his window seat. But he himself was far from pacified, with deep anxiety he kept stealing glances at the trapeze artist over the top of his book. Once such thoughts had begun to torment him, could they ever wholly cease? Must they not steadily intensify? Were they not a threat to his livelihood? And indeed, as the manager observed him in the apparently peaceful sleep into which he had sobbed himself, he thought he could see the first lines beginning to furrow the infant smoothness of the trapeze artist's brow.

A Little Woman

IT IS A LITTLE WOMAN that I now speak of; though quite slim by nature, she is also tightly laced; I always see her in the same dress, it is made of yellowish-grey material, something the colour of wood, and is trimmed with certain tassels or knot-like attachments of the same colour; she is always hatless, her dull-blond hair is smooth and not untidy, but kept very loose. Despite being tightly laced she is supple in her movements; in fact she exaggerates this mobility, she likes to put her hands on her hips and suddenly flip the upper part of her body sideways with surprising swiftness. The impression that her hand makes on me I can only convey by saying that I have never yet seen a hand which has the individual fingers so clearly marked off from one another as in her case; and yet her hand has by no means any anatomical peculiarities, it is a perfectly normal hand.

Now this little woman is highly dissatisfied with me, she always has some fault to find with me, I am always doing her an injustice, I annoy her at every turn; if it were possible to divide up one's life into the smallest of its parts and judge each part separately, there is no doubt that she would find every smallest part of my own life offensive. I have often wondered why it is that I should offend her so; it may be that everything about me runs counter to her aesthetic feelings, her sense of justice, her habits, her traditions, her hopes—such mutually incompatible natures do exist, but why does this cause her so much pain? There is absolutely no sort of relationship between us that might force her to suffer on my account. She need only decide to regard me as the complete stranger that I in fact am—and as which I should not oppose her decision but warmly welcome it; she need only decide to forget my existence, which I have never thrust upon her nor ever would thrust upon her—and then all her sufferings would obviously be over. In saying this I pay no regard to myself and to the fact that her behavior is naturally awkward for me as well; I pay no regard to that because I fully recognize that all the awkwardness I may feel is as nothing compared to what she has to suffer. At the same time, however, I am well aware that there is no spark of affection in her suffering; she is not in the least concerned with really improving me, and in any case the things about me which she objects to are not the kind of things which might affect my getting ahead in my career. But she does not even care about my getting ahead either, she cares only for her personal interest, that is to say: avenging the torment which I cause her and avoiding the torment which I threaten to cause her in future. I did once try to point out to her how one might best put an end to this continual distress of hers, but that provoked such an outburst on her part that I shall not repeat the attempt.

One might say that I do also have a certain responsibility in the matter, for however strange the little woman may be to me, and however true it is that the sole connection between us is the irritation that I cause her, or rather the irritation that she derives from me, nevertheless I can hardly remain indifferent to the physical ill-effects which visibly accompany it. From time to time I hear reports, more and more often recently, of how she has once again appeared in the morning with her face pale from lack of sleep, with a splitting headache and almost totally unfit for work; her condition is a source of anxiety for her relatives, they keep searching for the cause of it and have so far found no answer. I am the only one who knows that; it is the same old and ever-renewed irritation. Now of course I do not share the anxiety of her relatives; she is strong and resilient; anyone capable of such powerful irritation is likely to be able to get over its effects as well; I even have a suspicion that—at least to some extent—she only pretends to be suffering so as to direct public suspicion at me. She is too proud to declare openly how much my existence torments her; she would consider it degrading to seek the support of other people against me; it is sheer repulsion, endless repulsion, that constantly drives her to occupy herself with me; to go so far as to discuss this sordid matter in public, that would be too shameful for her to contemplate. But it is also too much for her to keep entirely quiet about the matter, which presses upon her without ceasing. So with her woman's cunning she tries a middle course; silently, only by the outward signs of a secret sorrow, does she seek to bring this affair before the court of public opinion. Perhaps she even hopes that if the public once gains a clear view of me, then a general public displeasure will emerge and use all the great powers at its disposal to condemn me for good and all, far more firmly and rapidly than she could ever do with her own relatively feeble private displeasure; and then she will retire into the background with a sigh of relief and turn her back on me. Well, if that is really what she hopes for she is deluding herself. The public will not take over her role; the public will never find such an infinity of faults in me, even if it subjects me to the most exact scrutiny. I am not such a wholly useless creature as she thinks; I have no wish to boast, and especially not in this connection; but even if I do not stand out as being especially worthwhile I am surely not conspicuous in the opposite sense either; only to her do I appear so, only to those eyes of hers, with their almost pure white gleam, do I appear so; she will never succeed in convincing anyone else. So perhaps I can feel quite reassured in this respect? No, I cannot; for if it really does become known that I am making her positively ill by my behaviour—and there are some diligent observers, precisely the most energetic newsmongers, who are on the point of perceiving this fact or at least they give that impression—and if then the world comes along and asks me the question: why is it that I so torment this poor little woman with my incorrigibility, and whether I perhaps intend to drive her to her death, and when am I going to show enough sense and simple human compassion to stop it—if the world puts that question to me it will be hard to find an answer. Ought I then admit that I do not much believe in those symptoms of illness, and ought I by so doing create the unpleasant impression of being a man who tries to avoid blame by blaming others, and in a most ungentlemanly manner at that? And could I, for instance, say quite openly that I should feel no flicker of compassion even if I did believe she was really ill, because the woman is a complete stranger to me and the relationship between us is entirely of her making and only exists from her point of view? I don't say that people would not believe me; more likely they would neither believe nor disbelieve; they would not even get to the stage where that question might arise; they would simply take note of the answer I had given, in respect of a frail and sickly woman, and that would hardly count in my favour. For here as with any other answer I should come up against the obstinate fact that the world cannot refrain, in a case like this, from suspecting that there must be a love affair behind it, although it is abundantly clear that no such relationship exists, and that if it did it would more likely come from my side rather than hers; for indeed I really should be quite capable of admiring the little woman, for the trenchancy of her judge-

ments and her tirelessness in pursuing her arguments, were it not for
the fact that I am the very one against whom these virtues are constantly being used as weapons. But at any rate there is no trace on her
side of a friendly relationship towards me; in that respect she is upright and truthful; therein lies my last hope; not even if it suited her
plan of campaign to foster belief in such a relationship would she so
far forget herself as to do anything of the kind. But the public, utterly
insensitive in such matters, will stick to its opinion and invariably decide against me.

So really the only thing left for me to do would be to alter myself
in time, before the world can intervene, sufficiently at least to mollify
the little woman's indignation somewhat, not of course eradicate it entirely, which would be unthinkable. And indeed I have frequently
asked myself whether I am actually so well satisfied with my current
state that I have no wish to alter it, and further, whether it might not
be possible to initiate certain changes in myself even if I did not do so
because I was convinced of their necessity, but purely in order to pla-
cate the woman. And I have made an honest attempt to do this, not
without effort and care; I even found it congenial, I almost enjoyed it;
some individual changes resulted, they were plain for all to see, I had
no need to draw the woman's attention to them, she notices all that
kind of thing sooner than I do myself, she can even perceive my intention as expressed in my manner; but I met with no success. And how
could I have done so? For her dissatisfaction with me is, as I now see,
a fundamental one; nothing can remove it, not even the removal of
myself; her transports of rage if she heard, let us say, of my suicide
would be beyond all bounds. Now I cannot imagine that she, sharp-
witted woman that she is, does not see this as clearly as I do, by which
I mean not merely the futility of her own efforts but also my own innocence, my own inability to meet her requirements even with the
best will in the world. Of course she sees it, but being a fighter by nature she forgets it in the heat of battle, whereas my own unhappy disposition—which I cannot do anything about, since I was born with
it—inclines me to whisper a gentle word of warning to anyone whose
howls of rage go beyond all limits of volume. In this way, naturally, we
shall never come to terms. I shall go on stepping out of my house, perhaps in the joyful hours of early morning, only to meet that disgruntled face, disgruntled on my account, that morose curl of the lip, that

searching look which knows in advance what it will find, which sweeps over me and misses nothing, however fleeting the glance may be, that bitter smile furrowing the girlish cheek, that plaintive raising of the eyes to heaven, that planting of the hands on the hips to gain support, and then that paling and trembling which accompanies the outburst of fury.

Recently—for the first time ever, as I realized to my amazement at the time—I dropped a few hints about this affair to a close friend of mine, just in passing, casually, only a word or two; I reduced the importance of the whole thing, which does indeed mean little enough to me in the end as far as the outside world is concerned, to a point slightly below the truth. It was curious that all the same my friend did not ignore it; in fact he actually made more of it on his own account, refused to be side-tracked and insisted on pursuing the matter. And what was still more curious: he did after all underestimate the matter in one important respect, for he seriously recommended me to go away for a while. No advice could have been more foolish; certainly the situation is simple enough, anyone who takes a closer look can get the hang of it, but it is still not so simple that my going away could resolve everything, or even the most important things about it. On the contrary, going away is precisely what I must avoid; if there is any sort of plan that I ought to follow then it is certainly this: to contain the affair within its present narrow limits, which so far do not include the outside world; in other words to stay quietly where I am and not permit the affair to give rise to any large-scale, conspicuous consequences; and that means, among other things, not mentioning it to anyone else; and all this is necessary not because it is some kind of dangerous secret, but because it is a minor, purely personal thing, and as such a light burden to bear despite everything, and because that is how it should stay. To this extent the remarks of my friend were not without value; while they have taught me nothing fresh they have strengthened me in my basic opinion.

And on closer reflection it does appear to be quite generally the case that those changes which the state of affairs seems to have undergone in the course of time are not changes in the matter itself, but merely developments in my attitude towards it, in so far as this attitude has been growing, on the one hand, calmer and more manly and getting closer to the heart of the matter, while on the other, as I have to admit, a certain jumpiness has been creeping into it, under the influence of the constant series of shocks, petty though they may be, which I cannot get over.

I am becoming calmer about the whole affair now I think I can recognize that a final decision, however imminent it may seem at times, is probably not yet in the offing; one is much inclined, particularly when young, greatly to overestimate the speed with which decisions arrive; whenever my little judge, grown faint at the very sight of me, sank sideways into a chair, holding on to the back of it with one hand and plucking at her corset strings with the other, while tears of rage and despair rolled down her cheeks, I used always to think that the decisive moment had come, and that I was on the point of being called to account. But not at all, no question of a final decision, no summons to account, women feel faint often enough, the world has no time to attend to every case. So what, then, has really happened in all these years? Simply that such episodes have recurred, sometimes with greater, sometimes lesser severity, so that now their sum total is greater. And that people now hang around in the vicinity and would gladly interfere, if only they could find a way of doing so; but they can find none; so far they have relied on their scent alone, and while scenting things out is enough to keep a nose fully occupied it serves no other purpose. But that is how things have always been, in essence; there were always these useless loiterers standing about, using up the atmosphere and excusing their presence in some crafty manner, preferably by claiming relationship; always they would be on the lookout, always they had their nostrils full of some scent or other, but as a result of all this they are just standing there still. The only difference is that I have gradually come to recognize them and distinguish one face from another; once I used to believe that they were steadily gathering from all over the place, that the matter was assuming ever greater proportions and that this in itself would force the final decision; today I feel pretty sure that it was all just the same from the very beginning, and that it has little if anything to do with the approach of the decision. And the decision itself, why do I give it such a weighty name? If it should ever happen—and certainly not tomorrow or the day after tomorrow and probably never—that the public comes to concern itself with this matter, which as I shall never tire of repeating lies beyond its competence, I shall certainly not emerge from the proceedings unharmed, but all the same it will probably be taken into account that I am not unknown to the public, that I have always lived fully in the public eye, trustful and earning trust in return, and that therefore this sorrowful little woman, who has emerged as a latecomer—and whom, let me say in passing, any other man would perhaps long since have recognized as a tiresome clinger and crushed under his heel well out of public earshot—that this woman could, at the very worst, only add a little ugly flourish to that diploma in which the public has long since certified me as one of its respected members. Such is the state of affairs at present, which is thus hardly of a kind to make me feel uneasy.

The fact that I have, all the same, grown a trifle uneasy in the course of the years has nothing to do with the actual importance of this matter; one simply cannot endure being a constant source of irritation to someone, even if one sees quite clearly that the irritation is groundless; one becomes uneasy; one begins, as it were in a purely physical way, to watch out for decisions, even if one has the good sense not to put too much faith in their coming. In part, though, it is simply a matter of advancing age; everything sits well on the young; unattractive features are lost to view in the constant surge of youthful energy; if one had a somewhat wary eye as a youngster, that was not taken amiss, it went quite unnoticed, even by oneself; but the things which survive into old age are remnants, each one of them is needed, none can be renewed, each is watched over; and the wary eye of an ageing man is now quite plainly a wary eye, and not at all hard to detect. But here again it cannot be said that things have really got worse in fact.

So from whichever angle I consider it, it always becomes apparent—and from this I will not budge—that if only I keep this little matter just lightly concealed with my hand I shall remain free for a long time to go on living my life as hitherto, untroubled by the world, despite all the raging of this woman.

A Fasting-artist

PUBLIC INTEREST in exhibition fasting has suffered a marked decline in recent decades. While one used to be able to make good money by mounting independent productions of this kind on quite a large scale, today that is quite impossible. Times have changed. In those days the fasting-artist was the talk of the town; from day to day of his fast enthusiasm grew; each day everyone wanted to go and see the fasting-artist at least once; during the later stages people with specially reserved seats used to sit in front of the little barred cage all day long; there were even showings at night as well, by torchlight to heighten the effect; on fine days the cage was carried out into the open, and it was then in particular that the fasting-artist was shown to the children; while for the grown-ups he was often no more than a joke, in which they took part because it was fashionable, the children stood open-mouthed, holding one another by the hand for safety's sake, and watched him as he sat there on the straw that had been spread for him, for he spurned even a chair, a pale figure in his black leotard, ribs grotesquely protruding, now nodding politely, now answering questions with a laboured smile, sometimes even stretching an arm through the bars for them to feel how skinny he was, but then withdrawing completely into himself again and paying attention to no one, not even to the striking of the clock, which meant so much for him and was the only piece of furniture in his cage, but merely staring ahead of him through half-shut eyes and taking an occasional sip from a tiny glass of water to moisten his lips.

Apart from the spectators who came and went there were also permanent watchmen there, men selected by the public—strangely enough they were usually butchers—whose task it was, operating three at a time, to observe the fasting-artist by day and night and make quite sure that he did not, perhaps by some kind of secret device, take nourishment after all. But this was a pure formality, introduced to reassure the masses, for the initiates knew well enough that the fasting-artist during the period of his fast would never, under no circumstances, not even under compulsion, have eaten the smallest morsel; the honour of his art forbade it. Not every watchman, of course, was capable of understanding this, there were often groups of watchmen on the night shift who were very lax about the watch they kept, deliberately getting together in a corner and absorbing themselves in a game of cards, with the obvious intention of allowing the fasting-artist a little refreshment, which in their opinion he could obtain by drawing on some kind of secret supply. Nothing was more of a torment to the fasting-artist than such watchmen; they reduced him to misery; they made his fasting hideously difficult; sometimes he would summon up what strength he had and sing during their watch, for as long as he could keep it up, so as to show these people how unjust their suspicions were. But that was of little use; they were merely amazed by his skill in being able to eat even while singing. Far more to his taste were the watchmen who sat close up against the bars, who were not satisfied with the dim night lighting in the hall, but kept him in the beams of the electric torches which had been issued to them by the manager. The glaring light did not bother him at all, he was unable to sleep in any case, and he could always doze a little whatever the light or the hour, even when the hall was crammed full of noisy people. With such watchmen he was quite prepared to spend the entire night without sleep; he was prepared to exchange jokes with them, tell them stories of his wandering life and then listen to their tales in turn, anything just to keep them awake, to demonstrate to them over and over again that he had nothing to eat in his cage and that he was fasting as not one of them could fast. But he was happiest when the morning came and a lavish breakfast was brought them, at his own expense, on which they flung themselves with the appetite of healthy men after a weary night's vigil. There were even people who tried to represent this breakfast as an attempt to exert undue influence on the watchmen, but that really was going too far, and when they were asked if they would care to take over the night watch without breakfast, just for the sake of the cause, they soon drifted away, though they stuck to their insinuations all the same.

But this was just one example of the many suspicions that are quite inseparable from fasting. After all, no one was capable of spending all his days and nights keeping an unbroken watch over the fasting-artist, so no one could know from his personal experience whether the fast had really been an unbroken and faultless performance; only the fasting-artist himself could know that; only he, therefore, could be at the same time the completely satisfied spectator of his own fast. But he again was never satisfied, for a different reason; perhaps it was not his fasting at all that had made him so extremely emaciated that many people, to their sorrow, had to forego his performances because they could not bear the sight of him; perhaps what had so emaciated him was simply dissatisfaction with himself. For he alone knew, something that no other initiate knew, how easy fasting was. It was the easiest thing in the world. He made no secret of this, either, but people would not believe him, they put it down at best to modesty, but mostly to publicity-seeking, or they even took him for a fraud, for whom no doubt fasting was easy because he knew how to make it easy, and he even had the audacity to half admit the fact. He had to put up with all that, indeed as the years went by he had grown accustomed to it, but inwardly this dissatisfaction of his kept gnawing at him, and not once, not at the end of a single fasting period—so much one had to grant him—had he voluntarily left his cage. His business manager had appointed forty days as the maximum time for fasting, beyond this he would never allow a fast to run, not even in the great cities, and there was a good reason for it. Experience had shown that in any town interest could be spurred on for about forty days, by gradually stepping up the publicity, but then the audience fell away, a substantial drop in attendance was recorded; naturally there were small variations in this respect as between the different towns and regions, but it remained the rule that forty days was the limit. So then, on the fortieth day, the gate of the flower-bedecked cage was opened, an enthusiastic throng of spectators filled the amphitheatre, a military band played, two doctors entered the cage to carry out the necessary measurements on the fasting-artist, the results were announced to the audience through a megaphone, and finally two young ladies stepped forward, overjoyed that the lot had fallen to them, with the intention of leading the fasting-artist out of his cage and down a few steps, where a carefully chosen invalid meal was laid out on a little table. And when this moment arrived the fasting-artist always resisted. He would go so far as to surrender his bony arms to the outstretched hands of these ladies, as they bent solicitously down to him, but stand up he would not. Why, after forty days, should he call a halt now? He could have kept going for much longer, for infinitely much longer; why stop just now, when he was at the very best pitch of his fasting, indeed when he had not yet even reached his best? Why did they want to rob him of the glory of fasting on, not just the glory of being the greatest fasting-artist of all time, which he probably already was, but the further glory of surpassing himself to achieve the inconceivable, for he felt that his capacity to fast was boundless. Why must this crowd which claimed to admire him so much have so little patience with him; if he could put up with more fasting, why should not they? And besides, he was tired, he was sitting comfortably in the straw, and now he was supposed to hoist himself up to his full height and proceed to a meal, the mere thought of which provoked such feelings of nausea that it was only with great difficulty, out of regard for the ladies, that he could avoid giving expression to them. And he looked up into the eyes of the ladies, so friendly in appearance, so cruel in reality, and shook the head that weighed all too heavily on that feeble neck. But what followed then was what always did follow. Up came the manager; silently—for the band made speech impossible—he raised his arms over the fasting-artist, as if he were calling on heaven to look on its handiwork down here on the straw, on this pitiable martyr, which indeed the fasting-artist was, though in quite another sense; grasped the fasting-artist round his meagre waist, seeking by his exaggerated delicacy to make plain how frail an object he had to deal with; and passed him over— not without a covert shake or two, so that his upper and lower parts lolled helplessly about—to the care of the ladies who had now grown pale as death. By this stage the fasting-artist had submitted completely; his head lay on his breast, as if it had rolled there and inexplicably come to rest; his body was all hollowed out; his legs were pressed tight together at the knees, by some instinct of self-preservation; yet his feet were scrabbling at the ground, scrabbling as if this ground were not the real one, the real ground was what they were seeking; and the whole, admittedly modest weight of his body rested on one of the ladies, who, looking around for help, with her breath coming in gasps—this was not how she had envisaged her position of honour— first stretched back her neck as far as she could, so as to prevent her face from coming into contact with the fasting-artist, but then, when she found this impossible, and her more fortunate companion did not come to her aid, contenting herself instead with carrying before her in her trembling hand that little bundle of bones that was the hand of the fasting-artist, then she burst into tears, amid the delighted laughter of the audience, and had to be replaced by an attendant who had been posted in readiness well in advance. Then came the meal, with the manager spooning a little food into the comatose, almost unconscious fasting-artist, to the accompaniment of a cheerful patter designed to distract attention from the artist's condition; and after that a toast to the public was proposed, a toast that had allegedly been whispered to the manager by the fasting-artist; the band set the seal on everything with a great fanfare, the whole company dispersed, and no one had any cause to feel dissatisfied with the show, no one, that is, save the fasting-artist, always just him alone.

So did he live for many years, with regular little rest periods, in apparent glory, honoured by the world, yet for all that mostly in sorrowful mood, which became increasingly sorrowful because no one was able to take it seriously. And indeed, how could they have comforted him? What more had he to wish for? And if once in a while some kindly soul came along who felt sorry for him, and tried to explain to him that his sadness was probably the result of his fasting, then it would sometimes happen, especially if his fast was well advanced, that the fasting-artist responded with an explosion of rage, and to universal alarm began to rattle like a wild beast at the bars of his cage. But for such outbreaks the manager had a means of correction which he was fond of employing. He would apologize to the assembled audience on the fasting-artist's behalf, would admit that the fasting-artist's behaviour could only be excused by the irritable condition brought on by his fasting, a condition by no means easy for well-fed persons to understand; and he would go on in that connection to speak of the fasting-artist's claim, which also required some explanation, that he was capable of fasting for much longer than he did fast; he would praise the high aspiration, the admirable intentions, the great measure of self-denial undoubtedly implicit in such a claim; but he would then seek to refute this claim by the simple enough means of producing photographs, which were simultaneously offered for sale to the public, for these photographs showed the fasting-artist on the fortieth day of one of his fasts, lying in bed almost at his last gasp from utter exhaustion. This perversion of the truth, which though familiar enough to the fasting-artist always sapped his strength anew, was too much for him. What was the consequence of the premature ending of his fast was here presented as its cause! To fight against this obtuseness, against this world of obtuseness, was impossible. Up to that point he always clung to his cage, listening eagerly and in all good faith to the manager, but each time the photographs appeared he would leave hold of the bars to sink back with a sigh on to his straw, and the now reassured public could approach again to inspect him.

When a few years later those who had witnessed such scenes recalled them to mind, they often found their own behaviour incomprehensible. For in the meantime that reversal already mentioned had taken place; it had happened almost overnight; there may have been deeper reasons for it, but who wanted to discover them; at all events one day the pampered fasting-artist found himself deserted by the pleasure-seeking crowds, who went streaming off to other exhibitions instead. For one last time his manager went chasing round half Europe with him, to see whether something of the old interest might still be found here and there; all in vain; as if by some secret agreement a positive revulsion against exhibition fasting had set in everywhere. In reality, of course, it cannot have come about so suddenly, and people now remembered with hindsight a number of warning signs that had been inadequately noted and inadequately dealt with in the intoxication of success, but by that time it was too late to take any countermeasures. Of course one day the time for fasting, like other things, would surely come round again, but that was no comfort to the living. What, then, was the fasting-artist to do? The man who had been acclaimed by thousands could not appear as a sideshow at village fairs, and as for taking up another profession the fasting-artist was not only too old but above all too fanatically dedicated to his fasting. So he took leave of his manager, his associate throughout an unparalleled career, and found himself an engagement with a great circus; in order to spare his own feelings he did not even glance at the terms of the contract.

A great circus with its vast quantity of personnel and animals and contrivances, all constantly balancing one another out and supplementing one another, can find a use for anybody and at any time, even a fasting-artist, assuming of course that his demands are sufficiently modest, and furthermore in this particular case it was not just the fasting-artist who was being engaged but also his old and famous name; indeed, in view of the peculiar nature of this artistic skill, which does not decrease with increasing years, one could not even say that here was a superannuated artist, past his best, seeking refuge in a peaceful circus job; on the contrary the fasting-artist maintained, and there was every reason to believe him, that he was fasting just as well as ever; in fact he even claimed that if they let him have his way, and this was promised him without hesitation, he would actually begin to produce justified amazement in the world for the first time, although this claim of his, considering the current mood, which the fasting-artist was apt to forget in his enthusiasm, provoked no more than a smile from the experts.

Fundamentally, however, the fasting-artist had not become blind to the real circumstances and he accepted it as perfectly natural that he should not, for example, be placed with his cage in the middle of the ring as a star attraction, but instead accommodated outside, in what was moreover a most accessible site close to the menagerie. Large, brightly coloured placards surrounded his cage and proclaimed what was to be seen there. When the public came thronging out during the intervals of the performance to look at the animals, they were almost bound to pass the fasting-artist's cage and stop there for a moment; perhaps they might even have stayed longer had not those pressing behind them in the narrow gangway, who could not understand this blockage on their way to the keenly awaited menagerie, made any more protracted and leisurely inspection impossible. That was also the reason why the fasting-artist, though he naturally longed for these visiting hours as the justification of his existence, trembled at their prospect as well. At first he had hardly been able to wait for the intervals; he had watched enraptured as the crowd came surging up, until it was all too soon borne in on him—even the most obstinate, almost deliberate self-deception could not obscure the fact—that the entire crowd consisted, at least as far as their intentions went, every single time, without exception, of people on their way to the animals. And that first sight of them from the distance always remained the best. For as soon as they came up to him he was deafened by the shouting and cursing of the two contending factions which kept forming: those who wanted—and the fasting-artist soon found this group the more distasteful—to be allowed a quiet stare at him, not from any real interest but from pigheadedness, just to satisfy a whim, and on the other hand the group who wanted to push straight on to the menagerie. Once the main flock had gone by, along came the stragglers, but in fact these, with nothing to prevent them from stopping for as long as they liked, hurried past with long strides, with hardly a sideways glance, so as to be sure of getting to the animals in time. And it was an all-too-rare stroke of luck if some father of a family turned up with his children, pointed a finger at the fasting-artist, explained in detail what it was all about, told stories of earlier years when he had witnessed similar, but incomparably more splendid performances, and when the children then, owing to the inadequate preparation that school and life had given them, still indeed remained uncomprehending—what was fasting to them?—and yet, by the brightness of their inquisitive eyes, revealed a glimpse of new, future, more merciful times. Perhaps, the fasting-artist sometimes said to himself, everything might be a little better after all if he were not located so very close to the animals' cages. That made the choice too easy for people, to say nothing of the fact that the stench emanating from the menagerie, the restlessness of the animals at night, the carrying past of raw lumps of flesh for the beasts of prey, the roars at feeding time, all distressed him and weighed on him constantly. But to complain to the management was more than he dared; after all, he had the animals to thank for the troops of visitors, among whom there might always just be one who was destined for him; and who could tell where they might hide him away if he tried to remind them of his existence, and hence of the fact that he was, strictly speaking, no more than an obstruction on the route to the animals.

A small obstruction, admittedly, an obstruction growing smaller all the time. It was becoming a habit to think it strange, nowadays, for anyone to claim attention for a fasting-artist; and with that habit his fate was sealed. He might fast as well as only he knew how, and so he did, but there was no longer anything that could save him; people passed him by. Just try to explain to someone what the art of fasting is. No one who does not feel it can be made to grasp what it means. The beautiful placards became dirty and illegible, they were ripped down, no one thought of replacing them; the little board showing the tally of days fasted, which at first had been scrupulously changed each day, had now long stayed unaltered, for after the first few weeks the staff had grown weary of even this little task; and so the fasting-artist did indeed go fasting on, as he had once dreamed of doing, but no one counted the days, no one, not even the fasting-artist himself, knew how great his achievement was, and his heart grew heavy. And if once in a while some casual passer-by should stop, ridicule the outdated number of the board and talk about fraudulence, that was in its way the stupidest lie that ever indifference and inborn malice could invent, for it was not

the fasting-artist who was cheating, he was working honestly, but the
world was cheating him of his reward.

But again many days went by, and there came an end to that too. One
day an overseer happened to notice the cage, and he asked the attendants why this perfectly good cage, with rotten straw in it, should be
left unused; no one could say until somebody, prompted by the tally-
board, recalled the fasting-artist. They poked around in the straw and
they found the fasting-artist underneath. 'Are you still fasting?' the
overseer asked, 'when on earth are you going to stop?' 'Forgive me,
everybody,' whispered the fasting-artist; only the overseer, with his ear
to the bars, could understand him. 'Of course,' said the overseer, tapping his forehead to indicate to the others the state that the artist was
in, 'we forgive you.' 'I always wanted you to admire my fasting,' said
the fasting-artist. 'And we do admire it,' said the overseer obligingly.
'But you shouldn't admire it,' the fasting-artist said. 'All right, we
don't admire it then,' said the overseer, 'but why shouldn't we admire
it?' 'Because I have to fast, I can't help it,' said the fasting-artist.
'Whatever next,' said the overseer, 'and why can't you help it?' 'Because,' said the fasting-artist, and he lifted his head a little and spoke,
with his lips pursed as if for a kiss, straight into the overseer's ear, so
that nothing might be missed, 'because I could never find the nourishment I liked. Had I found it, believe me, I would never have caused
any stir, and would have eaten my fill just like you and everyone else.'
Those were his last words, but in his failing eyes there still remained
the firm, if no longer proud conviction that he was fasting on.

'Now then, clear things up!' said the overseer, and they buried the
fasting-artist, straw and all. Into the cage they then put a young pan-
ther. It was a relief that even the dullest sense could feel to see this
wild creature leaping about in the cage that had been barren for so
long. He lacked for nothing. The food that he liked was brought him
by his keepers, without much reflection; he seemed not even to miss
his freedom; that noble body, furnished almost to bursting point with
all that it needed, seemed to carry freedom itself around with it too;
somewhere in his jaws it seemed to be hidden; and the joy of life
glowed so fiercely from the furnace of his throat that the onlookers
could scarcely stand up against it. But they mastered their weakness,
surrounded the cage, and simply refused to be dragged away.

Josefine, the Songstress
or:
The Mouse People

OUR SONGSTRESS is called Josefine. Anyone who has not heard her has never felt the power of song. There is not one of us whom her singing does not transport; and that says all the more since on the whole we are not a music-loving people. For us the best music is peace and tranquillity; our life is hard, and even when we have tried for once to shake off all our daily cares, we still cannot rise to things so remote from our normal lives as music is. Yet we do not lament it much; we do not even get that far; we consider our greatest asset to be a certain practical cunning—of which indeed we have the most urgent need—and it is with the smile of that cunning that we are used to console ourselves for everything, even supposing—though this doesn't happen—that we should feel a yearning for such happiness as perhaps music may provide. It is only Josefine who is the exception; she loves music, and knows how to convey it as well; she is the only one; with her departure music will disappear—for who knows how long—from out of our lives.

I have often reflected on the question of what this music really means. After all, we are wholly unmusical; how is it that we can understand Josefine's singing, or rather—since Josefine denies that—imagine that we can understand it. The simplest answer must be that the beauty of her song is such that even the dullest ear cannot resist it; yet this answer fails to satisfy. If it were really so, then her singing would have to give one the instant and lasting impression of being something out of the ordinary; the feeling that something was sounding from this throat that we had never heard before and were not even capable of hearing, something that only this unique Josefine and no one else could enable us to hear. But that is precisely what, in my opinion, does not occur; I do not feel it, nor have I observed any such reaction in others. In our own circle we openly admit that Josefine's song, as song, does not represent anything out of the ordinary.

Is this in fact singing at all? Despite our unmusicality we have some tradition of song; in the ancient days of our people song was known; legends tell of it, and certain songs have even been preserved, though admittedly no one can sing them any longer. So we do have some vague conception of what song is, and the truth is that Josefine's art does not actually correspond to this conception. Is it in fact singing at all? Is it not perhaps simply a piping? And piping is of course something that we all know, it is the particular skill of our people, or rather no skill at all but a characteristic expression of life. We all pipe, but naturally no one dreams of calling that an art, we pipe without paying any attention to it, indeed without noticing it, and there are even many among us who are quite unaware that piping is one of our characteristics. So if it should be true that Josefine does not sing but only pipes, and even, so it seems to me at least, hardly rises above the level of our usual piping—indeed perhaps her strength does not even quite suffice for this usual piping, whereas a common worker of the earth can produce it effortlessly all day long, on top of his work—if all that should be true, then Josefine's alleged artistry would indeed be refuted, but then the enormous effect that she has really would present a puzzle.

But it simply is not mere piping that she produces. If you stand a good way away from her and listen, or still better put yourself to the following test: if Josefine should happen to be singing along with other voices, and you set yourself the task of picking out hers, then you will invariably distinguish only a quite ordinary piping, standing out if at all by its fragility or weakness. And yet if you are placed in front of her, it is not mere piping; in order to understand her art it is necessary not just to hear her but to see her as well. Even if this were simply our own workaday piping, we first have to face the peculiar fact that someone is here solemnly standing up to do nothing more than the perfectly normal thing. It is in all conscience no great art to crack a nut, and therefore no one will make so bold as to assemble an audience and come forward to entertain it by cracking nuts. But if he should do so, and if he succeeds in his aim, then it cannot just be a matter of pure nut-cracking. Or alternatively it is a matter of nut-cracking, but it turns out that we have been overlooking this particular art because we were such pastmasters at it, and this new nut-cracker is the first to show us what it really consists in, in which case it might even enhance the effect if he were slightly less efficient at nut-cracking than the majority of us.

Perhaps it is much the same with Josefine's singing; we admire in her what we do not in the least admire in ourselves; in the latter respect, by the way, she quite agrees with us. I was present on one occasion when someone, as of course often happens, drew attention to our common folk-piping habit; it was only a discreet reference, but for Josefine it was just too much. A smile so sarcastic, so arrogant as she then put on I never saw; she, who in appearance is the very soul of delicacy, strikingly delicate even among a people rich in such feminine types, showed up at that moment as positively coarse; she must no doubt have recognized this at once, with her great sensitivity, and controlled herself. So at all events she denies any connection between her own art and piping. For those who are of the opposite opinion she has only contempt, and probably unacknowledged hatred. Nor is this common vanity, for the opposition, to which I myself half belong, certainly admires her no less than the great crowd, but Josefine does not want just to be admired, she wants to be admired in exactly the manner she prescribes, admiration in itself is of no interest to her. And when one is sitting in front of her, one understands her; opposition is only possible from a distance; sitting in front of her one knows: this piping of hers is no piping.

Since piping is one of our unthinking habits, one might suppose that there would be some piping in Josefine's audience too; her art gives us a sense of well-being, and when we feel like that we pipe; but her audience does not pipe, they are as quiet as mice; almost as though we had become partakers of that longed-for peace, from which our own piping does hold us back somewhat, we remain still. Is it her song that enchants us, or is it not rather the solemn stillness which enfolds that small and feeble voice? On one occasion it happened, while Josefine was singing, that some foolish young thing started in all innocence to pipe up too. Well now, it was just the same as what we were hearing from Josefine; out there in front that piping, still modest for all its slickness of routine, and here in the audience that self-forgetful infantile peeping; it would have been impossible to put one's finger on the difference; and yet at once we hissed and whistled for the interrupter to pipe down, although there was no need for it, for she would surely have crept away anyhow in fear and shame; meanwhile Josefine, quite beside herself, struck up her triumphal piping, with her arms outflung and her neck stretched up as far as it would go.

But that is what she is always like; every little thing, every chance occurrence, every nuisance, a creaking floorboard, a grinding of the teeth, something wrong with the lighting, she considers appropriate to heighten the effect of her song; in her view she is singing to deaf ears in any case; there is no lack of enthusiasm and applause, but she has long since abandoned hope of real understanding as she conceives it. So that is why every disturbance is most welcome to her; anything coming from outside that contrasts with the purity of her song and that can be defeated easily, even without a struggle, can play its part in awakening the crowd and informing it, if not with understanding, at least with some measure of awe and respect.

But if small things can serve her so well, how much more do the great ones. Our life is a very uneasy one, every day brings its surprises and alarms, its hopes and terrors, so that it would be impossible for any individual to bear it all unless he always had, by day and night, the support of his fellows; but even so things often become hard enough; sometimes the shoulders of a thousand tremble under a burden that was really meant for one alone. Then it is that Josefine believes her time to have come. There she stands, the delicate creature, quivering in an alarming way just below the breast; it is as if all her strength had gathered itself into her song; as if everything about her that did not immediately serve her song, every power, almost every means of subsistence had been stripped from her; as if she had been laid bare, exposed, committed solely to the care of good spirits; as if, while she thus resides, so totally exposed, in her song, one single cold breath in passing would be sufficient to destroy her. But it is precisely when we see her like this that we, her alleged opponents, tend to say: 'She cannot even pipe; look what a terrible effort she has to make to wring out of herself, not song—let us not speak of song—but even something approaching our customary piping.' So it appears to us; and yet, as already mentioned, this inevitable impression is a fleeting one and it rapidly vanishes. Soon we, too, are plunged in the feeling of the crowd as they listen, body pressed warmly to body, with reverently bated breath.

And in order to gather this crowd of our people around her—a people that is almost always on the move, scurrying to and fro for reasons that are often none too clear—all Josefine usually needs to do is to adopt that stance, with her head tilted back, mouth half-open, eyes raised to the skies, which indicates that she intends to sing. She can do this where she likes, the place need not be visible from far off, any secluded corner chosen on the spur of the moment will do just as well. The news that she is going to sing spreads at once, and soon whole processions are on the move. Occasionally, however, difficulties arise; Josefine sings for preference in troubled times, and then a variety of anxieties and hardships force us to travel by devious routes; with the best will in the world we cannot assemble as quickly as Josefine would like and she may perhaps have to stand there for some time in her impressive pose without a sufficient audience—then of course she gets furious, then she stamps her feet, she swears in a most unmaidenly fashion, indeed she actually bites. Yet even this sort of behavior cannot damage her reputation; instead of trying to curb her extravagant demands a little, people make every effort to meet them; messengers are dispatched to bring the listeners in; she is kept in ignorance of this manoeuvre; on all the routes round about one can then see sentries posted, waving on the new arrivals and urging them to make all speed; and this goes on until finally a tolerable number has been gathered.

What is it that drives our people to make such efforts for the sake of Josefine? A question no easier to answer than the question of Josefine's song, with which it is indeed connected. One might be able to strike out the first of these questions and unite it wholly with the second, supposing one could assert that our folk is unconditionally devoted to Josefine on account of her song. But that is just not the case; unconditional devotion is practically unknown among us; among this folk of ours, which is attached above all to a kind of cunning, a harmless kind, to childish whisperings, to superficial and quite innocent tittle-tattle, such a folk is simply unable to devote itself unconditionally; and that is probably what Josefine senses, too; that is what she is fighting against with all the might of her feeble vocal chords.

Of course it would be wrong to take such general statements too far; as a people we are indeed devoted to Josefine, certainly we are, only not unconditionally. For example, we should never be capable of laughing at Josefine. It may be confessed: there are plenty of things about Josefine that invite laughter; and laughter is itself something that we are always prone to; despite all the miseries of our existence a little quiet laughter is, so to speak, always at home with us; but we do not laugh at Josefine. Sometimes I have the impression that our people sees its relationship to Josefine rather like this: that she, this fragile, vulnerable, somehow distinguished creature, in her opinion distinguished by her song, has been entrusted to us and that we must look after her; the reason for this is not clear to anyone, only the fact seems to be established. But what has been entrusted to one's care one does not laugh at; to do so would be a breach of duty; the utmost spite that the most spiteful among us can vent on Josefine is when they sometimes say: 'When we see Josefine it is no laughing matter.'

So the people takes care, then, of Josefine, much as a father looks after a child whose small hand is stretched out—one cannot tell whether pleading or demanding—towards him. One might think that our people were not fitted to perform such fatherly duties, but in fact we do discharge them, at least in this case, in exemplary fashion; no individual could do what in this respect the people as a whole is capable of doing. To be sure, the strength of the people is so vastly much greater than the strength of the single person that it has only to draw the one committed to its charge into the warmth of its immediate presence and there he will find protection enough. Admittedly, no one dares mention such things to Josefine. 'Don't you speak of protecting me,' she then says, 'or I'll soon spoil your piping.' 'Ah yes, you know about piping,' we think. And in any case, she is not seriously trying to refute us when she rebels like that; it is rather a thoroughly childish, a childishly grateful way of behaving; and the way of a father is to pay no attention.

And yet there is something further that is involved here, something less easy to explain in terms of the relationship between the people and Josefine. The point is that Josefine takes the opposite view: she believes that it is she who protects the people. Whenever we are in grave trouble, political or economic, it is allegedly her song that saves us; it is supposed to achieve nothing less than that; and even if it does not avert our misfortune, at least it gives us the strength to bear it. She does not express the matter in so many words, or in any other words, indeed she never says much at all; she is the silent one among the chatterers; but it flashes from her eyes; from her closed lips—there are not many of us who can keep their lips closed, but she can—it is plainly to be read. Whenever we get bad news—and many a day it comes pouring in, thick and fast, with lies and half-truths included—she rises up at once from the weariness that otherwise drags her down, she rises up and cranes her neck and tries to survey her flock like a shepherd before the storm. It is true that children make similar claims, in their wild, impulsive fashion, but Josefine's claims are not quite so unfounded as theirs. Of course she does not save us, and she gives us no strength; it is easy to set oneself up as the saviour of a people which, accustomed to suffering, unsparing of itself, swift in decision, well acquainted with death, only seemingly anxious in the atmosphere of recklessness in which it constantly lives, and in addition to that as prolific as it is courageous—it is easy, I say, to set oneself up as a saviour of this people, which has somehow always managed to save itself, be it at a price that makes the historian—in general we neglect historical study entirely—grow cold with horror. And nevertheless it is precisely at such times when we are in our direst straits that we listen to Josefine's voice more attentively than at others. The threats that hang over us make us stiller, more humble, more submissive to Josefine's dictatorial behaviour; gladly do we come together, gladly huddle close to one another, especially since the occasion is one so remote from the single great, tormenting issue; it is as if we were drinking in all haste—oh yes, haste is necessary, Josefine is all too apt to forget that—a communal beaker of peace before the battle. It is not so much a recital of songs as a folk-gathering, and what is more a gathering where all, save for the faint piping up at the front, is completely silent; much too solemn is the hour for it to be spent in chattering.

Josefine, however, could never be satisfied with a relationship of this kind. Despite all the touchy discontent that fills her because her position always remains so ill-defined, there is much that Josefine fails to see, blinded as she is by her self-conceit, and she can be brought without much difficulty to overlook a great deal more; a bevy of flatterers is constantly at work to this end, and thus in fact performing a public service;—but just in order to sing as an incidental attraction, unheeded, in some corner of a folk-gathering, just for that, though in itself it would be no small thing, she would most certainly not sacrifice her song.

But she does not have to do that, because her art does not go unheeded. Despite the fact that we are at bottom preoccupied with quite other things, and that the silence which prevails is by no means due to her song alone, and that many a listener does not even look up but instead buries his face in the coat of his neighbour, and that Josefine therefore appears to be wearing herself out up there in front to no purpose, all the same something of her piping does—there is no denying it—irresistibly come through to us as well. This piping which rises up, when all others are enjoined to silence, comes almost as a message from the people to each individual; the thin piping of Josefine in the midst of grave decisions is almost like the pitiful existence of our people amid the tumult of the hostile world. Josefine makes herself felt, this mere nothing of a voice, this mere nothing of an achievement makes itself felt and forces its way through to us; it does good to remember that. If ever a true exponent of the art of song should emerge from among us we would certainly be unable to endure him at times like these, and would by common consent reject any such performance as absurd. May Josefine be spared the awareness that the fact that we listen to her is a proof that she is no true singer. Some suspicion of this she probably has, why else would she so passionately deny that we do listen to her, but she keeps on singing her way, piping her way free of this suspicion.

But there might be a further consolation for her as well: to some extent we do really listen to her, after all, in the sort of way that people presumably listen to true singers; she achieves effects that a true singer would seek in vain to achieve with us, and she owes these effects precisely to her inadequate powers. No doubt this hangs together above all with the kind of life we lead.

Among our people there is no such thing as youth, and hardly even the briefest spell of childhood. Demands are always being made that special allowances should be made for children, that they should be given special consideration, that their right to a little freedom from care, a little mad romping about, a little play, that this right should be recognized and attempts made to ensure it; such demands are made and nearly everyone approves them, there is nothing one could approve of more, but equally there is nothing more impossible to grant, given the reality of our daily lives; the demands are approved, some efforts are made along these lines, but quite soon everything is back again where it was. The truth is, our life is such that as soon as a child can run about a little and make out its surroundings a little, it has to fend for itself just like an adult; the territories on which we are forced, for economic reasons, to live dispersed are too vast, our enemies are too numerous, the dangers that lie in wait for us everywhere are too incalculable—we cannot shield our children from the struggle for existence; if we did so, it would mean that they met an early end. Beside these depressing reasons, however, there is also an uplifting one: the fertility of our race. One generation—and each is numerous—presses on the heels of the one before, the children have no time to be children. Other peoples may tend their children with great care, they may set up schools for their little ones, and from these schools the children, the future of the race, may come pouring out; but with these other peoples it is the same children, over a long period, who keep coming out like that each day. We have no schools, but the countless swarms of our children come pouring out of our people itself, at the briefest possible intervals, merrily chirping or peeping so long as they cannot yet pipe, rolling or being bowled along by the throng so long as they cannot yet run, clumsily sweeping all before them by their sheer mass so long as they cannot yet see,—our children! And not, as in those schools, the same children; no, always new ones, ever and again new ones; without end, without a break; hardly does a child appear than it is a child no more, while behind it the new childish faces come crowding, so many and so fast that no one can tell them apart, all pink with happiness. Of course, however delightful this may be and however much others may envy us for it, and rightly so, it still means that we cannot give our children a proper childhood. And that has its consequences. A certain perennial, ineradicable childishness pervades our people; in direct contrast to our greatest virtue, our infallible practical common sense, we sometimes behave with the utmost foolishness, and it is exactly the same kind of foolishness that children display: a crazy, extravagant, grandiose, irresponsible kind of foolishness, and often all for the sake of a little fun. And although the enjoyment we get from it cannot of course be as whole-hearted as a child's enjoyment, yet something of this does survive in it without a doubt. And one who has profited from this childishness of ours from the very beginning is Josefine.

But as a people we are not only childish, we are also in a sense prematurely old; childhood and age appear with us in a different way from elsewhere. We have no youth, we are grown up all at once, and then we stay grown up for too long; as a result a certain weariness and hopelessness runs through the nature of our people, tough and confident though this is at bottom, and leaves its mark. And that is probably connected with the fact that we are so unmusical; we are too old for music, its excitement, its upsurge does not suit our heaviness, wearily we wave it away; we have fallen back on piping, a little bit of piping here and there, that is the right thing for us. Who knows if there might not be some with a gift for music among us; but if there

were, the character of their fellows would suppress the gift before it
could unfold. Josefine, on the other hand, can pipe or sing or whatever
she cares to call it as much as she likes, that does not disturb us, that is
quite acceptable, that we can put up with; if there should be any musical content in what she produces it is reduced to the barest minimum;
a certain musical tradition is preserved, but without this being in the
slightest degree burdensome to us.

But our people, given this disposition of theirs, get something else
from Josefine. At her concerts, particularly when times are threaten-
ing, it is only the very young who are interested in the singer as such;
it is only they who gaze in astonishment at the way she puckers her
lips, expels the air between her dainty front teeth, swoons in wonder-
ment at the sounds she is herself producing, and then uses this sinking
down to inspire her to fresh heights of achievement, which seem to
her ever more incredible; but meanwhile the main body of the audience—this is plain to see—has withdrawn into itself. Here in these
brief interludes between their battles our people dream, it is as if the
limbs of each were loosened, as if each single, anxious individual were
allowed for once to stretch out and relax to his heart's content in the
great warm bed of the people. And into these dreams falls now and
again the sound of Josefine's piping; she calls it rippling, we call it
thrusting; but at all events it is here in its right place, as nowhere else,
it finds just the moment that is awaiting it, as music hardly ever does
otherwise. Something of our poor brief childhood is in it, something
of a lost happiness that can never be found again, but it also has something of our busy life here and now, of that little admixture of unfathomable gaiety which persists and cannot be extinguished. And all this
is certainly not expressed in a loud and imposing tone, but softly, whis-
peringly, confidentially, sometimes a little hoarsely. Of course this is a
kind of piping. How could it not be? Piping is the speech of our people; it is only that some pipe their whole life long without knowing it,
while here piping is freed from the fetters of everyday life and can free
us from them, too, for a little while. No, we would on no account wish
to forego these performances.

But from there to Josefine's assertion that at such times she gives
us new strength, and so on and so forth, it is a very long way. For ordinary folk, that is; not for Josefine's flatterers. 'How could it be otherwise?'—so they say with quite shameless audacity—'how else could
one explain the massive attendance, especially at times of imminent

danger, when precisely that full attendance has often prevented adequate measures being taken to avert the danger in time?' Now this last point is unfortunately true, though it hardly counts as one of Josefine's claims to fame, particularly not if one adds that Josefine—when such gatherings have been unexpectedly broken up by the enemy and many of our number have perished as a result—that Josefine, who was responsible for it all and whose piping may indeed have actually attracted the enemy, was herself invariably occupying the safest place, and was also the first to disappear, protected by her escort, very silently and at maximum speed? But everyone really knows this too, and still they come running the next time Josefine takes it into her head to rise up and sing, at whatever time or place she pleases. One might conclude from this that Josefine stands almost beyond the law, that she is allowed to do as she likes, even if it puts the community at risk, and that all will be forgiven her. If this were so, then even Josefine's claims would be quite comprehensible; indeed, one might see in such a licence granted her by the people, in such an extraordinary favour bestowed on no one else and actually in contravention of our laws, an admission of the fact that our people—just as she alleges—does not understand Josefine, but instead gapes at her art helplessly, does not feel worthy of it, and hopes to make good the pain thus caused to Josefine by a positively desperate sacrifice on their own part, namely by placing her person and her wishes as far beyond their jurisdiction as her art lies beyond their understanding. Well, that is simply not true at all, perhaps in matters of detail the people may capitulate too readily to Josefine, but they capitulate unconditionally to no one, and hence not to her either.

For a long time now, perhaps since the start of her artistic career, Josefine has been fighting to be excused all work on account of her song; all the cares about gaining her daily bread and about everything else involved in our struggle for existence should be taken off her shoulders and—presumably—transferred to the people as a whole. Anyone prone to instant enthusiasm—and there have been such enthusiasts—might conclude merely from the oddity of this demand, from the mentality capable of framing such a demand, that it must be inherently justified. But our people draw different conclusions and calmly turn the request down. Nor do they take overmuch trouble to refute the arguments on which it is based. Josefine argues, for instance, that the strain of work adversely affects her voice, that while the strain of work is admittedly a mere trifle by comparison with the strain of singing, it still makes it impossible for her to get sufficient rest after singing and strengthen herself for fresh song, so that she has to exhaust herself utterly by her singing and yet can never, in these circumstances, rise to her very highest achievement. The people listen to her arguments and take no notice. This people of ours, so easily moved, is sometimes not to be moved at all. Their refusal is sometimes so harsh that even Josefine is taken aback, she appears to submit, does her proper share of work, sings as best she can, but all that only for a while, then with renewed strength—for this purpose her strength seems unlimited—she takes up the fight again.

Now it is clear that what Josefine is really after is not what she literally demands. She is sensible; she is not work-shy, which is anyhow something quite unknown among us; she would, even if her petition were granted, certainly not live otherwise than before, her work would not in the least hinder her singing, nor indeed would her song become any more beautiful—no, what she is after is simply public recognition of her art, a recognition that is unambiguous, that outlasts all ages, and far surpasses anything known hitherto. But while almost everything else seems to be within her grasp, this persistently eludes her. Perhaps she should have taken a different line of attack from the beginning, perhaps she recognizes the mistake herself by now, but now she can no longer retreat, any retreat would amount to a self-betrayal, now she must stand or fall by this demand of hers.

If she really did have enemies, as she maintains, they could follow her campaign as amused onlookers without having to lift a finger. But she has no enemies, and even if she may meet with objections here and there, this struggle in which she is engaged amuses nobody. For the good reason that in this instance the people adopts a cold, judicial attitude which it otherwise rarely displays. And even if one may approve it in this case, the mere thought that the same attitude could be adopted towards oneself rules out all pleasure. For what really matters here is neither the refusal of the demand nor the demand itself; it is rather that the people as a whole should be capable of presenting such a stony, impenetrable front to one of their own comrades, a front that is all the more impenetrable because otherwise they care for that same comrade with fatherly—indeed more than fatherly, with humble concern.

Let us imagine a single individual in place of the people: one might suppose that this man had been giving in to Josefine the whole time with the constant, burning desire to bring all this conceding to a full stop at last; that he had conceded a superhuman amount in the firm belief that concessions were bound to find their proper limit in the end; indeed, that he had conceded more than was necessary simply in order to speed things up, simply in order to spoil Josefine and encourage her to ask for more and more, until she really did come out with this final demand of hers, whereupon of course he, being well prepared in advance, could counter quite shortly with his ultimate refusal. Well, that is most certainly not how things stand; the people have no need of such wiles, and besides their admiration for Josefine is sincere and well established, and anyhow Josefine's demand is so monstrous that any simple child could have told her what the outcome would be; nevertheless it is conceivable that the above suppositions do colour Josefine's own view of the matter, and so add a further bitterness to the pain of being refused.

But even if she does entertain such suppositions she does not let them deter her from pursuing her campaign. Recently this has even been intensified; whereas previously she fought with words alone, now she has begun to use other weapons, weapons that in her opinion are more effective but in our opinion more dangerous for her.

There are some who believe that Josefine is becoming so importunate because she feels she is growing old, her voice is showing signs of weakness, and so it seems to her to be high time to wage her final battle for recognition. I do not believe it. Josefine would not be Josefine if that were true. For her there is no growing old and no weakening of her voice. When she demands something she is not impelled by outward circumstances but by an inner logic. She reaches for the highest crown not because it happens to have dropped down a little lower, but because it is the highest; if it lay in her power she would hang it higher still.

This contempt for external difficulties does not, however, prevent her from employing the most unworthy methods. Her rights are to her beyond question, so what does it matter how she secures them; especially since in this world, as she sees it, the worthy methods are precisely the ones that fail. Perhaps indeed that is the very reason why she has shifted her campaign for justice from the field of song to another which is of little importance to her. Her supporters have put about statements of hers to the effect that she does indeed feel perfectly capable of such song as would give true delight to the people, at all its levels and into the furthest corners of the opposition—true delight, what is more, not by popular standards, for the people claim they have always delighted in Josefine's singing, but by the standard of Josefine's own ambition. But—she adds—since she can bring herself neither to falsify what is noble nor pander to the vulgar, her singing must remain as it is. But when it comes to her fight to be exempted from work, it is a different matter; naturally her singing is at stake here as well, but here she is not using the precious weapon of her song directly, and hence any method she chooses is good enough.

Thus for example the rumour was spread abroad that Josefine intended, if her demand were not granted, to shorten her coloraturas. I know nothing about coloraturas and have never noticed any sign of coloraturas in her song. But Josefine is going to shorten her coloraturas; not, for the time being, to cut them out entirely, simply to shorten them. Allegedly she has carried out this threat, although I for one have observed no difference from her previous performances. The people as a whole listened as usual, without passing any comment on the coloraturas, nor has there been any change in the treatment of her demand. It cannot be denied, incidentally, that Josefine, who has a certain graciousness about her person, occasionally displays something of the same kind in her way of thinking. Thus for instance she announced after that concert, as if her decision in respect of the coloraturas had been too harsh or too sudden, that on the next occasion she would be singing the coloraturas once more in their entirety. But after the next concert she changed her mind yet again, it was now definitely all over with the full-scale coloraturas, and until a decision favourable to Josefine was reached they would never return. Well, the people simply turn a deaf ear to all these announcements, decisions and counter-decisions, much as a grown-up turns a deaf ear to the chattering of a child, fundamentally well-disposed but beyond reach.

But Josefine does not give in. The other day, for example, she claimed that she had hurt her foot at work, so that it was difficult for her to stand up while singing; but since she was only able to sing standing up, she would now actually have to cut short her songs. Although she goes around with a limp, supported by her group of followers, no one believes that she has a real injury. Even if one grants that her small frame is exceptionally sensitive, we are after all a working people and Josefine is one of us; if we were to start limping every time we got a scratch the whole people would never stop limping. But even if she does allow herself to be led around like a cripple, even if she does display herself in this lamentable condition more frequently than usual, the people still listen to her singing in gratitude and enchantment as before; only as far as the cuts are concerned, they make no great fuss.

Since she cannot go on limping for ever, she invents something else, she pleads exhaustion, dejection, feeling faint. So now we get a theatrical performance in addition to the concert. Behind Josefine we see her supporters in the background, begging her and imploring her to sing. She would be happy to do so, but she cannot. They comfort her, they caress her with flatteries, they almost carry her to the chosen spot where she is due to sing. Finally, weeping tears that defy interpretation, she relents; but then, when she intends to sing, evidently at the end of her powers, enfeebled, her arms not spread wide as usual but hanging limply at her sides, which creates the impression that they may be a little too short—when she then intends to strike up, no, it is no use after all, a reluctant shake of the head tells us as much and she sinks down before our eyes. Admittedly she gets up again after that and sings, in my opinion pretty much as usual; perhaps the most discriminating ear might detect a marginal increase in emotion, which however only contributes to the effect. And in the end she is actually less tired than before; with a firm tread, in so far as her whisking and scurrying may be so described, she moves off, refusing all assistance from her supporters and measuring with a cold eye the crowd which makes way for her in awe.

That is how things were until recently, but the latest news is this: on one occasion, when her song was awaited, she had disappeared. It is not just her supporters who are looking for her, many others have joined the search, it is all in vain; Josefine has vanished, she refuses to sing, she will not even accept an invitation to sing, this time she has deserted us completely.

It is curious how badly she miscalculates, the clever creature, so badly that one might imagine that she did not calculate at all, but was merely driven onwards by her destiny, which in our world cannot be anything but a sad one. Of her own accord she withdraws from song, of her own accord she destroys the power she has won over our hearts. How could she ever have gained that power, since she knows these hearts so little? She hides herself away and declines to sing; but

meanwhile our people, calmly, without visible disappointment, as an
imperious and self-sufficient body, which can in all truth, despite ap-
pearances, only ever bestow gifts and not receive them, not even from
Josefine, this people of ours continues on its way.

But Josefine's path can only go downward. The time will soon
come when her last pipe sounds and fades away. She is a little episode
in the endless history of our people, and the people will get over their
loss. Not that it will be easy for us; how shall our gatherings take place
in utter silence? And yet, were they not silent even when Josefine was
there? Was her actual piping notably louder and more lively than the
memory of it will be? Was it even in her lifetime any more than simply a memory? Is it not rather that our people, in their wisdom, trea-
sured Josefine's song so highly just because in this way it could never
fade?

So perhaps we shall not miss so very much after all, while Josefine,
for her part, delivered from earthly afflictions, which however to her
mind are the privilege of chosen spirits, will happily lose herself in the
countless throng of the heroes of our people, and soon, since we pursue no history, be accorded the heightened deliverance of being forgotten along with all her brethren.